Haunting Thelma Thimblewhistle
The Chronicles of Dead Anna

A.J. GREA

Published/Created: Knoxville, TN: Oakberry & Inkwell, 2025.

Edited by R.M. Collins

Front and back cover design by A.J. Grea

Library of Congress Cataloging-in-Publication Data

Grea, A.J.

Haunting Thelma Thimblewhistle: The Chronicles of Dead Anna
by A.J. Grea – 3rd ed.

p. cm.

Summary: A young girl discovers she can communicate with the spirit world, who inform her she must prevent the return of the Boogey Man.

ISBN-13: 978-1-968152-08-6

1   2   3   4   5   6   7   8   9

[1. Horror — Fiction. 2. Ghosts — Fiction 3. Monsters — Fiction 4. World War II — Fiction]

OAKBERRY & INKWELL

Other books by A.J. ~~Giea~~

VICKIE VAN HELSING

Dedication

For every child who has ever been afraid of the Boogey Man, I dedicate this book to **you**. Smile in the darkness and know there is a certain magic in things that go *bump* in the night.

Griselda

May I tell you a story?

I've a wondrous tale for you about a little girl—one unlike any other—a little girl named *Thelma Thimblewhistle*. All good tales begin at the beginning, and since this is a very good tale, the beginning is exactly where we shall start.

In the year 1933, there lived an old gypsy woman who was known as Griselda. She lived in a small, quaint cottage in the middle of the city with a cat she named *Whiskus* and a fountain pen—a very special fountain pen—whom she called *Solomon*.

Each day Griselda made her living selling predictions about love, money and health to those who came seeking her insight. Each client would enter her home and, for a modest fee, Griselda would offer them tea and their future. Together she and her patron would sit facing one another at a small sitting table. Upon this table she would lay a small stack of parchment, an inkwell, and Solomon. She would then request her patron to ask his or her questions only once, and then remain silent. Taking Solomon into her hand, she would dip him into his ink and begin writing the answer to the query. Though she would never ever look at the paper as she wrote, her handwriting was never flawed. It was as if the pen could write on its own.

Once her predictions were completed, she would close the parchment with a single fold, seal it in an envelope, and hand it to her customer without reading what had been written.

Why would she read a future that was not her own?

Then she would bid her customer farewell, never allowing them to read what had been written in her presence. The future was the future—plain and simple. There was little Griselda could do to alter its course.

One dark evening, when the fog was thick in the air, Griselda turned on her porch lamp as she did each evening to indicate to passersby that she was open to accept business. The whistle of her teapot sounded, warning her to remove it from the heat of the stove. In her cup she placed a single teabag, with flavors of honey and cinnamon, and two teaspoons of sugar. Steam rolled from the spout as the boiling water filled the porcelain cup. Then she went to prepare the sitting table, gathering a small stack of parchment and resting Solomon in its center.

"Oh, Solomon," she sighed. "Old Griselda needs to find a new line of work!" She rounded the table and took a seat to await the doorbell. "Of course, I don't know what *you* would do, my old friend. I fear you may grow bored with only me to keep you company."

She took a careful sip from her cup, tasting the warm flavor as it covered her palate. Placing the cup onto its saucer, she couldn't help but notice a green glow falling on her white linen tablecloth. She sprang to her feet.

"Oh no!" she said to herself.

She ran to the window and looked into the sky. There it was: an *Emerald Moon*. She had heard the stories about Emerald Moons her entire life, but never thought she would live to see one. It was high in the night sky, diamond-like in shape, and the brightest green you had ever seen. It was so bright, in fact, that it was nearly like daylight.

A moon of emerald, bright and high, warns of wickedness nearby.

There would be no patrons that night, most definitely not.

As Griselda rushed to her door to turn off the porch lamp, she could see a newlywed couple arriving to inquire about their future together. They were holding hands and smiling lovingly at one another. Just as the young man was preparing to ring the bell, Griselda opened the door.

"Hello!" announced the young man. "We wanted to know if you could tell us…"

"I'm very sorry," Griselda interrupted. "But I cannot entertain tonight. My sincere apologies. Please, come back tomorrow and I'll write for you then…for free!"

"Uh, but…"

"I am sorry. Goodnight."

Griselda shut the door and turned off the porch lamp. She turned each lock tightly and returned to her table to put away the parchment.

"The Emerald Moon," she said to herself. "What could it mean?"

Rrriiiiing!

A stranger was at the door. At first, Griselda did nothing. *Maybe if I don't allow myself to be seen, they will leave.*

Rrriiiiing! Rrriiiiing!

Cautiously, Griselda peeked around the corner. She could see a small figure standing at her doorway.

Rrriiiiing!

Taking a deep breath, Griselda walked to the door and saw a young woman who was with child standing there with a frantic look upon her face. No one accompanied the young woman, who was elegantly dressed in expensive attire and jewelry. Obviously, she lived a very comfortable life.

Griselda pulled back the small lace curtain on the door's window. "I'm sorry. I'm not writing this evening. Please come back tomorrow."

"But, please…please. I need to see you," said the young woman.

"Not tonight. I'm not feeling well. I wouldn't want to give an illness to you or your baby. Come back tomorrow and…"

"Please," begged the woman. "I can pay you. I can give you this." The young woman held up a very large sum of money, much more than Griselda requested for her services.

Griselda was torn. The young woman was so distressed and the money was so substantial, it was nearly impossible not to allow it. Though she thought it unwise with an Emerald Moon present, what harm could a young expectant mother do? She unlocked the door and quickly ushered her inside.

"Thank you! Oh, thank you. I appreciate your assistance."

"You are very welcome. Please, come this way," Griselda said as she peered past the young woman into the foggy darkness. Griselda shut the door and locked it tight. She took the young woman's coat and then offered her a seat at the table. "Would you like tea?"

"No," the young woman replied. "No, thank you."

"Very well."

Griselda took the parchment from the small drawer and laid it upon the table along with Solomon.

"What a lovely pen!" said the woman.

"Thank you. Yes, he's been in my family for generations."

"He?"

Griselda smiled. "Sorry. I call him Solomon. I know it's silly of me to do such a thing. But he's been with me so long. Sometimes he's all the company I have."

Meow…

"Oh!" said the woman with a start. Whiskus rubbed against her leg. "What a lovely cat."

"Sorry, Whiskus. No, I'm not forgetting about you."

The young woman smiled. "So, if I may, how should we begin?"

Griselda explained her process to the young woman and then said, "Now, please proceed with your question."

"You see, I am to be married," explained the woman. "I do love my fiancé, though our wedding is somewhat unplanned." She rubbed her stomach. "I fear that he believes I only want his money. But I assure him that I love him for the man he is. I want to know what the future holds for our marriage and for my unborn child. Will we be happy?"

Griselda took Solomon into her hand, dipping him into his ink, and waited for the writing to begin. Curiously, it did not. She closed her eyes and willed her hand to move, but it would not respond. Typically, it was second nature, requiring no effort or thought at all. Within moments of a question being posed, her hand would begin to flow effortlessly across the pages, dictating the answer in explicit detail. Regrettably, this time that was not the case.

"Is there a problem?" asked the woman.

"No, no. My apologies. I fear my mind may be wandering."

"Well," said the young woman, her tone becoming sharp, "I suggest you concentrate. This is a large amount of money."

Griselda took exception to her tone, though she did her best to not show it. She took a deep breath and cleared her mind. Then she began to write. However, for some reason, this time she read along; she felt she must. The more words that appeared, the more anxiety knotted in her throat. She could not believe what she was seeing. Once the premonitions were written, Griselda dropped Solomon to the table.

"What? What is it?" asked the young woman. "What? You must tell me."

Griselda folded the paper in a single crease just as she always did. She quickly stuffed the paper in an envelope and handed it to the girl.

"Now, your answers are inside. Please…I must bid you good night. You may keep your money."

The young girl stood up in a panic. "But what does it say?"

"Now, now," Griselda said. "Just as we discussed, you must read the telling on your own."

"Let's read it now."

"No, please…"

The young woman opened the paper and began to read. Her expression was one of total astonishment as she paced around the sitting room, carefully reading the predictions and then reading them once again. "Is this true? You're saying this is my fate, old woman?"

"You need to leave this house immediately!" demanded Griselda.

"You don't know me! You have no right to say any of this!"

"I didn't say anything."

The young woman glanced down to Solomon. "Oh…so you say it's the pen's fault? The pen predicted this?" She snatched Solomon from the table top.

"Stop! Get out of here…now! Your future is yours. I, nor the pen, have any say in it!"

Then the young woman began to calm herself. She sat back down at the table and began to sob. Suddenly, Griselda felt pity for her and her terrible future.

"I can't believe this. I mean…it's hopeless," cried the woman.

Griselda sighed. "Oh, honey, you can't take my word for anything. Who am I? I'm just an old gypsy lady with a musty cat who talks to a fountain pen!"

The young woman laughed. "I'm sorry. I'm sorry. If you don't mind, I'd like some tea before I leave, if I'm still welcome."

Wanting to appease the woman and send her on her way quickly, Griselda said, "Of course! I don't mind at all."

Griselda stepped to the cupboard and took out another cup and saucer, her hand shaking nervously. This was the exact reason fortunes were never permitted to be read in her presence. A customer on an Emerald Moon—what else could she have expected?

"You know, sometimes I wonder about stopping all of this nonsense," rattled Griselda. "I don't want to do this forever, of course. It's not a very lucrative career choice, as you could well imagine." She poured the water into the cup. "You have to have a certain understanding for the human condition. Some people, such as yourself, are simply too distraught to…"

The blow came quickly and quietly.

Griselda had not noticed the young woman approaching her from behind armed with the poker from the fireplace. As her lifeless body lay in the glow of the emerald moonlight, Whiskus walked up to meow to her as if she could still respond. The cat rubbed her face affectionately and curled up beside her to enjoy the warmth as it began to leave her body. And into the darkness, a murderess made her escape with knowledge of a future she could not change and an enchanted fountain pen named *Solomon J. Inkwell.*

The Peterson Estate

The doors groaned as they creaked open allowing the last remaining rays of sunlight to invade the dank, dusty room. The crisp November wind blew leaves around four shadowy silhouettes that stretched across the pale marble floors.

"Is this not awesome?" her father asked.

Thelma stepped around him and into the foyer. "Oh yeah," she replied with a hint of sarcasm. "This is just...I mean...wow."

"Now, Thelma," her grandmother, Mimi, warned as she followed her inside. "No one likes a smarty pants."

"I *love* a smarty pants, Thelma," called Norma Underwood, Mimi's best friend. "Here—get these bags, sweetness, before I pop a lung!"

Thelma took the bags from Norma and sat them on the floor. It was hard to believe that the Peterson Estate, the creepy mansion that had always held fascination for her, now belonged to the Thimblewhistles. She couldn't quite explain how it happened. Only a few short weeks before, she was in her room in Indiana surrounded by familiar things, things she had always known. In the blink of an eye, it seemed, she was whisked away to the land of *Raven Den, Tennessee.*

Raven Den.

What a freaky name. Thelma had always thought so. The rural town had always been the home of her fun-loving, eccentric grandmother, Marilyn, whom everyone had always lovingly referred to as *Mimi*. In fact, when Thelma was learning to speak as a child, it was easier for her to say "Mimi" than it was to say "Grandma." Besides the mountains and Mimi, there wasn't much she enjoyed about Raven Den. For as long as she could remember, they had come to visit each fall during football season when everything in the town was smothered in the colors of orange and white…including Mimi.

During every stay, Thelma would get a terrible case of the sniffles. However, she tried to look past that and focus on the wondrous autumn mountains, how they blazed with colors of gold and copper in the distance. The air was much crisper here than in the big city, and it was elating to see a deer scamper through Mimi's backyard, or a fuzzy bunny hop through the brush.

Okay…maybe Raven Den was not so bad, but she still loathed the sniffles.

Her father, Edwin, had always loved Raven Den. It was his hometown and the place he had lived until his mid-twenties. Sometimes Thelma wondered how he had survived here so long. Now she wondered if she would survive.

"So, what d'ya think?" Edwin asked as he shut the squeaky French doors and sat their luggage down.

Thelma studied the inside of the massive house as she took off her jacket. "Well, it's certainly freaky enough."

"I know!" Mimi exclaimed. "Isn't it great?"

"With all those scary movies you sneak around and watch behind my back, this should be right up your alley," Edwin replied with a grin as he tossed Thelma's backpack to her.

"Right." Thelma smiled sarcastically and sat her pack on the floor.

Thelma gazed at the grand space before her, which needed a little dusting. Above her head she could see two crystal chandeliers hanging from the cathedral ceiling. The marble floor was in very good condition. Before her, there were two curved staircases on either side of the room, which converged on the landing of the second floor. Yards and yards of wine-colored fabric and white chiffon draped the oversized windows on the second level. It was the most spectacular thing she had ever seen. She couldn't help but smile. It was just spooky enough to be intriguing, mysterious—just the way she liked.

"Mimi, old gal," Norma barked. "Let's say you and I head to the kitchen and put on a pot of tea. I've got a mess of cookies longing to be eaten! Then we need to get some pictures taken for the scrapbooks."

"Sounds good to me!" Mimi replied. "Thelma, wanna come with?"

"Would you guys mind if I take a look around?" Thelma asked as she looked to her father.

"Sure. No problem. The moving van won't be here for about another hour or two," he said. "But keep your phone on you and answer it if it rings!"

"Yeah, yeah, yeah," Thelma replied as she picked up her backpack.

Mimi and Norma disappeared through the swinging kitchen door. It was difficult to determine where to begin exploring first; there were so many choices. As her father began carrying in other items from their vehicle outside, Thelma began to investigate the main level. To her left was the remarkable sitting room. It had a marble fireplace and in front of it laid a thick, soft, cream-colored rug. Directly alongside the sitting room was a dining area that had another crystal chandelier, just like the two in the foyer, hanging above a long, stately table.

Across from the sitting room, on the opposite side of the foyer, there was a bathroom for guests. Next to it, Thelma could see a set of double doors. She slid them open to find a vast library filled with dusty books—books as far as the eye could see. They lined the walls on massive bookcases that stretched from the floor to the ceiling. Attached to a brass rail, there was a ladder that slid around the bookcases so that you could reach books on the upper shelves. Toward the back of the room, there was another fireplace with a distinguished oak desk in front of it. She walked over and climbed into its bulky leather chair that squeaked as she situated herself. A wide smile crossed her face. Books were some of her favorite things, and a library this big was bound to have tons of interesting reading material.

The desk had many drawers. Naturally, she was very curious as to what could be inside them, but alas every drawer in the desk was tightly locked. She wondered if her father had the key. As she studied the desk, she noticed that in the lower left-hand corner of the desktop there was a strange symbol, an emblem of sorts, which was carved into the wood—an eight-pointed star cupped on either side by crescent moons—possibly an insignia from the manufacturer.

She stood and began to make her way back to the foyer when she heard a *thud*. The dust was settling around a thick book, bound in leather, which had apparently fallen to the floor from the top of the desk when she had stood. She walked over and bent down to pick it up. It was quite heavy. Engraved into the leather of the cover with detailed artistry was the same emblem she had seen on the desk. She rubbed the skin of the book, feeling its coolness as her fingers traced the outline of the mark. She tried to open it, but it was sealed tight by a brass lock. Searching the desk, she soon found a tiny brass key; its tip was adorned with the same emblem as the desk and the book's cover.

"I guess you two go together," Thelma said to herself.

She unlocked the book and opened it wide, only to see that each of its aged pages were absent of any print. Yet, it was fascinating. She thought if nothing else it would make a wonderful diary. With such a large book, she could record the rest of her life. She unzipped her pack and stuffed it inside.

Thelma made her way back to the foyer. From the kitchen, she could hear the voice of Edwin interlacing with Mimi's and Norma's as they discussed how the mansion's interior was to be designed. Making her way to the second level, she could see that there were two hallways, one to the left and one to the right. There were a total of seven rooms in all, including six bedrooms and a spacious bathroom. As she walked down the hall to the right, she found two of the rooms completely empty. The final bedroom at the end, however, was enormous and even had its own bathroom. It had obviously been claimed by her father as she could see his things already resting in the floor.

"That's my room," Edwin said.

Thelma jumped. "God!" She took a deep breath prompting her father to giggle. She playfully smacked his arm. "Yeah, I kinda figured you'd take the best room."

"Oh…really? Come here." Thelma followed her father to the left hallway. "You ready?"

Thelma nodded. As he opened the door, she gasped. It was amazing. The room needed a little dusting, but overall it was astonishing. There was a huge bed with a canopy, like a queen's bed. To the right of the bed there was a baroque-style wardrobe that reminded Thelma of her favorite book, *The Lion, the Witch and the Wardrobe*. In front of the picture window there was a bench that overlooked the grounds where she could not wait to relax and read.

"Oh, my God! Dad, it's great!" She set down her pack, walked over to the bed, and fell forward into the softness of its plush mattress and its new sheets.

"You like it?" Edwin laughed.

"Uh…no!" Thelma said. "I *love* it!" Thelma sat up on the bed. "But…where's my bathroom?"

"It's down the hall. Don't get cheeky."

Thelma laughed. She stood and walked to the wardrobe opening it wide. "Okay, Dad, why did the Petersons leave all this junk behind? I mean, look at this thing! And this bed. And downstairs there's a library filled with all kinds of books. And a big, old desk, which I'm sure is worth a ton."

Edwin chuckled. "Good. We're gonna have to sell it to pay the mortgage!" He walked over and sat down on the window seat. "You know, I'm not sure. Peterson's son just said they had already taken what they wanted, and the rest they were leaving. Guess they didn't want to be bothered."

"Huh," Thelma huffed as she shut the wardrobe doors. "Well, I'll take it!"

Thelma and Edwin joined Mimi and Norma in the kitchen where tea and cookies were being consumed.

"Hey, honey, what do you think?" Mimi asked as she poured a cup of tea for both herself and Norma.

"Creepy enough for ya?" Norma asked.

"Eh…we'll see," Thelma replied.

"You'll get used to it," Edwin said with a sly grin.

"Oh, hush up, Eddie," Mimi said as she sat down the teapot. "Here, honey, I got you something for your birthday. Sorry it's late." Mimi presented Thelma with a large gift bag. "His name is Bartholomew Bear."

Thelma smiled and pulled the tissue paper from the bag. Inside was a beautiful stuffed bear. She really wasn't a teddy bear kind of girl any longer, but she smiled just the same. "Thank you, Mimi," she said giving her grandmother a huge hug.

"You're welcome, honey. Oh, we are gonna have so much fun! Just think, Thelma—all these years we've been telling stories about this old place and now it belongs to you!"

"A glutton for punishment, if you ask me," Norma chimed in. "I'd never live across from your grandma. She'd drive me nuts. I tell ya, Eddie, I think you're losing it."

"Woman! Hush your mouth," Mimi said. "Eddie has always been Momma's little boy." Mimi caressed Edwin's cheeks.

Thelma laughed.

Edwin rolled his eyes. "Norma, I think you're right."

"I do love the stuff they left here, though, especially the library books," Thelma commented.

"Yes, one thing the Petersons never had to worry about is money, dear," Mimi said.

Norma giggled. "Boy, ain't that the truth! At least Peterson kept my father in a job back in the day. You know, Henry Peterson was a good old guy, really. He was always good to me and my family."

"Your dad worked for Henry Peterson? I didn't know that, Norma," Edwin said as he pulled a soda from the refrigerator.

"Sure did! He was the head groundskeeper here for years. Henry hired him before the house was finished, right after he bought the land from old lady Evermoore." Norma took a careful sip from her hot tea cup.

"Mrs. Evermoore. Lord, there's a story for ya," Mimi said in her usual sympathetic southern tone. "Bless her heart."

"Bless her heart," Norma agreed.

And the ladies stopped there.

Mimi and Norma would never gossip unprovoked. To do so was rude. Granted, they always wanted to continue, but one had to urge their story forward.

"Okay…so who is old lady Evermoore and what was her deal?" Thelma finally asked.

"Well," Mimi leaned in as if she didn't want to be overheard. "Old lady Evermoore owned all of this land, before Henry bought it from her, back when Norma and I were just little girls. Her family had owned it for years."

"Generations," added Norma.

Mimi continued. "True. Love her soul, her son died in the war. Nearly destroyed her. He left behind his young wife and baby."

Norma pointed at Edwin and Thelma. "Worse yet, not two years after her son passed, the daughter-in-law died of pneumonia! Left that poor old lady with a baby to look after."

"Old lady Evermoore couldn't handle taking care of a baby, naturally," Mimi said. "She was sickly and tired, forgetful, too. I think she had a touch of what Dorothy Chester had, Norma, what was that?"

"Dementia."

"Dementia! That's it. So, she had to sell this land off, and move into a home."

"Sad!" Norma said.

"Sad," agreed Mimi.

"So, that's when Peterson stepped in," said Edwin.

"Yep," Mimi continued. "He was so nice. He gave her double what she was asking for this land and the little old shack that was on it."

Norma put another lump of sugar in her cup. "Sure did. Her only request was that he leave the cemetery be."

Thelma's ears perked up. "Cemetery?"

Mimi looked at Edwin. "Yes. At the edge of the grounds in the back, close to those overgrown woods, there's the old family graveyard that belonged to the Evermoores."

"And you need to stay out of it," warned Edwin. "I'm sure it's nasty and filled with God knows what."

Thelma smiled, knowing she would visit the cemetery in due time. "Okay, so what happened to Peterson?"

Mimi grew solemn as Norma patted her hand. "Well, Henry and his family moved in—him, his wife, their two sons, and Anna, their youngest daughter. It was before I had met old Norma here. Anna and I hit it off. She was such fun. Lord, the imagination that girl had! Just like you." Mimi touched Thelma's nose. "We were fast friends. We had the same birthday and everything. That pool out there…the two of us practically lived at that pool."

"I still can't believe it," Norma said.

"What?" Thelma asked becoming interested.

Norma and Mimi looked at one another, and then to Edwin.

"Anna had gone out to swim one day," Edwin said. "No one really knows what happened."

"We think she hit her head," Norma added.

Thelma eyes widened. "She died?"

Mimi patted Thelma's hand. "Yes. Oh, it was awful. I was heartbroken."

"We met at her funeral," Norma said.

"That's right, we did." Mimi smiled as she playfully waved a napkin in Norma's face. "Well, after Anna passed, Henry completely changed. He was never the same…totally lost his zest for life. Finally, he moved the family away and left this old place vacant. But he never thought about selling it, even though he had plenty of offers. It reminded him of Anna too much. His decision to keep this old place drove his family to distraction. They couldn't see the point in it. But Henry couldn't let it go."

Norma grinned. "That's why your Grannie flipped her bonnet when it finally hit the market."

"Someone was going to snatch it up if we didn't move quickly. No sooner had that *For Sale* sign hit the yard than an offer was on the table," Mimi said slapping the countertop.

"Thus came the Great Bidding War," Edwin said stretching his arms forward. "It about drove me crazy!"

"But we outbid them," Mimi chuckled.

Edwin sat down. "No, they just got sick of us. I was almost sick of it, myself. If they would have countered our offer one more time, I swear I would've walked away."

Mimi got up and kissed Edwin on the head. "I'm so happy you hung in there, honey."

Happy?

Thelma wasn't certain that *happy* described how she was feeling. Inexplicably, there was only one word that entered her mind:

Beware…

Shadows

T helma felt absolutely silly hiding in her blankets. Scary movies and ghost stories were her playground, so the dark had never been something she had feared. She rather enjoyed the mystery that hid in the shadows. Then again, there was no reason to fear the familiar shadows that lurked inside her home in Indiana. She knew them well. But, these shadows were new…strange, even.

And fear is not fun when it is real.

Her father had offered to let her room with him during their first night in the massive old mansion. Thelma, however, felt it was a ridiculous suggestion for a girl who was the ripe old age of *eleven*, so she declined. She regretted her decision now that the house was beginning to speak to her. Not necessarily in audible words, mind you, but in creaks, groans, and mysterious pops that made her insides shiver. She could see the thick clouds through her window as they slowly moved across the dark sky. A storm was approaching.

"Why did I let him talk me into this?" she whispered to the nothingness as if it would answer.

It had been quite a busy day. While the moving men were unloading their truck, Thelma managed to slip through the backdoor undetected to explore the grounds…and, of course, the cemetery. The fact that she had been warned not to do so made it even more appealing.

The immense back yard was in desperate need of cleaning. There had once been a great garden that was now overgrown with all sorts of weeds and brush, brown and wilted from the bitterness of the fall. In front of the garden was the swimming pool. Thelma stepped to its edge. It was filled with years of rain water. She was certain it would be in need of repair. However, once it was cleaned, it would be very lovely. Thick ice covered the murky water, which was filled with leaves, vines, and other debris. She tried not to dwell on the fact that a girl around her age had died there.

In the distance, she could see what appeared to be a quaint wrought iron gate. This had to be where the Evermoore cemetery remained. The high weeds touched her fingertips as she strolled through them. In reality, the graveyard was very small. Its gates were broken and tattered. The entryway was completely gone leaving only a few rusted, crooked sections impaled into the dry ground. The headstones were modest and obviously made by hand. She wandered around them, trying to make out names on the ones the weather had not destroyed over time.

Some were simple:

Marybelle Evermoore ~ Beloved Grandmother
Born July 1891, Died June 1956

Some were funny:

Gustus Evermoore – The Old Drunk
Here Lies Most of Poor Gustus
The Bear Took the Rest of Him

Some had different last names:

Zachary & Pearl McGucken - Together
Forever

Then Thelma found a grave she assumed belonged to Mrs. Evermoore's son and his wife:

Markus Evermoore ~ Defender of Freedom
WWII

Born January 1917
Died April 1945
Maria Evermoore ~ Beloved Wife & Mother
Born October 1919
Died August 1947

Thelma was startled by the ringing of her cell phone. Knowing it was her father, she began to run out of the graveyard and back to the mansion.

"Hello?" Thelma said out of breath.

"Get in here and help Mimi and Norma put the kitchen together. You better not be in that graveyard, young lady."

"I'm not, Dad," Thelma lied.

She could hear Mimi in the background.

"Ed! Leave her alone and let her explore. Good gravy!"

Mimi—right now she was the primary source of positivity for Thelma. Now that her mother was gone, Mimi was the only woman in her life.

An entire year. That Christmas would mark one year since her mother's accident. *Juliana.* It was such a lovely name. Sometimes Thelma would whisper it to herself while looking into her bedroom mirror just to hear it aloud. Sometimes, she would write it on white paper so she could remember that at one time her mother had existed; a time that was not so long ago, yet seemed like an eternity. Her father didn't show his sadness much, but the sudden desire to relocate to Tennessee proved to her that he was running away from painful memories he could not bear to recall.

Rattle…squeeeeaal…shake, Bump, RATTLE!

From her gloomy room, she could hear the iron gates that surrounded the property as they beat fiercely in the wind like a creature was tearing them, trying to break through. All the talk of graveyards and haunted mansions was beginning to eat at her. She thought about taking her father up on his offer and going to his room, but the following morning would be his first day at his new job. He would certainly be upset if she awoke him for a simple case of the *shivers*.

After winning the contract for the estate, her father had secured a new job as Vice President of a local bank, Hallow Savings & Loan. It was a big step forward in his career and he was incredibly excited about the opportunity. Thelma had not been so enthusiastic. She hadn't been thrilled about relocating at all, as a matter of fact. It all happened so quickly. Just a month before, all she had been concerned with was turning eleven. Then, in a matter of days, she was moving to a new place to start a new life. Inside she knew it was what her father needed. She could understand that feeling, the desire to get away…to fly. On rare occasions, she could see the anguish in her father's blue eyes even though his smile tried to hide it. For him, she would not complain. For him, she would do her best to be positive.

Whoooooooooooooooo! Hisssss. Whoooooooooooooooo!

The wind cried as it whipped through the trees outside of her window. She pulled the blankets tighter around her. Farewells had not been too difficult. Luckily, Thelma didn't have to say good-bye to friends, because she did not have any. She stared through the window and thought of how nice it would be if she actually could make friends in Raven Den. At least there were children in the neighborhood. She had seen them earlier that day, scattered about, riding bicycles and skateboards. One girl caught her eye, an *odd* girl. She was wearing a large pair of rollerblades, which looked way too big for her, and struggling to make her way onto the sidewalk. She had long, wavy brown hair and wore glasses that she kept pushing up her pronounced nose as she concentrated on the pavement. Thelma waved to her as they passed. The girl smiled and returned the gesture, but as she did, she lost her balance and fell headfirst into the grass. Thelma giggled—she couldn't help it.

BANG!

A muffled shriek escaped Thelma's lips as the wind dislodged a small branch from the tree near her window, hurling it at the window pane. She threw the blankets over her head and tried to calm herself. Without thinking, she pulled Bartholomew Bear close to her and felt just a bit safer with him beside her.

From under the blankets, she could see a soft glow of light entering the room. She slowly pulled the blankets from her eyes to see the entire bedroom was cast in a bright green hue. Looking through the window, she could see the clouds had broken and through them shined the emerald glow of the moon. She had never seen a green moon before, especially in such an odd shape. She had to get a closer look.

She quickly scampered across the cold floor to her window bench to get a closer look. It was almost shaped like a cat's eye or a diamond, and was very, very bright…brighter than any full moon she'd ever seen.

"What is that?" she whispered to herself.

Then she heard something curious—the sound of laughter, a girl's laughter, swirling in the wind. The glow of the odd moon was bright enough

to completely illuminate the back yard. Thelma's eyes began searching for any signs of a stranger, but there was no one there. Then she heard the laughing again.

The room suddenly felt cooler, much cooler, nearly frigid. Suddenly, she was deathly afraid. Then the giggle broke into a wild laugh, which was all the motivation Thelma needed to move away from the window. She slowly climbed down from the bench and was about to run toward the safety of her bed when she heard:

Snooooooooooort!

Of course, any laugh with such a violent snort did not seem evil at all. The ridiculous noise made her smile. Slowly she walked back to the bench and looked outside once again, barely peeking over the windowsill.

Pow!

Something hit the pane of glass directly in front of Thelma's face. She gasped and started to run back to her bed. Then she heard something else.

Knock, knock, knock...

Someone, or something, was knocking on her window. She stood there motionless, afraid to turn around. Her room was nearly three stories from the ground, so she could not imagine who could have been there. Carefully, she turned her eyes back to the window and saw that nothing was there at all. Then condensation began to appear on the windowpane as something that couldn't be seen blew its breath upon the glass. She couldn't move. The glass began to squeak as an invisible finger wrote:

Hello, Thelma
I'm Dead Anna

Thelma sprang back into her bed and encased herself in covers. And then there was silence. Logic began telling her that she was seeing things; it was simply her imagination running away with her. That was all. Allowing one eye to peer from the blankets, by the light of the green moon she could see the mysterious message slowly beginning to fade away.

Again, that word entered her mind:

Beware...

Ignacio Ignacio

Dealing with an alarm clock again was problematic for Edwin, as he had grown accustomed to these past few days free of wake up calls. The excitement of beginning a new job had made it very difficult to fall asleep the night before, so he was still quite tired. Today, he would be meeting his new boss, Victor Von Hallow, for the first time. The recruiter who had met with Edwin barely mentioned Von Hallow during their *unusual* interview—an interview that was so strange Edwin was shocked to learn he had been awarded the position.

The recruiter, Marty Mulligan, spent the entire interview trembling nervously. He winced at any sound, after which he would push his oversized glasses back up the bridge of his bulbous nose. He didn't provide Edwin with much information other than he was to call Victor "Mister Von Hallow" at all times. Edwin was convinced that the whole interview was a failure. Nevertheless, a letter arrived the day before his daughter's birthday that read:

Dear Mr. Thimblewhistle;

It is with great pleasure that I offer you the position of Vice President at Hallow Savings & Loan. Attached you will find that your salary requirements have been exceeded. From what I understand, your interview was very interesting. Therefore, I would like to apologize for Mr. Mulligan's behavior during your meeting. He is...well, an anxious fellow. We expect that you will be able to begin at the start of the fourth quarter, preferably on Friday, November 30th. Please arrive before 8:00 AM on that day so that my assistant can show you to your office. You and I will meet later that afternoon. Should you have any questions, please contact Ignado Ignacio at 555-666-3845.

Goodie for you;

V. V. H.

Edwin arrived at the bank at seven twenty-seven in the morning. Luckily, a receptionist was already on site. She advised him to wait in the lobby until she returned. He stood there with his computer bag on his shoulder, gazing about the waiting area, studying the surroundings. The office was very quiet. Though he had not noticed it during his previous visit, hanging on the wall to the right of the lobby was a large portrait of Victor himself. He appeared to be a large fellow, broad shouldered. "Dark" was the only word that came to Edwin's mind. The man had a noble chin. A thick black moustache lined his upper lip. His nose was pointed, yet regal. Thick eyebrows accented his ice blue eyes and wavy black hair.

The painting almost seemed *real*. Edwin was compelled to stretch out his hand to touch it, as if his touch would confirm it was canvas and not flesh. His fingers were less than an inch away from the painting; they were so close, in fact, that he could almost feel the heat from Victor's skin on his palm.

"Very life-like, isn't it?" muttered a voice from behind him.

Startled, Edwin turned to see a small balding man with large, buggy eyes. His hands were folded neatly in front of him. He stood slightly hunched over, as if his back was in pain. The subtle exaggeration of some of his facial features nearly reminded Edwin of a Christmas elf of sorts: the bucked teeth, the slightly pointed ears…bizarre.

"Y…yes. Very," Edwin replied.

"Ignado Ignacio," said the small man outstretching his hand. "Pleased to make your acquaintance. You must be Mr. Thimblewhistle. We spoke on the phone."

"Yes. Please, call me Ed," said Edwin.

"Very good. You may call me Iggy. If you will follow me, I will show you to your office. Mr. Von Hallow is anxious to meet you."

Edwin began to follow Iggy down the corridor to the elevator at the end of the hall. As they approached the elevator doors, he could not help but notice the distinct limp that Iggy attempted to conceal. Edwin felt it rude to inquire, though it was curious.

"How was your trip?" Iggy asked.

"Very well. I'm very excited to be here. We still have a great deal of unpacking to do, but things are coming along fine"

"Good, good."

As they entered the elevator, Iggy produced a small key from his pocket. He inserted it into a lock at the base of the keypad on the elevator board. As if things could not get any stranger, once he turned it, a button to the *thirteenth* floor appeared. The elevator quickly began to rise. Edwin could feel the tension in his stomach tighten in anticipation.

"On the way to floor thirteen: Sporting goods, Electronics and Fitness Equipment," Iggy said with a giggle. "So, I can't recall from your resume. Where did you graduate from?"

"I graduated from the University of Tennessee, located in Knoxville," Edwin replied.

"Nice. Go Big Orange," Iggy said with a smile.

"Oh, yeah. Orange and white. And what about yourself? Where did you go to school?"

"Actually, I was privately tutored. Believe it or not, I majored in Literature. Business never interested me, yet here I am."

"You know, I can tell that about you. You seem like a literary fellow," Edwin confirmed, attempting to be pleasant.

"Really? Well, thank you. I'll show you to your office," replied Iggy as the elevator opened.

Edwin saw an environment unlike the comfortable surroundings of the offices below. The whole area was quite dark and dimly lit. There were no windows at all, which Edwin found odd. The floor appeared to be covered in black carpet. There were only three offices and the one directly in the middle had a large, extravagant set of doors. Across the top of the door it read *Victor Von Hallow, President*. Edwin could not help but shudder at the sight—it was almost chilling.

"This, of course, is Mister Von Hallow's office, if you could not tell," Iggy stated, with another wheezy cackle. "My office is to the right, and yours is this way."

Edwin began to follow him toward the office to the left of Von Hallow's. Iggy opened the door and as they entered, Edwin saw barren walls and a large desk with a computer in the center of the room. Edwin walked to the desk and sat his case down.

"We apologize for the lack of decor. You see, Lillian Carlton, the previous V.P., left rather suddenly and her tastes were, well, eccentric. It took some time to get her things removed. Feel free to make this space your own. You may visit the Facilities office on the third floor and choose from a wide array of artwork and other items. Or you may bring your own. Though, we do ask that you refrain from displaying items of a religious nature. We try to maintain a very neutral environment in that manner. I am certain you understand."

"Of course," Edwin replied.

"Well, I will leave you to get settled. You will meet with Mister Von Hallow at ten o'clock. He will ring you when he is ready," Iggy stated. He reached into his jacket pocket and pulled out a key just like the one he had used on the elevator and walked to Edwin's desk. "Here is your elevator key. Please keep it secure as there is sensitive information on this floor."

"Certainly," Edwin replied.

"One last thing," Iggy began, "we believe that we have found and removed all of Lillian's belongings. Should you find anything of hers, you will be certain to let me know as soon as possible, won't you? We wouldn't like any sensitive information lying about."

Once Iggy was gone, Edwin breathed a sigh of relief. *What in the world is this place?* He was looking for a change, not a total alteration of life. This was definitely not the type of bank in which Edwin was used to working. It was indeed strange. Nevertheless, both he and Thelma needed the new surroundings and the higher income. A single parent was a hard thing to be, even harder than Vice President of a bank.

The Message in the Window

"You look like you haven't slept in days, child," Mimi said to Thelma, who sat at the breakfast table like a zombie. Thelma was floating somewhere between weariness and curiosity. She could not rid her mind of thoughts of her strange visitor. Even more, she couldn't quite determine if what she had seen was real or just a figment of her healthy imagination. "I didn't sleep well."

"Aw, I'd expect that on the first night in a new house. I would've been afraid, too. Did you sleep in your father's room?"

"No, I wanted to sleep in my room."

"Brave." Mimi scooped the sizzling bacon from the stovetop and placed it on a small platter. She looked at Thelma, noticing how her features were beginning to shed their child-like appearance, becoming more like a woman's, more like Juliana's. Mimi smiled. "Honey, you're growing up so fast. Your father did, too, you know. Where does the time go?" Mimi sat a plate of eggs, bacon, toast, and jam in front of Thelma. "Wanna play Scrabble in a bit?"

"Maybe. I don't know," Thelma replied.

Mimi sat down at the counter with her. "Honey, what's wrong. Tell me."

Any child knows that telling adults about unbelievable things often leads nowhere. But Thelma understood that Mimi was not like other adults. The thing she loved most about Mimi was her ability to see life through the eyes of a child. So, with a deep breath, Thelma reluctantly said, "I think…I think I heard things last night."

Mimi paused. "Well, this is a big old house and big old houses make all sorts of rude sounds during the night—just like *big old women*." Thelma tried to smile at Mimi's humor. "Actually, these old houses make the same noises all day; you just notice it more when it is dark and quiet, when your mind wanders."

Thelma moved her food around on her plate showing little interest. "No, it was something else."

Mimi looked at her inquisitively as she poured herself a mug of hot coffee. Then she sat down and touched Thelma's hand. "Well, okay, what was it?"

Thelma sighed. "Never mind. You won't believe me. I don't even believe me."

"Won't believe…? Lord, I never! Of course, I will."

Thelma sat her fork on her plate. "The moon looked weird, so I got up to get a closer look and I heard someone laughing—a girl, I think.

"Laughing?" Mimi asked.

"Yeah it sounded like she was outside, in the back yard. Then, my room got cold."

"I see. Honey, it could've been anything, really. I've heard birds before that sound like they're talking. Why…I heard one say my name once, plain as day. Lord, I about passed out. And the cold? Woo! This place can really get frigid. I wouldn't…"

"No, Mimi, I saw something. It knocked on my window…" Thelma began to explain.

"Thelma, honey, you could've just had a dream," Mimi suggested.

Growing upset, Thelma said, "Mimi, it's true! It knocked on my window and then…then it breathed on it and wrote…"

Mimi patted her hand. "Thelma, now I know you may think…"

"Oh, forget it!" Thelma huffed. "I shouldn't have said anything."

Mimi leaned back and cocked her eyebrow in a familiar way. "Now, you wait just a minute, young lady. You won't take that tone with me. I don't care *what* you think you saw."

Hurt, Thelma got up from the table and began to walk away. "Never mind," she muttered. "It's stupid."

"Now wait, Thelma. I am not saying that I don't, or I won't be…" Mimi began, but it was too late.

Thelma marched to the foyer and climbed the steps to her room. She had hardly touched her plate. Mimi took a deep breath and began straightening the kitchen and packing away the leftovers. In a way, she felt Thelma's overactive imagination regarding the Peterson Estate was her fault. Mimi had told stories to Thelma nearly every time she visited. Of course, if she had known that one day Thelma would live in the old house she would have never done such a thing.

Luckily, Edwin did not inherit Mimi's love for the macabre. He never cared that the Peterson house was the place the neighborhood children dared each other to visit on Halloween night. Why would he? Even Mimi knew it was all nonsense, just scary stories to tell in the dark…nothing more.

She shuddered to think that any of the Peterson Estate folklore could be real. The neighborhood had always been alive with ghost stories of the mansion. An old, abandoned house where someone had died—how could there not be a multitude of fantastic fabrications? It even had its own graveyard! All the kids told stories about the ghost of the little girl who drowned, the ghost they called *Dead Anna*. Even Mimi herself thought she had heard things, whispers in the darkness, familiar voices. But her adult mind could easily explain the events out of existence. Loving ghost stories was one thing—believing they were real was another thing altogether.

As the warm water from the sink flowed through her fingers, her mind began to walk to mysterious places where paranormal possibilities were breathing with life. What if the stories were true? What if witches did fly on brooms and cast evil spells? What if monsters did hide in closets and under beds? What if somewhere in the darkness…something was *waiting* for us?

BANG!

An old stray cat leapt from one of the trashcans by the back door causing it to tumble to the ground. Mimi jumped with fright as she let out a muffled yelp. Then she giggled in spite of herself. Wiping the water from her hands, she smiled and shook her head. Obviously, frightening oneself was fairly easy. She refilled her coffee and began to climb the steps in the foyer.

She tapped on Thelma's door and then stuck her head inside. "Are you still mad at me?"

Thelma sat peering out of the window into the cold winter morning. "No, Mimi. I'm not mad. It was just…so real. I saw it right here. It wrote, 'Hello, Thelma. I'm Dead Anna,'" Thelma placed her palm on the window. "Maybe I'm just losing it."

"Aw, honey, you're not losing it…you never *had* it," Mimi smiled.

Thelma smiled. "Well, I get that from you. You told me all those stories."

Mimi laughed. "True, but those stories aren't half as bad as those movies we sneak and watch behind your father's back." Mimi sat her coffee cup on the dresser and took a seat with Thelma at the window.

Thelma looked down and shook her head. "I know. I don't believe it either, but, Mimi, it's true. I swear. You know I wouldn't lie."

Mimi sighed then gave Thelma a playful nudge. It was a fact that though Thelma had a vivid imagination, she was not prone to lies. "So, you say it was at this window?"

"Yeah," Thelma said.

"This window right here?"

"Yes!" Thelma laughed. "Right there." Thelma sighed, got up, and began to walk to the door. There was a part of her that was comforted by the thought that it was all her imagination. "Never mind, Mimi. Let's just forget it. I scared myself is all."

"Now, hold on," Mimi said. She examined the windowpane for a moment, and then slowly climbed on top of the window seat to reach the window's lock. It took some force for her to loosen the old latch, but she was finally able to open it to the inside. The brisk wind whirled through the room, blowing the curtains to and fro.

"Mimi, what are you doing?" asked Thelma. "You don't have to jump. I forgive you."

"Ha, ha…you say whatever it was wrote on the glass, right?" Mimi asked as she stepped down to the floor.

"Aw, come on. Let's go downstairs. I'm hungry."

"Wait now, you're giving up too easily. Hand me that coffee."

Thelma handed her the warm coffee cup. "Mimi, if you fall Dad will kill me."

Mimi took a sip of hot coffee and held it in her mouth. Then, she knelt down to the icy glass and blew her hot breath upon it. Slowly, the writing faded into view, just as Thelma said. The two of them were motionless, captured by the sight.

Crash!

Thelma jumped as Mimi's coffee cup shattered on the floor.

Ring!

"Ah!" they both screamed, surprised by the phone.

"Dear Lord! Thelma…uh…would you grab a towel for that?" Mimi was shaken by what they had seen. "I'm sorry I made a mess on your floor. Let

me…let me get the phone." Mimi scampered to the hallway and picked up the phone. "Hello? Oh, oh, Eddie, it's you!" she said with an uneasy laugh. "Oh, everything is just wonderful. Couldn't be better."

As she mopped up the spilled coffee with a hand towel from the bathroom, Thelma could hear Mimi talking to her father on the phone. Now, not only could Mimi believe her, she could believe herself.

"Thelma, honey," Mimi called. "Your father's on the phone for you." Thelma walked into the hallway smiling. Mimi covered the receiver. "Young lady…don't mention this to your father. He'll put me in a home!" Mimi handed her the phone and then went to the bedroom to tend to the broken cup.

While Thelma spoke with Edwin, Mimi finished picking up the last pieces of the broken coffee mug. She closed and locked the window, then took a seat on the window bench studying the words on the glass as they began to fade away. Her adult mind began to seek explanations.

"So," Thelma said returning to the room.

"What?" Mimi replied.

"You believe me now?"

Mimi sighed. "Thelma…did you write on that window?"

"No!" Thelma said.

"Are you sure?"

"Mimi, how would I have reached that latch?"

Mimi thought for a moment. "Then it was one of the kids from the neighborhood. They're telling those Dead Anna stories all the time. They just wanted to scare the girl in the haunted house is all."

"But I didn't see anyone there. It's nearly three stories from the ground! I would've seen a ladder or something."

Mimi sighed. "Lord, I don't know."

Thelma sat down on her bed. "Come on, Mimi…don't you think it could be possible? You of all people?"

"What? Ghosts?"

"Yeah! What about all of those stories you've heard, the ones you've told us—couldn't just one of them be true?"

"You're so silly," Mimi said dismissively. Then she smiled. "Lord knows if ghosts did exist and this house had one, it would be Anna. She wouldn't allow another spirit near it!"

Suddenly, there was the scent of flowers—violets to be exact. Their subtle fragrance wafted throughout the entire room. Every now and then when Mimi felt alone or afraid, she would notice the smell of violets, even when there were none around. Anna had loved them.

Thelma could see nostalgia in Mimi's eyes. "I'm sorry she died."

Mimi took Thelma's hand. "Oh, honey, it's alright. That was forever ago. I met Anna when I was about your age. I met her the day Henry came out to sign the deal for this land with Mrs. Evermoore. Anna was such an adventurer, so brave. You think I have an imagination? Anna was something else. The stories she would make up! She had the type of imagination that got us into all sorts of trouble." Mimi pointed down from Thelma's window to the pool. "We practically lived at that swimming pool. It was where we spent most of our time in the warmer months. That was before she was…well, before the accident."

"How old was she?" Thelma asked.

Mimi stood up and sighed. "She was thirteen. Over the years I watched all these new houses come to be, all the new people arrive…and I watched this old place die. It broke my heart. After your daddy moved away and your grandpa passed, it got a little lonely. I think that's why I was so excited when this place came up for sale."

"Do you believe I am telling the truth?" asked Thelma sincerely.

Mimi turned to her and smiled. "I believe you're convinced that what you saw was real, and in that, yes I do believe you. We'll have to remain open to all possibilities and wait to see what is actually true. It's only fair. Am I right?"

Thelma thought for a moment and then smiled. "Yeah, I can live with that."

"Now," Mimi said walking toward the door, "an imagination must always be open to unimaginable things. You need to be brave, honey. Don't be scared. Who knows, if ghosts do exist and one is here, it may be more afraid of you than you are of it."

"Well, what should I do if it comes back?"

Mimi thought for a moment, and then smiled. "Say, 'Hello…'"

The Curious Victor Von Hallow

After his conversation with Thelma, Edwin hopped into the elevator to visit the Facilities Department. There he packed up a box of essentials that included various office supplies, including file folders, paper clips, note pads, pens, binders, and a plethora of other items. He used his "special key" to get back to the thirteenth floor. After fumbling through his office door, he walked to his desk and dropped the box on top of it. Then he rounded the desk, took his seat, and began organizing his workspace.

He had a format for where common things were to be placed. This way, he could reach for them without having to think. Staplers always rested to his upper right. Pens were kept in a coffee mug to his left. His desk calendar always faced him. Out of habit, paperclips were hidden in the drawer. At his other bank in Indiana, paperclips were nearly like currency. They were so rare that you could almost bargain with them. Therefore, he always kept them safe and hidden away from thieving eyes.

Opening the drawer to his left, he began to put the large box of clips inside when his elbow caught the edge. The box tumbled from his hand, scattering his precious paperclips around his feet. Mumbling in aggravation, he got on his knees and began fishing for them. With a *bang*, he whacked his head on the open drawer as he began to rise, causing him to grumble louder.

When he stood up, he noticed something in the drawer, something shiny. He reached in and retrieved a small pair of reading glasses. They were made of brass, it seemed, thin, elegant in appearance, obviously belonging to a woman. The lenses were a pinkish-red hue. Naturally, he concluded that they must have belonged to his predecessor. He sat down at his desk, unfolded them, and put them on. He could barely see a thing. He gazed at himself in the reflection of his window.

"That is just a hot mess," he said to himself with a giggle. He removed them and tossed them into the orange Facilities box so he could turn them in, just like the odd Iggy had requested.

The phone rang, causing the red indicator light to blink. He looked at the clock—ten o'clock precisely. He picked up the phone.

"Hello, Edwin Thimblewhistle," he said confidently.

"Ah, Edwin. This is Victor," said a sly voice.

"Good morning, Mr. Von Hallow."

"Yes…well, it is now time for our first meeting and you are two minutes late."

"Pardon?" Edwin said with a panic.

"Just kidding, ol' boy. Just kidding. Please step to my office. You can't miss it."

"Yes, Mr. Von Hallow."

He quickly gathered his new note pad and pen and bolted for the door. He hurried down the hallway to the large set of doors, but oddly, there were no doorknobs or handles with which to open them. Edwin was puzzled—he hadn't noticed that fact before. So, he tried pushing them, but that didn't work. He wondered if he needed another strange key. Suddenly, from the other side of the door, he heard a voice say, "Enter." Edwin stepped back as the doors began to creak open.

The space was magnificent, commanding, and foreboding. The scent of exotic incense filled the air. A massive fireplace was the focal point of the room. Above it was an enormous sculpture of a serpent made of porcelain. On top of the fireplace mantle were numerous ornaments, photographs, and wooden boxes. Displayed in the center was what appeared to be a very large, sophisticated apothecary chest with bulky doors and a silver keyhole. Seated directly in front of the fireplace at a beautifully expensive cherry wood desk was Victor himself. His chair was like a throne. He sat glaring at Edwin, who must have seemed like a small mouse shivering in front of a hungry cat.

"Come in, come in," the deep voice cooed.

Edwin entered trying to smile. "Hello, Mr. Von Hallow," he said stretching out his hand.

Victor's cold skin accentuated the icy disdain of his manner as they shook hands. "Please, call me Victor."

Edwin cocked his eyebrow with surprise. "Well, thank you, Victor."

"You seem stunned."

"Well, yes. I was told not to call you 'Victor.'"

"Rubbish. By whom?"

"Well, a few people, actually." Edwin replied.

"Well, those *people* aren't the new Vice President of this financial institution, are they now?"

"No, sir," Edwin said.

"Splendid! Now, take a seat, Edwin. Let's get to know one another."

Edwin took a seat in front of the desk as Victor rose, gracefully making his way to the fireplace. He opened one of the small boxes and extracted a cigar. He appeared to be extending the box towards Edwin.

"I'm sorry, Victor, I don't smoke."

"I didn't offer," Victor replied in a shrewd manner. "So, Edwin, are you liking your new home?"

"Yes, very much. It's such a wonderful old house; full of history. According to my mother, who's lived beside it all of her life, it's been there for over fifty years," Edwin proudly said.

"Fifty-seven to be exact," Victor corrected. "Before that ostentatious house was constructed, the land had previously been in use by the same family for…my, I believe nearly two hundred years."

"Really? Do you have an interest in the house? It sounds like you know a lot about it."

"Not really…only the land. Yes, yes. I was actually in the market to purchase it until you were awarded the contract," Victor stated.

This revelation made Edwin uncomfortable, to say the least, so he tried to be humorous by saying, "Well, you were a fierce competitor, Victor. If not for my mom's help, I don't think we would have been able to bid on it." Victor didn't respond to the awkward comment. "Uh…were you planning to remodel it?"

"Oh, yes…yes, indeed. I was going to knock it down and erect a grand shopping center. But, no matter. Bravo to you, Edwin. Are you from Indiana?"

"Actually, I'm from here."

"Really? Intriguing. Why did you move away from *little ol' Raven Den*?"

"Actually, it was because of my wife. She was originally from Indiana and attended college at the University of Tennessee at the same time I did. We both moved to Indiana when we married after graduation."

"You're married? How lovely," Victor stated, retrieving a bulky silver lighter from his desktop.

"Actually, my wife passed away."

"Oh," Victor solemnly replied. "Well…marriage is overrated, dear boy. There are things far worse than death…like *divorce*." He sat back down at his desk and blew a large cloud of smoke into the air. "So, go on, go on."

"Well," Edwin continued, confused by Victor's lack of sentiment. "After my wife passed last year, we decided to move here to be near my mother."

"We? You and…your daughter?"

"Yes, how did you know?"

"Oh, I do know some things about you, Edwin. The important things, at least," Victor said devilishly. Edwin was obviously unsettled by the statement. "I searched your professional biography on the *Googie* and found it posted on your previous bank's website," he finished.

"Google," Edwin corrected without thinking.

"Yes, that's what I said. Google. So, your daughter?"

Edwin leaned back. "Thelma."

"Thelma…what a lovely name. Thelma."

"Yes, she just turned eleven last month."

"Eleven! Well, my, my. She will be starting her collegiate studies before you know it," Victor laughed.

"Yes, I'm sure," Edwin said. "So, what about you, Victor?"

"Yes?"

"Tell me about yourself."

"Oh, what is there to tell, really? Nothing much, nothing much. I run this modest little bank."

"I don't know if I would call it modest, Victor. Hallow Savings & Loan is the top banking institution in this region. Since Highwater National Bank took you under their wing, your stock has maintained the largest growth of any bank in this part of the state, outbidding other National lenders in the area. It is a very crucial part of the banking industry in Raven Den," Edwin stated proudly. Victor appeared to be impressed. "I use Google, too."

"Really? Oh, you flatter me, Edwin. I hadn't noticed. I don't keep up with all the specifics of this bank," Victor said, laughing proudly. "That is why I hired you."

"Well, I've worked in the banking industry my entire professional life, Victor. I plan to do a good job," Edwin said.

Victor crushed his cigar. "Goodie. I am so glad to hear it. Now, there is a task that I would like for you to do for me today. I need to know the details on how our Merchant Processing Division is doing these days. I will need the last twelve months of volume, expense, and profit for the division. Additionally, I need to know how many merchant accounts we carry that process over $500,000.00 annually in electronic payments. You can see Miss Maggie Jordan in the Facilities Department who should be able to obtain the files for you. Do you know where it is?"

"Yes, I just picked up some supplies earlier. When do you need the report?" Edwin asked scribbling in his notepad.

"By Monday afternoon?"

"No problem. I'll get started on it now."

Edwin rose from his seat and Victor turned to him. Edwin smiled and outstretched his hand.

"I look forward to working with you."

"Oh, me too, me too, Edwin. Carry on," Victor sang. Edwin and Victor shook hands and Edwin turned to leave. But once again, the doors would simply not cooperate with Edwin. He looked back at Victor with a smile. "Oh, yes, my apologies. *Exit*," Victor muttered with a wave of his hand.

The doors opened and Edwin stepped into the hallway. As the doors shut, Victor sat down and began drumming his fingers on the wood of his desk, pondering, plotting.

"We are going to have to take care of this little girl, Iggy…this…*Thelma*," Victor said.

A shadow on the floor floated to Victor's desk and began to stand upright. As it took shape, it began to speak.

"Yes, master. Yes, I was listening. Thelma, it was," replied the figure.

"Yes, exactly," Victor said peering at the black object. The blackness stood motionless, hovering beside Victor's chair. "Oh, for the love of cheese and rice, Iggy, stop being so dramatic! You know I hate talking to you when you drift like that!"

With a small poof, Iggy appeared, taking the place of where the blackness once stood. His subtle facial characteristics were now more pronounced and elf-like: ears sharply pointed, eyes slanted, almost ghoulish.

"Sorry, master," Iggy replied. "Solomon said the girl would be trouble. Have you been able to locate him?"

"Blast it, no. I have not seen Solomon. Crafty thing he is."

"He has been missing for two days now."

Victor rolled his eyes. "I am aware of that, Iggy. Luckily, he doesn't have all of the information."

"But he does know some things. He could use them against us. Last night was the Emerald Moon, just as he predicted! He said that the little girl would arrive on the eve of the Emerald Moon. He said…"

Victor motioned for Iggy to cease rambling. "Yes, I am aware of the Emerald Moon, Iggy. As for what Solomon may know, I have protection from his accusations—he cannot even write my name. He'll be able to tell no one." Victor rose from his desk and began to pace. "It is no coincidence that this Thelma has taken ownership of the land of Evermoore on the very evening the Emerald Moon arose in the sky. Yet, I feel no power from her," Victor replied rubbing his beard.

"Yes, but Solomon said she would be the Defender," Iggy nervously replied.

"But Solomon said a great many useless things. Regardless—Felix and I have made assurances to one another, and I intend to deliver. I cannot allow anything to stand in the way of our arrangement. Especially not this child."

"I will miss you, Master," Iggy lied.

"I'm sure," Victor skeptically replied. "But it will soothe you to know that after Felix grants me the power I deserve, I'll be with you *forever*…wherever you go." An eerie grin stretched across Victor's face.

Iggy did not like his expression. "So…so, what do we do?"

"We must take care of her immediately. We cannot risk this child being the Defender of the Dead. Now, as we know, the wicked cannot step onto the soil of Evermoore and the girl is protected from harm while in the house. So, unfortunately, I will have to rely on you."

"But I'm far too wicked to step onto the land," Iggy said.

Victor shot him an impatient gaze, then walked to his desk, opened a drawer, and pulled out a fuzzy object with a cotton tail and long floppy ears. "Iggy…what is this?"

"It's a Snugglebunny…"

"A Snugglebunny," Victor cooed. "And where did I find it?"

"In my desk."

"In your desk." Victor tossed the toy back into his drawer. "You are as wicked as a butterfly. That is why you are useful to me. You are evil because I *want* you to be."

Iggy gulped. "So, what do I do?"

Victor walked to the fireplace mantle and pulled a crystal bottle from one of the boxes that rested upon it. A churning, dark substance was inside. "Simple. All you have to do is go to the house and open this bottle. What is contained inside will do the rest."

"Just open it?"

"Just open it. That should be simple enough." He handed the bottle to Iggy and then looked down to him. "Sadly, all of this could have been avoided." The comment made Iggy tense. "We would not be going through this right now if you had been watching Lillian. We could have secured the contract on the home after that old fool, Peterson, kicked the bucket. If I owned that property now, we would never have to worry about this girl. There would be a lovely bull dozer tearing that house to shreds right now. I would be throwing that loud-mouthed writing desk in the wood chipper. No. Worries. At all."

"But, master, I tried, I did," Iggy said. "But Lillian didn't submit the final offer. It was all *her* fault. Thimblewhistle signed. There was nothing else I could do. I even doubled the price. I told…"

"Hush, hush, my dear Iggy. I was just pointing out the obvious. No matter now. I no longer need Solomon. And that foolish, lying Lillian? Well, let's just say she is no longer a bother, she nor any other member of the Board. We will take care of Edwin's daughter tonight and then we will run him out of the house and destroy it." Victor sat back down at his desk. "We need to be attentive to *Mister Timberwassle*. He will need time to grieve after all."

"Thimble…*whistle*," Iggy corrected.

"Yes, yes, yes. That's what I said!"

As the sinister meeting between Iggy and Victor continued to unfold, Edwin was on his way back to the Facilities Department to return his supply box and meet with Ms. Jordan as instructed. Something was definitely odd about this Victor character, though Edwin could not place his finger on it. All the same, any fool could see that there was something outlandish, something distinctly bizarre about Von Hallow, about the entire bank.

Edwin was shocked that someone would want to buy that wonderful old house only to rip it down, all that history just gone in the blink of an eye. Victor did not appear to be one who was moved by history at all. Was Victor actually untrustworthy or simply an eccentric character with too much time and power on his hands? Only time would tell.

Regardless, one of the most unusual things was the missing V.P. who had previously held Edwin's office. What had she done to be terminated? What happened to her? Was she whisked away by aliens to another planet? Was she locked away in a dungeon guarded by dragons?

It was just one of the many mysteries Edwin was beginning to uncover.

The 1st Death

The grandfather clock in the foyer showed twelve minutes after nine. Thelma could see it from her location in the sitting room. She and Mimi sat together patiently waiting on Edwin. Thelma scribbled in her new diary while listening to music, and Mimi read the newspaper, the two trying to pass the time. It was terribly late for her father to still be working. They had tried to contact his office phone and his cell phone, but there had been no answer.

Thelma could envision that familiar scene replaying over and over again in her mind: the doorbell ringing, Mimi answering the door to a policeman who would let them know that Edwin was gone, a victim of yet another tragic accident.

Then what would Thelma do?

In many ways, she had not completely accepted losing her mother. That tragedy was something buried deep in the soil of her mind. Subconsciously, Thelma forced herself to believe that her mother was simply away, on a trip bound to return at any moment—a reunion that unfortunately would never take place. It would be far too traumatic for her to lose her father, too—especially now. Edwin was her protector, her hero, but she would never admit she was still her father's *little girl*. In reality, she could not imagine life without him.

Tick-tick-tick…the minutes crept by. Through the window Thelma could see that the moon had returned to its normal state. Then her eyes fixated on the brass second hand of the clock. She noticed that when it would point downward to the number six, light would brightly reflect from its polished surface. As she became hypnotized by it, her mind unwillingly began to drift back to the horrors of the previous year.

It was two days before Christmas, which happened to fall on what Thelma knew as *Chocolate Cake Night*, her favorite night of the week. Her mother made the cake from scratch with a recipe that could not be duplicated. Snow had begun to fall, but her mother knew that Thelma would have been disappointed if there was no cake, so she decided to quickly run to the store to get some missing ingredients.

As time began to slip away, Thelma noticed her father growing increasingly worried. Outside the snow peppered down like confectioner's sugar while Thelma sat staring out of the living room window, waiting for the glow of headlights to shine through the white snow and twinkling Christmas lights.

Edwin paced back and forth in front of the fireplace lined with stockings. He kept attempting to reach Juliana on her cell phone, but there was never an answer. He even began calling family and friends, asking if she had stopped by to visit and wait out the bad weather, but everyone said they had not seen her.

Eventually, Thelma saw headlights slowly approaching from the end of the street. She could feel joy well up inside her as she leapt from the couch and ran through the living room nearly knocking Edwin to the ground.

"Dad," Thelma shouted. "Dad, Mom is home! I see her coming!"

Thelma was so enthusiastic that Edwin immediately believed her. They looked from the window and saw the headlights pulling into the driveway. Edwin walked toward the door, preparing to help Juliana with groceries. Oddly, the doorbell rang before he reached the door.

Why would her mother ring the doorbell?

Thelma thought that maybe her mother had armloads of bags and could not open the door. From the look on his face, her father was not expecting that to be the case. The doorbell rang once again, but he did not answer. He laid his hand on the doorknob and took a deep breath. As the door finally opened, Thelma could hear a man's voice.

"Are you Mr. Thimblewhistle?" the voice asked.

"Yes," her father replied.

Edwin stepped out to the landing and pulled the door closed behind him. Thelma stood there, waiting, feeling as if her legs were made of fire. For some reason, she was ready to run—from what, she was unaware. What she did know

was that at any moment she might need to get away…and quickly. It felt like hours passing instead of minutes, but her limbs failed to respond. She stood there, motionless, helpless.

In the following days, the adults didn't tell Thelma much, only that her mother was entering the highway as the snow began coming down. There was a truck, one of the big trucks, which could not stop in time. It was an accident, a tragedy. The family spent that Christmas at the hospital waiting for Juliana to open her eyes. There was no Christmas. Before the New Year arrived, her mother was gone forever…and Thelma did not understand. She was allowed to look upon her mother one last time. Thankfully, the tubes and wires had been removed. Though there was no life, her mother's hand was still warm. It was the very definition of peace—calm and serene. And at that moment, a hole was torn into the fabric of Thelma's heart.

The doorbell rang, startling Thelma from her thoughts. Looking down at her diary, she had written nearly an entire page without realizing it. Anxiety pulled her from the floor as she removed her headphones. Mimi knew what was going through Thelma's mind, because it was going through her mind as well.

"Now, honey, just calm down and sit," Mimi said with a smile.

Thelma sat back down. Mimi straightened her dress and walked to the foyer toward the front doors. Thelma leaned back on the sofa as far as she could to be able to see. Mimi was almost to the doors when the doorbell rang again. Thelma's throat felt tight and her skin unusually cold.

Mimi unlocked the bolts, grabbed the handle, and opened the doors. A sudden rush of heat covered Thelma's body as she saw Edwin stumbling into the house with papers overloading his arms.

Edwin struggled with his briefcase and computer bag. "I *never* thought I was going to get out of there!"

"Oh! Thank goodness you're home! We were beginning to get worried. Why are you so late?" Mimi asked as she shut the doors behind him.

Edwin dropped his overflowing armload of paperwork to the table and sat his cases on the floor. Then he slowly walked into the sitting room and fell onto the sofa where Thelma sat. She leapt for his neck, hugging him tightly.

"Ouch!" he said, acting as if her embrace hurt. "Your father has been put through the ringer today, Pumpkin."

"You should have called," Thelma mumbled into his shirt.

"I know, and I didn't hear you call because my phone was on vibrate, and I was trying to get these files…" Then, guilt fell upon him. He realized that he had frightened his daughter by not calling, and after the loss of Juliana, that was unacceptable. He closed his eyes and hugged her tightly. "I'm…I'm sorry, Pumpkin. Okay? Promise—from now on, I'll always call. Cross my heart."

Thelma leaned back and smiled at him. "So, how as the first day of school?"

"Awful! That's what it was," he said with a sigh.

Rattle, rustle…

Though she couldn't be certain, Thelma believed that her father's briefcase made a noise.

"First," Edwin began, "there is this little freaky looking dude name Iggy…"

Rustle, rustle…

With a *pop* the case rattled again and fell completely open, sending papers sailing across the floor.

"Oh, and it just keeps getting better! I swear, I can't keep this thing closed! There's a rat in my briefcase," Edwin said with defeat.

"Good! Now we can get a cat!" Thelma said with a huge smile.

"Pumpkin, I know you want a cat, but you know how allergic I am. Why not a puppy or a pony? Don't girls want ponies anymore?" he pleaded as he began rounding up papers.

"Puppies turn into dogs and dogs stink. And a pony? Dad, really. Do I look like a pony-type of girl? A horse can't cuddle in my bed with me," Thelma said.

"Well, you could sleep in the stable with it instead," Edwin replied. "That would be better, actually. We could just throw down some hay for you."

Mimi laughed as she helped Edwin gather up his papers and get them tucked neatly into his briefcase. "Did you meet your boss today?"

"Oh, yes! Yes, I did."

"And what do we think about him?" Mimi asked.

"We think he is two sandwiches short of a picnic, that's what we think," Edwin said with a smile.

Out of the corner of her eye, Thelma saw a glimmer, a reflection of light from an object that was scampering toward the library, like a little *silver mouse.* She walked to the edge of the door and peered into the foyer to get a closer look, but nothing was there.

Edwin proceeded to tell them about the day: the odd elevator, the strange little assistant, the missing V.P., and, of course, the sinister Von Hallow. "It's going to be like working in a funhouse! Don't get me wrong; all other areas of the bank itself are normal and run efficiently. For example, I met with the

Senior Manager of Facilities, Maggie, and she was perfectly fine—not a thing out of place. Her floor was neat and her department operated like any other Facilities area I have been in. But the madness happening on my floor—*the thirteenth floor*, nonetheless—well, it's just crazy. I felt like *Alice in Wonderland*."

"Man…I want to go to work with you, Dad!" Thelma laughed.

"Lord, me too!" Mimi chimed in.

"Oh, I wish, ladies," Edwin said. "But, unfortunately, Lillian Carlton, wherever she is now, has left the Merchant Division in a huge mess. That's what all this stuff is. Believe it or not, I have to go through all of this paperwork and there is yet *another* file that Maggie is trying to locate for me."

They gathered into the kitchen where they enjoyed Mimi's pot roast, Italian bread, and mashed potatoes. They all sat at the huge island in the kitchen with their plates and listened to Edwin confess even more details about his strange day, especially more particulars of the enigmatic Mr. Von Hallow. They talked and laughed until nearly eleven o'clock that night. Thelma wasn't to start her new school until after the holidays, so Edwin didn't mind her staying up later in the evening, which was fine with Thelma, who was too distracted to sleep. It had been an interesting day, to say the least.

Mimi stretched. "It's getting late. Why don't you see your old grandma out, dear."

The cool air filled Thelma's nose as they opened the front door. "Mimi," Thelma said. "What should I do tonight?"

"Darling, that's up to you. But I think you need to sleep in your father's room tonight, just until we can see what all of this truly is, you know? But, like we agreed, we have to remain open either way. Right?"

Thelma knew Mimi was absolutely correct. "Yeah, okay. What if I see something again? What if it says, 'Thelllmmmaaa'?" she moaned, waving her arms above her head like a phantom.

"Well…offer it something to eat. Give it some tea. Be polite. Remember, you *are* Southern, after all."

Her father was perfectly fine with her rooming with him that evening. Together they walked down to his room and she climbed into his large bed. Now that she had the security of his company, Thelma's fatigue finally overwhelmed her. It was not difficult at all to go to sleep. As a matter of fact, she drifted away in a manner of minutes, even before he had returned from brushing his teeth. He smiled and tucked the blankets around her. He, too, was fast asleep before long.

Later into the night, a voice through the darkness awoke her. She rubbed her dry, tired eyes and looked around the room. Her father was beside her snoring loudly. Focusing her vision, she immediately looked to the window and saw nothing there. She sighed and flopped back down on her pillow.

"Thelma?"

She sprang to full attention. Indeed it was a voice—the voice of her mother.

"Thelma, where are you?" Juliana called.

Carefully, she crawled from the bed and left her father's room. She could still hear her mother outside calling to her. It sounded as if she was in the back yard. Though her mind was wary, her heart forced her forward; she felt compelled to find her mother. She quickly ducked into her room and slid on her coat and shoes and then down the steps she went.

"Thelma, help me. I need you…"

Thelma slowly opened the door and stepped onto the front porch. "Mom?" she called out after she shut the door behind her.

"Thelma…I'm here…in the garden."

A dense fog surrounded the area in front of her making it nearly impossible to see ahead. She stepped from the porch and began to warily make her way around the house. "Mom, is that you?"

"Yes, Thelma. I need you to help me. I'm trapped…"

Thinking her mother was in danger, her pace quickened. She stretched out her arms, feeling into the fog for Juliana. "I'm coming! Mom, hold on. I'm coming!"

She stumbled through the fog for what seemed like an eternity. Then she heard another noise.

Hissssss…

It sounded like snakes slithering along the ground around her feet. Then out of the shadows came a horrible laughter and a different voice. It mocked her.

"Poor, poor, Thelma," it croaked.

"Who's there?" Thelma called. "Mom?"

"Mom? Mommy…I want my mommy…"

"Shut up!" Thelma shouted.

"Shut up!" it called in a mocking tone.

The fog became thicker, surrounding her. She called for Juliana once again, but there was no answer, only the voices obnoxiously calling back to her. Suddenly, she heard a crack, as if a pane of glass was buckling under her weight.

"*Thelma! Open your eyes…now!*" said yet another voice she had never heard before, the voice of a girl. "*Open your eyes, Thelma. Now!*"

The fog began to lift away from her and she could see she was standing in the middle of the dark, frozen swimming pool, the ice cracking around her feet. She began to panic. What was she going to do? It seemed like with every breath she took, another crack would appear. She slowed her breathing and stood perfectly still.

"Hello?" she softly called to the voice, but there was no answer. Whoever it was simply had to help her.

Crack…snap…crack!

"Help!" Thelma shouted. The ice crunched further with the force of her cry. It seemed no matter how cautious her movements were the ice was bound to give way. "Dad! Dad, help…Ahhh!"

The ice broke away, sending her plunging into the icy waters below. She tried very hard to hold her breath, but the iciness overwhelmed her. She kicked and kicked, trying to make it back to the surface, but the water was littered with large vines and leaves. They seemed to grab her, hold her, as if they wanted her to drown. She could not break away from their tangling grip. The cold water filled her lungs for the first time and she began to cough, but it did her no good. There was no air, only water. Through the bubbling liquid, she could hear the taunting voices again, laughing at her.

Then her panic began to subside. Thelma began to feel oddly tranquil, almost at peace. At that moment, she realized she was dying. Through the water a gloomy, slithering creature came toward her. It studied her for a moment and then bit into her chest. It pulled and tugged at her soul, tearing her spirit from her body as it prepared to devour it.

Out of nowhere, with a sharp slice she could see the blade of a sickle sever the creature's black head from its body. Screams resonated through the waters as the thing dissipated into the liquid allowing her soul to be freed. Through the murky waters she could see a dark, cloaked figure near her. It took her gently by the hand, and as it did, she could feel the warmth of life leaving her body, dispelling into the liquid around her. And remarkably, she did not feel afraid. She simply felt…peaceful.

Slowly and steadily, Thelma's eyes began to close. The figure did not leave her side. She could see that the figure was dressed in a black, flowing robe with a large hood that hid its face. It continued to hold her by the hand as it led her. A light began to appear before Thelma. Brighter and brighter it grew. The gloom dissipated before it; the cruel voices cried out in pain and faded away.

The light grew so intense she could no longer look into it. Warmth enveloped her like a blanket.

She no longer felt nervous.

She no longer felt afraid.

She only felt peace.

Suddenly, Thelma was standing before three entryways. She noticed that the door to the left led down and the door to the right led up. Something was approaching her from the door in the center. Figures made of iridescent light floated around her, helping to guide her to a new destination. They looked like they were made of clouds. She did not know where they were taking her, but she felt as if she belonged there in the comfort of the light for eternity. Juliana was somewhere waiting for her—she knew that. As they led her into the entryway in the center, Thelma found herself on a road, surrounded by light and white flowers of every kind. She was compelled to walk forward, towards the source of the light.

As she began to do so, something stopped her. She turned to see figures standing on either side of her. They gently took her by the arms, advising her to remain still. Then she noticed a shadow moving in front of her, a small figure approaching from the distance. The intensity of the light dimmed slightly, and as it did she could see a tiny, little man.

"Hello, hello, hello, little girl," said the petite man.

He was dressed all in white with a white moustache that was nearly larger than he was. His white hair was thinning on top and he had small spectacles that sat regally on his quaint button nose. Embroidered on his jacket was the odd emblem of the star and moons that she had seen on her new diary and the desk in the library.

"Allow me to introduce myself. I am Beauregard Whittleton—Director of Arrivals to the *Neither Realm*."

Thelma cocked a suspicious eyebrow. "The Neither what?"

"The Neither Realm. It means you're neither *here*, nor *there*. And if you're not here, well, you can't be there neither. Understand?"

"Oookay. If you say so."

He presented a small white book bound in gold thread. He opened it and began flipping through the pages. "Ah! And you are one Miss Thelma Thimblewhistle, correct?"

"Yeah," Thelma responded confidently.

"Oh, my, my, my. It says here that you're *very early*. Very early, indeed," replied the shocked Beauregard. "Typically, if a child is scheduled, I like to meet

him or her beforehand. Sometimes the transition can be very scary for a child, more so than for an adult."

"Okay…so, out of curiosity, how early am I?" Thelma asked.

"Now, that is for me to know, Miss Thimblewhistle." He rustled through his book, adjusting his glasses and studying deeply. She watched patiently. "Oh…interesting. I see. Emerald Moon. It is *you*, after all. You're going to be quite busy, quite busy indeed. Says here we have some work to do before you return home. *Anna* will be assigned to you. But for now, you will need to come with me." Beauregard took Thelma gently by the hand. The figures let go of her and allowed her to follow.

"What is the Emerald Moon?" Thelma asked.

"Important. Very important. This way."

Thelma continued to follow. "Okay…who's Anna?"

"You will find out about her soon enough. Trust me. The girl drives me to distraction."

"Why did those people not have faces? Can they talk without a mouth?" Thelma asked as she followed Beauregard.

"They do, they do. It is *you* who cannot see their face or hear their words…at least not yet, anyway," he replied. He stopped her in front of a large elegant white door with a golden handle. "The room before you is the Neither Realm's *Room of Arcanum* for which I have no key. Inside is an influence or gift, if you will, for special souls."

"So, why are we here if you don't have a key?"

"Well, *you* can open it. Inside will be your influence, your special gift. It is different for everyone who is to acquire it. It will unlock at your touch."

Thelma looked at him oddly. She didn't quite understand, but then again, she didn't grasp anything that was taking place. So, she stretched out her hand and took hold of the large door knob. The cracking of unlocking bolts sounded through the air. The door swung open to reveal a circular room of white stone with a large pillar in its center. Atop the pillar was a large, swirling, iridescent light. It was almost as if it was spinning within itself. Beauregard took her by the hand and led her inside and together they walked to the pillar.

"Behold, child. It is the *Secret*, the substance of all things wonderful in all worlds. You'll need to touch it for it to work."

Though she was afraid to do so, she raised her hand and inserted it into the mass. It felt as if her skin was being touched by thousands of butterflies. She giggled. The sensation was so peculiar that she withdrew her hand at first. Then, looking to Beauregard, she once again took hold of the light. It began to move over her body like a warm blanket. She could see nothing but the brightness, but it did not hurt her eyes to look at it.

Thelma felt confident, radiant.

And most importantly—she felt *alive*.

Resurrection

"She'll be fine, Mr. Thimblewhistle. We want to keep her for the next forty-eight hours to make certain she doesn't develop pneumonia, of course."

"Sure."

"She is a very lucky little girl. It is hard to tell how long she was gone. In all actuality, it was the frozen water that probably saved her."

"Can you tell if there is any…damage?"

Thelma could hear her father's voice and another she did not recognize. She was suddenly aware of the world around her but was unable to move or open her eyes.

"It is uncertain, really. We never know until the patient is fully cognizant. Then we can measure brain abnormalities, if any. She is a young girl, Mr. Thimblewhistle. Her EKG and EEG came out normal and we are awaiting the results of her MRI. I feel fairly confident that she will be just fine. But, we will need to run some more tests."

"Thank you, Doctor."

"Ed, I'll sit with her. You go down and get something to eat," Mimi said.

Her father agreed and Thelma heard him leave the room with the doctor.

Brain damage?

Thelma hoped she didn't have anything like that. Her chest did feel very sore and her lungs felt sensitive and raw. However, all in all, she felt fairly relaxed. She was simply overjoyed to still be alive after the accident. Now if she could only remember what had happened. There was so much she could not recall, so many scattered memories. Why had she been outside? Voices. She remembered voices. What did they say? Thelma heard Mimi move a chair closer to her bed and sat down beside her.

"Goodness, little girl, you certainly gave me quite a scare," said Mimi patting Thelma's hand.

Thelma found enough strength to move her hand under Mimi's. She even began to open her eyes.

"Thelma?"

"Hi, Mimi," Thelma replied in a very scratchy voice. Her throat was quite sore.

"Dear Lord, honey, how are you feeling?"

"Fine…I don't have brain damage, do I?"

Mimi chuckled. "Well, nothing beyond what was already there, I'm sure."

Thelma smiled. "How's Dad?"

"Oh, he's fit to be tied, your father. He was hysterical. He told me that he heard you yelling and by the time he got down there you had somehow managed to get out of the pool."

"I got out?"

"That's what he said. He said you were lying on the ground beside the pool, ice cold, and soaked to the bone. Of course, we're wondering what you were even doing *at* the pool at that time of the night…alone."

Then she could remember the pool. She had fallen into the pool. She remembered the cold water. If she was out of the water when she was discovered, she had either managed to climb out herself without realizing it, or someone (or something) had saved her. "I can't remember," she said. "I don't know what happened."

"Well, it's fine, honey. I'm just tickled purple that you're okay."

At that moment, Edwin entered the room carrying two cups of coffee and a couple of sandwiches. Noticing Thelma was awake, he immediately rushed to her bedside. He fumbled to hand the sandwiches and coffees to Mimi. "Thelma! How are you feeling? Are you okay?"

"Great news!" Mimi began. "She's certainly no sillier than she was before. So, her noggin is apparently intact."

Thelma smiled.

"Good, good. Thank God. How are you feeling?" Edwin asked again, smiling wide.

"Fine. My chest hurts a little and my throat is sore," Thelma muttered. "But I'm doing okay." She delivered a *thumbs up*.

Her father's eyes glazed with fresh tears and his strong voice cracked with the pressure of his emotion. "Wonderful!"

"Dad, I don't remember what happened. I don't know how I got out there."

"Shhh, shhh, now. You just rest. We'll talk about it later," he replied rubbing her head. He reached over, covered her with another blanket, and tucked her in tight. Mimi smiled. Thelma didn't think she had ever seen her father so thrilled to see her. It made her feel very warm inside. This man, who was so strong, so domineering, was wrapped around his little girl's finger. And she loved it. "You get some rest now. The doctor said that he wanted to keep you for a couple of days just to be on the safe side. Mimi and I are going to be right here with you."

Thelma began to stir. "But, your job."

"It is all taken care of. Don't you worry about that," he said. "Now, get some sleep. We'll be here when you wake up."

Thelma smiled. She nestled in the bed and closed her eyes. Edwin continued to stroke her hair. And she slowly drifted to sleep hoping to remember what had led her to this destination.

A Vast Celebration

Victor angrily paced the floor while Iggy cowered in the corner, hiding behind a plant. He would occasionally stop his pacing and turn to Iggy as if he were about to yell aloud. Then he would change his mind and continue to pace instead. "You!...I cannot believe!...What am I!?...OH!" he said falling into his chair with a thud, his face red with anger.

"M…M…Master, I tried, I promise," Iggy pleaded. "I opened the bottle, just as you said. The blackness came out and called to her. Once she was outside, it pulled her all the way down to the bottom of the water. She wasn't breathing! It had her soul—I saw it! Then something took her, something very scary that had on a dark robe with a big hood and…"

Victor's hand slammed the top of the desk. "And she lived! I can *feel* her power. She touched the Secret. I bet that pompous Whittleton just handed it to her, as if it were nothing. Her soul was to have been obliterated! But, *no*. Now, not only did she make it to the Neither Realm, she's been gifted! Felix and his Boogey Men are going to be furious! What am I to do?"

"Yeah, Whittleton probably gave her something cool," Iggy said without thought as he played with his sleeve.

"ARGHHH!" boomed Victor, rattling the walls. Fire exploded from the fireplace. He glared at Iggy with distinct hatred. Then he calmed himself with a graceful elegance. "Oh, my dear Ignacio…I am afraid you've gone and upset me. Just what am I going to do with you?"

Victor turned his back to Iggy as the room grew dim. The fire began to shrivel, sucking the light from the room. A low rumble vibrated the floor beneath them. Iggy grew terrified for he knew his end was imminent. A low hiss was heard from all corners of the dark room. Victor's foreboding shadow lay on the ground at Iggy's chair. Dark lines began to extend from within it, coming to life, wiggling across the floor toward where Iggy sat cowering.

"I do hate to do *thisss*…" hissed Victor.

The hair from Victor's head began falling to the floor chunk by chunk, section by section, and those familiar horns slowly sprouted from his brow. His body popped and cracked sounding like breaking tree branches.

"Master, please!" pleaded Iggy.

Victor spun around to reveal his true form—a horrid beast that was part reptile and part mammal: the nose flat to the surface, the skin brown and grey, great horns protruding from its head, fangs hanging far below its gaping jaws. It glared at Iggy, its forked tongue flicking in the breeze, then began to stomp toward him. Iggy tried to run. The beast wrapped its large paws around his neck and raised him to its face.

Iggy screamed, "But, Master, you need me. You need me! Who will be your slave now?"

"I will find another," the creature said in a deep, growling voice.

"But…but…no one else *likes* you!" cried Iggy.

Then much to Iggy's amazement, the monstrosity stopped. After a moment of silence, it dropped him to the floor. Quickly, Iggy scampered back to the corner and faded into a black smoke to conceal himself.

"Regrettably…you have a point," Victor said in his human voice. Taking a seat at his desk, he began organizing himself. "I am not very well-liked in general. And though you are an idiot…you are *my* idiot. Involving anyone else at this point is unthinkable."

Iggy faded in from the blackness. He scurried over to the desk with Victor and climbed into the chair opposite him.

"Yes, yes…exactly," agreed Iggy. "What do we do?"

"As I promised Felix, at midnight on the Eve of the Great Feast, I will sacrifice my earthly existence to release him and his brood from their prison in the depths of Perditia. And for that sacrifice, Felix has promised to grant me the eternal power of the Boogey Men! I cannot allow this child to cause me to break these promises. It is in her fate to die, after all, and she will not escape that fate."

"But she did die," Iggy pointed out. "Well, she was sort of dead, for a little while."

"Yes, but it will be so much more effective if she can *stay* dead, Iggy. Not *sort-of-dead-for-a-little-while*." Iggy fell silent. "And after the Boogey Men are again

unleashed on the world, Felix will lead us into victory. We will scour the earth, sucking fear from those who cower before us. No one will be able to stop us—not even the Defender of the Dead!"

"Oooh," Iggy said as he applauded. "That sounds like so much fun!"

Victor smiled. "Yes…it does, doesn't it? But! First thing's first—I have to find a way to get to the girl myself, get her to a place where wickedness has no limitations."

Iggy thought and thought. "A party!" he squealed with excitement. "Let's have a Christmas party."

Victor gawked at him with frustration, but then he began to see the brilliance of the suggestion. "Yes…yes, you witty little fool, I think you are onto something—a vast celebration. We will email the entire company to attend. The girl is safe on the land of Evermoore, but she is quite helpless away from the grounds. It will be evening and easy to hide in the darkness. There will be people everywhere and Edwin will be easily distracted while I snatch the girl from under his nose."

"But you can't hurt her in front of all those people," Iggy stated.

An evil sneer crossed Victor's face. He turned in his chair and stared into the fireplace. Patting his leg, he began to whistle and call out for something. The flames rumbled and cracked as out of the fireplace stepped an animal, engulfed in fire and ash, its eyes blazing. As its flames began to die away, Victor gently patted the hellish canine's head. "Yes, boobums. Daddy's little woogums."

Iggy leaned around the desk, his mouth hanging open. "That sure is one *ugly* dog."

The thing ferociously snapped in Iggy's direction causing him to jump backward.

"I don't have to *lift a finger* to kill the girl, you see." Snapping a finger from his hand, Victor tossed the treat to the dog, which snatched it in one bite. "I shall be inside at the party being my usual entertaining self. Unfortunately, Edwin's daughter will mysteriously disappear. Get the email out at once!" Victor looked over to the antique chessboard that sat on top of his desk. He began examining the pieces, turning them gently in his clawed fingertips as his missing finger reappeared. "It will be like setting up a complex chess board, planning your move, deciding exactly how you will invade and make the kill."

He extended his hand and gently tipped over the queen.

The Ghostly Nurse

Thelma had remained in the hospital for three days. Remarkably, she suffered no ill effects from her ordeal and felt very good overall—actually, better than she had felt in some time. She did suffer a bit of chest congestion from the cold water. All of the doctors and nurses were shocked that she was not worse than she appeared.

She and Mimi had played nearly every board game the hospital owned and had each won their fair share of rounds. As the scoring stood, Mimi owed Thelma a batch of fudge chocolate chip cookies. Thelma owed Mimi a foot massage and was tasked with brushing her cat, Riley, who was shedding…badly. It was a fair trade, Thelma thought.

During their games or comfortable silences, there were moments where she had begun to tell Mimi about the few details she could now recall from the night of her accident. Little by little, pieces were starting to return to her. She remembered hearing her mother's voice calling, going to find her, the water, being attacked by the shadow, and then the light, that bright light. And then the little man who spoke to her. What was his name? If only she could recall. Maybe none of it happened at all. Maybe she had dreamt the ordeal, walked outside in her sleep, and stumbled into the pool. It was a possibility—more possible than voices that were not there and little men dressed in white.

Her father had taken leave from work after Thelma's accident, but she had convinced him to go back against his better judgment. She was feeling perfectly fine and saw no reason to keep him from his new job. She was anxious to leave

the hospital, longing to return home and decorate her new house for Christmas. It would be strange to celebrate the holiday without her mother, but it was a part of the perfect life she once had. And now, more than ever, she needed normalcy.

Thelma looked at the clock and realized it was nearly time for a visit from one of the nurses. There were two of them, Betty and Eunice, who were in charge of Thelma—Betty during the day and Eunice in the evening. Betty was quite pleasant and very sweet; Eunice, however, was not overly friendly. Several times during each of their shifts they would check on Thelma, take her vital signs, and deliver medication and food. Sometimes Betty would stay with Thelma and Mimi to talk or play a quick hand of Go Fish. Thelma liked Betty a great deal. Eunice? Not so much.

Mimi and Thelma were in the midst of a checkers tournament when her doctor, Dr. George, came to visit in place of one of the nurses.

"How's my favorite patient today?" Dr. George asked with a smile, peeking his head in the door.

"Doc! Doing good," Thelma answered.

"Good, good, good," he said entering the room. "Have we seen reason for concern?" he directed to Mimi.

Mimi patted Thelma's leg. "Not at all. She has seemed perfectly fine. Her chest is still a little congested, but I think she's going to be okay."

Dr. George took out his stethoscope and touched it to Thelma's back for a listen. It was very cold and she jumped when he placed it against her skin. Afterwards, he took her temperature in her ear.

"Well, I can hear a little bit of fluid, but nothing out of the ordinary," he said. "Temp seems to be fine as well. All in all, I would say after tonight, you're free to go."

"Yay!" both ladies shouted.

"Yes," laughed the doctor. "Now, you just relax tonight. I am certain that Betty and Eunice will take good care of you. If you need anything at all, please let me know."

He opened the door and looked back at Mimi. "Please tell Mr. Thimblewhistle to call my office if he has any questions."

"Will do," said Mimi.

Knowing that she would be going home in the morning, the day went by slowly for Thelma. Edwin called while on his lunch break and said that he may be a little late getting to the hospital because he was having a long day, but he was excited that she would be able to go home the following day.

As the evening wound down, Mimi and Thelma decided to spend their last night relaxing and watching television instead of playing games. Mimi found an excellent cartoon for them to watch while she sipped her coffee. Thelma was growing tired of the same commercials over and over again. She didn't care how wonderful *Yippie Burger's* new chicken sandwich tasted.

The screen went black and then a colorful clown jumped onto the screen. "Now, it's time for Beauregard the Basset Hound!" the clown said excitedly.

Beauregard. The name sounded strangely familiar. She began wondering where she had heard it before. Then, for the first time since the accident, she remembered the little man whose name was *Beauregard Whittleton.* She felt her body run cold.

"You okay, kiddo?" asked Mimi.

"Uh…yeah. Yeah, I'm okay," Thelma replied with obvious uncertainty.

"Are you sure?"

Thelma thought for a moment and looked down at her lap, then to Mimi. "Mimi, what did Dad say about the night of my accident?"

Mimi turned off the television and turned toward Thelma. "Well, Eddie said that you walked outside in your sleep. He said he felt you get up, but he only thought you were going to the bathroom, so he didn't think another thing about it. It wasn't until he heard you scream and the splashing water that he knew you were outside. By the time he had gotten there, you had already made it out of the pool, but…well, you weren't breathing."

Thelma looked down. "Was I dead?"

"You know, I don't know for sure, honey. Just because someone isn't breathing doesn't always mean that they're dead, you know. But, if you weren't already, you would've been gone soon, I imagine. Eddie gave you CPR to push air into your lungs and said you coughed up a lot of ugly water. You were covered in vines and leaves. They were wrapped all around your arms and legs. Then, he carried you inside, called 9-1-1, and then called me."

"Oh," Thelma said softly.

Mimi looked at Thelma and could tell that something else was weighing on her young mind. "Do you want to tell me what happened now?"

"I'm not sure," Thelma replied. "I was dreaming, I think. I thought I heard Mom calling to me from outside. I went out to try to find her, but it was so foggy I couldn't see my hand in front of my face. Then I heard another voice, a different voice. I don't know…it sounded evil, I guess. I got lost in the fog and when it finally cleared I saw that I was standing on the ice in the pool. I don't know how I got there. I tried to carefully walk back to the edge of the pool, but the ice broke. The water was so cold."

Mimi squeezed her hand. "Oh, I am certain it was, honey."

Thelma began to grow upset as she remembered how frightening the event was. "And the vines, the vines wouldn't let me get out. I remember that. I think I was tangled up in the vines somehow. Then something was after me under the water and it bit me and…"

"Shhh," Mimi said trying to calm her.

"Hey there," said Edwin stepping through the doors causing them to nearly jump clean out of their skins with fright.

"Edwin, for Pete's Sake!" Mimi said.

"My, ladies," Edwin said with a laugh. "What were you doing? Telling ghost stories again? You better not have been watching horror movies."

Thelma situated herself in the bed. "Hey, Dad."

"Hey, Pumpkin, you okay?" he said, noticing she appeared to be a bit upset. "How are you feeling?"

"Fine, ready to be home," Thelma said as she forced a wide smile.

"I bet. I'm ready for you to be home, too" he said. "It's been so quiet…I've gotten so much accomplished."

Thelma smiled and smacked his arm.

"How was work?" Mimi inquired.

"Oh, how is work? That Von Hallow dude is going to be the death of me. I swear, every time I get one project done, he's got something else to keep me busy. If I didn't know better, I would think he wanted to keep me there forever!"

"Well, you are just too good at your job," Mimi said.

Edwin waved away the compliment. "Well, I don't know about that. And on top of everything, I got an email this afternoon saying that we're having a Christmas party. I didn't take ol' Vic to be the partying type. But sure enough, he is throwing one."

"Oh, Dad, that sounds like so much fun!" said Thelma.

"Come on, Pumpkin. I don't think you are up to a party. Let's just get you home," Edwin replied.

"Please, Dad? I've been cooped up here for days and I'm ready to do something fun that doesn't require my temperature being taken. If I don't have fun soon, I'm going to *freak* out."

Mimi chimed in. "She has been doing good, Eddie—no temperature or anything. You'll need to make an appearance. You are the new Vice President."

"Yes, with a sick daughter. I don't think they'll expect me to party."

"But I'm not sick," Thelma said.

Mimi smiled. "And maybe this party is just the thing you need to get over some of the awkwardness with your new boss and make some friends at work."

"Mom, it's not high school," Edwin snorted. "I don't know. It would be nice to take my two best girls out. We'll see. What I *do* know, however, is that I'm starving! Mom, you want to go to the cafeteria with me?"

"I would be glad to. I'm a little hungry myself," Mimi answered.

They both stood up and began to walk to the door. Thelma told them she wanted a chocolate malt; that was her favorite. As the door closed behind them, she began re-examining the events in her mind. Things were getting stranger and stranger by the second. For some bizarre reason, she began to grow uneasy in the hospital room all alone. She pulled her bed sheet around her for security. Where was Bartholomew when she needed him? She felt so strange. Something was different. There was an odd sensation on the surface of her skin that almost felt like electricity. It was unusual.

"How are we feeling tonight?" said a peculiar voice.

There was a nurse standing in her room, but not Betty or Eunice. She had never seen this woman before. Her nametag read "Angelica Miller, R.N." She was young and beautiful and dressed somewhat differently from the other nurses, crisper, all in white. All of the other nurses mostly wore brightly colored scrubs with an array of patterns, but not Angelica.

"I'm…doing okay," Thelma replied.

"Good, sweetheart. My name is Angelica. I'm supposed to check on you."

"I'm Thelma," Thelma replied kindly.

"What a lovely name. It is nice to meet you, Thelma." Angelica stepped around Thelma's bed and laid her hand on Thelma's forehead, and then felt her own forehead for comparison. Her hand was cool and very soft. She smelled of flowers—roses to be exact. "You don't seem to have a temperature."

Thelma thought this was a strange way to measure a temperature, no machine or thermometer of any kind.

"Uh…that's good," Thelma replied.

"Yes, that's very good, sweetheart," Angelica said. She sat down on the bed beside Thelma and took Thelma's wrist into her hand and began watching the clock.

"You like being a nurse?"

"Sure! My mother was a nurse, too."

"Really? Did you work here together?"

"Actually, we did, for a while during the war."

Thelma shifted in the bed. "That's cool. A friend of mine from my old school had a brother that fought in the war."

"Really?"

"Yeah. He got to come home from Afghanistan last summer when he hurt his knee. I bet working with your Mom was fun," Thelma said.

"Yes, it was pretty fun, I have to say," smiled Angelica.

"Is she still alive?"

"Oh, no, sweetheart. She isn't. She passed some time ago," Angelica said.

"My Mom is gone, too."

"I'm sorry to hear that…and so young. I don't think a child should ever be without a mom or a dad," Angelica said.

Thelma sat patiently as the nurse continued her evaluation. "How long have you worked here?"

"My, I've been here for a very, very long time, as long as I can remember. The Army needed a lot of nurses to care for the soldiers when they would come back home. I even went overseas to help."

Angelica sat with Thelma for a long time, telling stories of the war and her duties as a nurse. It was all so fascinating. Angelica described the war all in such great detail, detail that Thelma did not recall from what she had heard at school, seen on television, or read in the papers.

"Well, I do believe I have taken enough of your time," said Angelica rising from the bed. "I have some other patients to look in on."

They bid each other good night and Angelica left the room. Shortly after, Edwin and Mimi returned from the cafeteria with Thelma's chocolate malt. Edwin began telling them about his day. He would become so animated during the stories that Thelma and Mimi would laugh until it hurt.

Then the door opened and in walked Eunice for her nightly visit. "Hello, everyone," Eunice said as she entered the room. "I'm here to check on my patient."

"But someone just came and checked on me," Thelma said.

Eunice didn't understand. She looked at Thelma's chart. "I don't think so. If they did they didn't record it in your chart. I'm assigned to check you this evening."

"But, Angelica was just here," Thelma said. "She felt my temperature and everything."

"I don't believe we have any nurses by the name of Angelica," Eunice spat.

Thelma leaned up. "Uh…yeah, you do. Her name is Angelica Miller."

Eunice stopped in the middle of the room and looked at them strangely. "Angelica Miller?"

"Yes," said Thelma.

"Are you certain?" asked Eunice.

"Positive!"

"Thelma, it's alright. Just leave it alone," Edwin said. "Maybe there was a mix-up."

Eunice shook her head, left the room, and came back with a plaque. It was wooden with brass fittings, an award of sorts. She showed Thelma the picture at the top of the plaque. "Is this the person you're talking about?"

"Yes, that's her. See…that's her," Thelma said excitedly. It was. Thelma knew it. She was even dressed almost the same as in the picture. "Where is she? She'll tell you."

"Listen," said Eunice, "Angelica Miller, this woman here, is the nurse that this wing of the hospital is dedicated to. She was a nurse during World War II. She was the only nurse from this district who went overseas to help the soldiers. She was killed decades ago."

"What do you mean, killed?" Thelma said in shock. "Like dead?" Thelma looked to Edwin and Mimi. "Dad, you guys believe me, right?"

They didn't reply. Thelma felt sick to her stomach.

"Look…right here in black and white." Eunice handed her the plaque. At the bottom of the plaque was a small purple heart. In the center was George Washington, just like on a quarter. The bottom of the plaque read:

THE UNITED STATES OF AMERICA

To all who shall see these presents, greeting:

This is to certify that the

President of the United States of America

has awarded the

PURPLE HEART

Established by General George Washington

At Newburg, New York, August 7, 1782

To

ANGELICA ELIZABETH MILLER, RN

Haunting Thelma Thimblewhistle

For bravery and service to the soldiers

of World War II.

1916 - 1945.

Haunting Thelma Thimblewhistle

For bravery and service to the soldiers

of World War II.

1916 - 1945.

Fearful Festivities

Edwin knew that Thelma was still angry with him. A ghost nurse…one that provides check-ups? It was too much, certainly a tall tale. Mimi said she didn't believe the story either, but Edwin wasn't so certain. He got the impression that Mimi was far more open to the event than he had been, but Mimi always was more open to strange things. Nevertheless, his daughter had never been the type to be untruthful. Above all else, Edwin and Juliana had taught Thelma to be honest. Why would she begin telling lies now, especially about something so silly? He was convinced that the holidays were beginning to stir emotions within his daughter, memories of Juliana. It was possible both of them were dealing with feelings they had been keeping locked away.

He was jolted from his thoughts by the ringing of the phone.

"Thank you for calling Von Hallow Savings and Loan. This is…"

"Edwin, this is Maggie…from downstairs? The other day, you and I were looking for the Merchant Processing files that Lillian Carlton used to handle. I found that other file we were looking for."

"Oh…oh, yes. Thank you for that, by the way. I meant to…"

"Yes, yes. Edwin, I'm sorry to interrupt, but I think we need to talk, you and me. It's urgent," Maggie replied quietly, as if she didn't want to be overheard.

"Uh…sure. When would like for me to come to your office?" asked Edwin.

"I'm not in the office right now. But, I can meet you tonight at the Christmas party. You are going, right?"

"Well, I thought about it, but, you see, my daughter just got out of the..."

"Wonderful! I'll see you there, Edwin."

The call was over as quickly as it had begun. Edwin had not necessarily planned on going to the party that evening. Even though Thelma had been excited by the event, Edwin wasn't certain she was up to it so soon after her accident, no matter how well she appeared to be. Still, maybe a fun evening would get him out of the *dog house* with his daughter?

He needed coffee and the second floor had the best coffee in the building. The second floor was where the bank's Internal Technology team was housed. Edwin imagined that those who worked in that department had to stay up way into the night on some occasions, so they certainly needed premium caffeine. He exited his office and pressed "down" on the elevator keypad. As he stood thumbing his elevator key waiting for the elevator to arrive, his daughter's story turned repeatedly in his mind, and he tried to find a way to convince himself it was true.

"A dead nurse. What a crock," Edwin muttered to himself.

"A dead what?"

Stunned, Edwin turned to see Victor standing behind him, eerily glaring at him. "Oh, Victor. God, you scared me!"

"You know, I get that a lot," Victor smiled. "So, to where are you off?"

Edwin chuckled. "Oh, just going down to get some good coffee from the IT guys."

"Well, what is wrong with the coffee from this floor?" Victor asked in a serious tone.

"Uh...well, nothing...nothing at all. I just liked..."

"Oh, don't worry about it, dear boy. Iggy makes the coffee up here most of the time and he can't even *boil water* correctly. It is understood."

The elevator opened up and both of them stepped on.

"So, how are things with you?" asked Edwin.

"Oh, busy, busy, busy. Getting ready for the party, you know."

"Oh, yes, everyone's excited. Some employees were saying just the other day that the bank has always been too tight with mon..." Edwin cut his comment short noticing the expression on Victor's face. "They're pretty excited."

"Yes, I suppose we have had to be somewhat tight with the purse strings in order to stay ahead of the game. You understand, of course."

"Certainly! I didn't mean to…"

The elevator doors opened on the second floor. Edwin was surprised to see that Victor was actually stepping out with him.

"That is fine, that is fine. Honestly, we had a wonderful third quarter and, so far, the fourth has been even better. So, I felt it was about time to give a little something back—especially since we have a new Vice President who has not yet met everyone. You *are* coming this evening, aren't you?"

Edwin shifted nervously. "Well…"

"I won't take *no* for an answer, Edwin."

"Well, you know Thelma just got out of the hospital this morning."

"And how is Thelma?"

"She's doing great and…"

"Have you told her about the party?"

"Well, yes, and she was very excited. You know how little girls like to dress up and…"

Victor clapped his hands together. "Marvelous! It is settled then. And I will tell you what, Edwin. Just to be certain you have everything in line to attend this evening, why don't you leave now. Take the afternoon off. Tend to Thelma and assess her situation. I will see you this evening." Victor pressed the button for the elevator and the doors slid open.

"Oh…okay," replied Edwin nervously.

"And don't forget to have your lovely mother come as well. It will be a glorious time. See you this evening!"

Edwin stood there with his mouth slightly ajar, unsure of what had just happened. He dismissed the coffee and took advantage of leaving early. Regardless of what he told Victor, he had no desire to go to the party that evening. Excuses kept spilling into his head. He would just tell Victor something had arisen, that Thelma was not feeling well. And he could catch up with Maggie on Monday.

"Hello, ladies!" Edwin yelled as he entered the front door.

"Well, hello there, Eddie," yelled Mimi from the sitting room.

There was no reply from Thelma. Edwin initially thought she must be in her room, but was surprised to see her in the sitting room with Mimi.

"Hello, Pumpkin, I got off early," Edwin said to Thelma as he entered the room.

"Whoopee for you," Thelma replied coldly.

Edwin stood there for a moment. Thelma knew exactly how to get to him, and the *cold* treatment was awful. The only thing worse than that was the *silent* treatment. The silent treatment meant you did something nearly unforgivable. Therefore, the mere fact that she was speaking at all was hopeful. He took a deep breath, knowing exactly what would ease the tension in the room.

"Okay. You got me. What do you say we all get dressed up really fancy tonight…and go to a *party?*"

Mimi smiled. Edwin could see Thelma trying to fight back a grin, but finally she could not help herself.

"I can live with that!" Thelma said, jumping from the couch and giving him a hug.

Ah, sweet relief. In reality, if a party would help get him out of the doghouse with his daughter, then he would even offer to serve drinks while they were there. The remainder of the day was spent with Thelma and Mimi talking about what they were going to wear, their hair styles, and what shoes would best go with their outfits.

It was terribly boring.

Edwin could only guess what was happening with Maggie. Why was she so desperate to speak to him? Why so soon? Why couldn't he have simply gone to the Facilities Department and picked up the file?

By the time they were ready to leave, Edwin was nearly sick of hearing about hair-do's and dresses, but smiled tirelessly all the same. At least Thelma was in an incredible mood. He couldn't imagine what he would have done if she had not recovered from her accident. He could not have carried on.

Edwin found the December air quite refreshing as his suit was very warm. Parking was limited with the immense turn out for the event. Luckily, they found an acceptable space right by the door. As they pulled into it, Edwin saw it was reserved: "Reserved—E. Thimblewhistle, V.P."

"How impressive! Reserved parking. Goodness, everyone is here!" Mimi commented.

"Obviously," Edwin agreed.

An obnoxious receptionist was at the door taking coats and showing everyone where to go. The three of them turned in their coats and went into the main meeting hall where champagne and extravagant hors d'oeuvres were being served. Elegant Christmas decorations were draped over anything that would stand still. Everyone was dressed as if they were going to the Academy Awards, and Thelma and Mimi were having a wonderful time, unlike Edwin who could not have cared less.

He had nearly forgotten about the frantic call from Maggie Jordan and the *top secret* file she had for him, until he spied her out of the corner of his eye. Feeling it best to be inconspicuous, he tried not to make direct eye contact with her, but it couldn't be avoided. He gave her a smile and a nod and continued to sip his drink. She started towards him.

"Hello, Edwin. How are you?" Maggie asked.

"Oh, I'm doing well, really well."

Edwin introduced her to Thelma and Mimi, and the group exchanged a few pleasantries with one another about outfits and accessory choices—the typical feminine subjects. Of course, there were the few playful remarks about Edwin, as well as embarrassing "eligible bachelor" comments.

"Whew! It's terribly warm in here," Maggie began. "I think I need some air." Maggie passed by Edwin's ear and whispered, "Meet me by the large hedge at the edge of the walkway in five minutes. Make certain you aren't followed."

"Uh…okay," he replied.

What was this about? It was all very peculiar. Nevertheless, he did just as she asked. As he neared the hedge, he could see her standing there waiting, nervously looking around, trying her best to blend in with the landscaping, as if she feared she was being watched. In her hand she held a manila envelope.

"Did anyone see you?" Maggie whispered as Edwin neared.

"Not that I know of. Now, I've got to know what this is about, Maggie. Are you, like, a secret agent or something?"

Maggie looked around them once again and then handed Edwin the envelope. "After we talked about the Merchant accounts, I remembered this letter. I admit I hadn't been keeping much of an eye on the Merchant files since Lillian disappeared. The last time I saw her, she looked frightened to death, said she hadn't been sleeping, having bad dreams and all. She had suddenly become distant, hardly speaking to anyone at all. She said she was working on a large project with Victor, some kind of real estate deal and that's what was taking up her time."

Real estate. Edwin found this interesting. "Did she say what it was?"

"No, she didn't give any details, just that it was important and time-sensitive. The next day, it was announced that she had resigned due to 'stress-related' reasons. Everyone thought it was a nervous breakdown. But I didn't believe it, not for a second. I knew the truth—Lillian and Victor were *involved.* I don't think Lillian wanted to be with him anymore. As a matter of fact, she told me she was going to end it. Then she was gone. Part of my job in Facilities is packing up desks for employees who are terminated. They wouldn't even allow me into Lillian's office, let alone allow me to pack her things. Then two days later I got these papers from her in the office mail."

Maggie handed him the file. Opening the envelope, Edwin noticed that the pages appeared to be from a general Merchant file. "This is just a Merchant agreement."

"Yes, but look at this one." Maggie pulled a page from the middle and showed it to him. Handwritten at the top of the page, it read:

Your assistance is needed. In order to see, one must first look...

The remainder of the page was completely blank with exception of Lillian's signature at the bottom.

"So…I don't get it. It doesn't say anything," Edwin said.

"But that is what doesn't make sense," Maggie went on. "What does it mean? *Your assistance is needed?* And why send this to me buried in a Merchant file through inter-office mail? Why not just hand it to me? And look here," Maggie added pointing to a stain on the upper part of the page. "Is that blood?"

Edwin examined the page again. "Listen, Maggie, I really don't know. It could be a coffee stain? Maybe she didn't even mean to put this page in the file. Maybe it was included by accident. I mean, I agree something is definitely not right with all of this."

Maggie turned and looked over her shoulder. "I got a strange phone call the night before she left. I answered, but no one would reply. I kept saying, 'Hello?' The only thing I could hear was breathing and, like, *squeaks*, and clicking sounds, as if someone on the other line was trying to tell me something, but couldn't because they were choking."

"Have you talked to her lately?"

"No, I haven't been able to get hold of her."

Edwin didn't feel comfortable with any of it. "Have you talked to the police or anything?"

Maggie rubbed her eyes. "No, but I talked to her landlady. She said the day after Lillian was fired, she turned in her keys and said she was moving back to Pennsylvania."

"Well, there you have it, Maggie. She just left. Maybe she was having some kind of personal issue, emotionally, something you didn't know about."

"Edwin, Victor has done something with her, I know it," Maggie replied with conviction. "I haven't heard from Lillian since she left. She would have called me. She would have said something."

Edwin did not know how to respond to Maggie's claims, but he did believe something was terribly wrong with the entire situation. It was obvious that she believed Lillian was in danger. But could Maggie have been one of the things from which Lillian was trying to escape? The whole thing carried the stench of suspicion. Maggie looked down at the ground, ashamed. Edwin could tell she was beginning to cry.

"Do you have anyone you can call?" he asked, patting her shoulder.

"Yes, my mother—she thinks I'm crazy," she replied, trying to calm herself and dry her eyes. She laughed. "Edwin, maybe I am. I'm going to see my therapist again tomorrow. He'll get a kick out of this. And on top of everything else, I have to get the Williams report done before the end of next week." She took a deep breath and looked at him sincerely. "But, really, you have to admit that something strange was going on with Lillian."

"I do. Definitely," Edwin replied.

Again, Maggie giggled. "Look at me. People are going to begin wondering where we are, and I'm certain you need to go back to your family. If I walk into the party looking this way, they'll just have me committed on sight! You go back in first." She handed him the file. "Here, you take this with you. If you happen to think of anything, you'll let me know?"

Edwin smiled. "Of course."

Stopping briefly at the car, Edwin tossed the file into his briefcase and then began to venture inside. As he entered the doors, he heard that old familiar voice.

"Edwin, nice to see you. So, where were you?" Victor stood close to him, blocking his way.

"I was just outside getting some air…" Edwin began.

"And with whom?" Victor replied suspiciously.

"With no one, actually. I went alone. Had to make certain I rolled up my window."

"I see," said Victor doubtfully. He moved out of the way and allowed Edwin to pass. He walked alongside Edwin, speaking in a low, secretive manner. "You know, Edwin, I feel I must let you know of some…well…matters that have been taking place well before your employment. I am a very private person, so to speak. I despise those who attempt to warm up to me in hopes of advancing their own career. I feel as if my presence in the general population of the company would only provoke this type of behavior. Therefore, I moved to the thirteenth floor of the building many years ago and chose to simply be…an *image* to the employees. I find it better that way. However, as you can imagine, acting in this restrained manner has not prevented negative rumors to circulate about me and the way in which I choose to do business."

Edwin cleared his throat. "Well, people have always enjoyed gossip, especially when it's completely untrue."

"Precisely. Your predecessor turned out to be one of the main individuals spreading vicious lies about me out of sheer jealousy. Therefore, you shouldn't listen to rumors should you hear them."

"Certainly not."

"Good man," Victor said. "Now where is that daughter and mother of yours?"

"Right this way," Edwin replied.

"Mother," said Edwin to Mimi. "This is my boss Victor Von Hallow."

"So pleased to meet you, Mrs. Thimblewhistle," Victor said kissing Mimi's hand. "I am very glad to have your talented son on board with us."

"It's a pleasure to meet you as well, Mr. Von Hallow. I'm glad to hear that. And thank you for giving him the opportunity that allowed him to come back home!"

"And you must be the famous Thelma whom I have heard so much about," Victor said slyly, kissing Thelma's hand, too.

Thelma smiled. "That's me."

"Well, your father talks about you incessantly. He is a proud papa, I must say. Are you as proud of him?"

Thelma looked at Edwin. "Well…yeah."

Edwin and Thelma smiled at one another.

"Pictures!" Mimi exclaimed. "Let's get a picture for my scrapbook." She fumbled through her purse to locate her camera. They passed the camera to the receptionist and huddled together for some photos.

"So, where's Iggy?" asked Edwin. "I wanted to introduce him."

"Alas, Iggy had to run an errand at the last minute. He was supposed to bring back some more champagne, but he has not returned yet. I fear we may be running out soon."

Edwin looked around at the employees. They were all having so much fun being together. "Victor, it's truly a great party. I'm impressed. Everyone is having a wonderful time."

"Thank you, dear boy. That means a lot, especially coming from someone who has not been with us that long."

"Dad," Thelma interrupted, "where is the bathroom?"

Unfortunately, the large soda she had consumed before they left the house was beginning to catch up with her. Edwin pointed the way and she hurried off. She didn't want to miss anything. She was having such a great time. It was fun being dressed up and getting noticed, like a game she did not often get to play. She couldn't imagine what Edwin found odd about Mr. Von Hallow. To her, he was pleasant and charming. He did look slightly creepy, like a horror movie villain, but he seemed fascinating. She couldn't wait to get home and begin recording the experience in her diary.

As she exited the bathroom, she began searching the crowd for Edwin and Mimi. There were so many people about that it was difficult to locate them. She hunted and hunted, but there was no sign of them. When someone appeared friendly enough, she would ask them if they had seen her father explaining that he was the new Vice President of the bank, but no one knew where he was hiding. Suddenly, she spied her father near the front door.

"Dad!" she called. But he didn't turn around. The receptionist handed him his coat. "Dad, where are you going? Are we leaving?"

Surely he wouldn't leave without her. She ran outside without stopping for her coat and saw her father walking through the lot towards the shrubbery, which encircled the area. She called for him again, but he didn't respond. Then he was gone, vanished into thin air. An uneasy feeling began rising in her stomach. As she stood at the edge of the lot peering into the darkness, searching for him, she heard a rustle in the bushes.

"Hello?" Thelma called. But there was no reply. "Dad, is that you?"

Then slowly it emerged from the shrubbery. At first she thought it was a large dog, but it was unlike any dog she had ever seen before. It scrutinized Thelma with raging red eyes. Its large paws marched toward her with its slick, black claws glistening in the moonlight. From its fur, smoke rose into the air, as if the beast had been in flames. Her heart began to race. An inexplicable coldness hit her in the center of her chest and then ran over her entire body; she knew the feeling was fear. It petrified her. She couldn't move, but she knew she had to run. It studied her as drool dripped from the jagged fangs that lined its gaping mouth.

Thelma closed her eyes and began to mumble, "I know you're not real and I'm not afraid of you. You're not real…and I'm not afraid of you." Its low growl seemed to rattle the ground beneath her feet. "Go away," she whispered.

A piercing bark escaped its mouth and seemed to almost hit her in the chest, sending shivers down her legs. Then it lunged at her and began to chase her through the lot. Thelma screamed and ran as quickly as her legs could carry her. The claws of the beast grated the concrete behind her sending sparks scattering about. The cold air froze her airways, making it difficult to breathe deeply. Then she noticed she no longer heard the scraping of claws on the pavement—it had leapt into the air for her. She could feel it soaring closer and closer, its breathing growing very heavy. Losing her balance, she fell backwards with a *thud* to the ground. The beast was in mid-air, teeth bared, claws prepared to tear into her flesh.

And it was then she heard a voice.

"Thelma!" shouted Edwin from the doors.

At the exact moment Edwin's voice pierced the wind, the creature shattered into a fog and vanished into the night air. Thelma shrieked. She lay there on the ground in disbelief. It had gotten so close to her that she felt its sticky drool on her cheek.

"Thelma! Thelma, what are you doing?" Edwin said with aggravation. Everyone was coming outside to see the cause of the commotion. Edwin grabbed her, staring into her eyes.

"Dad…Dad, it was here."

"What was here, Pumpkin?"

"It was something…I don't know. A monster."

Edwin grew angry with embarrassment. "A monster?"

"Yeah, it was after me. I saw it, but then it disappeared."

Edwin put a hand over his eyes. "Like the ghost nurse, right? Seriously? Again?"

"But, Dad, it's true. It was there. Look—on my face…"

"*Stop!*" Edwin yelled causing Thelma to jolt. He had never been so fiercely angry with her. He took her by the arm and helped her up. "There's nothing on your face, Thelma! I swear…I think you're doing this on purpose!"

"Edwin, stop it!" Mimi shouted.

Thelma was frozen. Her father's anger cut at her, and she began to cry. At that moment, he realized what he had done. It didn't matter what had happened; he had no right to speak to his daughter in that manner. He pulled her close to him and she held him tightly, like she did when she was very small.

She sobbed into his jacket. After his anger had begun to subside, regret overwhelmed him. Mimi got their coats as Edwin carried Thelma to the car assuring her that Daddy was still there.

Tongue~tied

he *silent treatment*. It was certainly a step down from his previous residence in the doghouse. An entire weekend without his daughter speaking to him was a little more than Edwin could bear. When they had arrived home after the party, she had gone directly to bed. On Saturday, she spent the day writing in her new journal, which he was certain now said many negative things about him. By Sunday, he had managed to receive *yes* and *no* answers from her. With Christmas on the horizon, he had an idea of what might calm her anger. It would take planning, however, and coordination with Mimi, for he would have to be alone in the house for some time.

Fatigued from the emotional weekend, Edwin was not looking forward to work. Sleep was restless, but eventually came. He muddled through the morning in a disconnected state with his mind half present/half absent. By lunch he had begun to feel slightly better. He wanted to think about something else besides forgiveness from his daughter, so he began to think of Maggie Jordan's mystery.

Edwin ate in the cafeteria that day, the strange note running through his mind. *In order to see, one must first look.* He had searched the phrase on the internet, but turned up nothing but sites about weight loss, bird watching, and self-help theory. As he ate his dry sandwich, he opened the file and looked at the page once again, touching the strange stain at the top. True, it could be blood, but the only people whom he could tell would be the police. Did he feel comfortable enough to become involved on that level? Did he trust Maggie's intuition that greatly? The answer was no.

"Ah, Mr. Thimblewhistle," said a familiar voice.

Edwin turned to see Iggy standing beside him. "Well, hello, Mr. Ignacio."

"I haven't been able to get with you lately and see how you've been doing. So, let me officially ask now."

"I'm doing quite well," Edwin replied, hoping his weariness would not be apparent. "So, where were you during all of the Christmas festivities?"

"Oh, I had to run an errand for the *boss*, you know. I apparently returned just as you had left."

"Yes, and I am sorry. My daughter, Thelma, wasn't feeling very well at all, so we had to leave a bit earlier than we anticipated."

Iggy gave Edwin an inquisitive look. "Is she doing better?"

"Yes, she's doing fine."

"Good to hear. Keeping you busy around here?"

"Ah, never a dull moment," Edwin smiled

"That is certainly the truth. What do you have there?"

Iggy had noticed the file lying on the table. He was clearly the type of assistant that kept track of other employees in the company and provided explicit reporting to his superiors on a daily basis. A lump of tension entered Edwin's throat.

"Um…just doing a little research on some of this Merchant business while grabbing a bite," Edwin said. "Nothing important."

"Really? Interesting. What client?" asked Iggy delightedly.

"Um…actually," Edwin fumbled the pages together, hiding Lillian's mysterious note. "Um…Majestic Industries."

Iggy began to pick up the paper. "Oh, they're a big client. Big, big! How exciting."

Edwin tried to smile with sincerity. "Sure!" Edwin replied as he calculated his next move. "I was thinking of giving them a call." Thinking Iggy may be able to provide some information, he decided to throw Iggy some bait to see if he would take the opportunity to bite. "Lillian sure left this stuff in a mess. I understand no one has heard from her since she left."

Iggy sighed. For a moment he said nothing, but then he leaned into Edwin. "I agree, Edwin, she left things in an awful mess. She had *issues*. She made my job so much more difficult. I mean, I can't go into details, but a couple of days after she left, she contacted me about her medical benefits package telling me she was going to be…hospitalized. You know, for…" Iggy tapped his head to indicate something of a mental nature.

"Ahh," Edwin agreed.

"Yes, nasty business. I'm sure she's quite embarrassed about it. I wouldn't want anyone to know I was locked up in the cuckoo's nest!" A giggle escaped Iggy's mouth. "Well, I will run along now. You have a pleasant day!"

Iggy left Edwin to his lunch. *Hospitalized?* That would definitely explain why no one had heard from Lillian. There was indeed a nut among them—be it Lillian, Maggie, or even Victor! Maybe confidentially informing Maggie of Lillian's medical predicament would soothe her nerves.

He put his tray away and made his way back to his office. Edwin had to reach out to Maggie as soon as he could to comfort her worry. The elevator reached the thirteenth floor and as Edwin stepped off of the elevator, he noticed something very strange. Victor's office door appeared to be *open*—an extraordinary event that Edwin imagined never occurred, not with Victor's excessive need for privacy. He warily stepped toward the door.

"Victor?" he called.

There was no sound except the crackling of the fireplace. As Edwin got closer, he could see what had prevented the door from closing: the doorstop that was hinged to the base of the door had accidentally dropped down, keeping it from completely closing. Edwin called out for Victor once again, but there was only silence.

He placed his palm on the wood of the door and gently pushed it open for a clearer view. Seated with her back to the door was Maggie, sitting silently, facing the fireplace. She did not look in Edwin's direction.

"Hey, Maggie, is that you?" Edwin whispered, even though he had not doubt it was her. "I was just about to call you. Come see me when Vic…"

"Might I ask what you think you are doing?" Victor growled from behind him.

"Victor!" Edwin said spinning around to meet him.

"I hope you realize this behavior is *not* tolerated within this company, Mr. Thimblewhistle."

"Oh, sorry. But, the door was open. I thought something may be wrong," Edwin attempted to explain. But, Victor was not interested.

"What is *wrong* here is that you have just displayed a genuine disregard for my privacy. Miss Jordan and I are having a private meeting and I stepped away to get a cup of coffee. *Do not* ever enter this room uninvited. *Ever.* The only time you will be in this area is when I *want* you here. If I so much as find you outside of this door without me calling for you, I will have you escorted out of the building immediately. Is that understood?"

Edwin was completely frozen with humiliation. "Yes," he said meekly.

"I said, is that understood?"

"Yes, it is."

Victor pushed passed him, grabbing the door. "Get out and go home for the remainder of the day. Tomorrow I want the Tuesday OSI Report on my desk by 10:00. Hopefully, when you arrive in the morning, we will have forgotten about this little…*embarrassing* episode."

"Yes, sir," Edwin said.

Edwin's temper was boiling over. He walked into his office and abruptly shut the door, cursing Victor in his mind. He was not going to put up with it any longer. It took only a moment to make up his mind that when he returned in the morning, he would officially be giving Victor his resignation along with the Tuesday OSI Report. Gathering his things, he picked up the phone to call Mimi and let her know he was coming home unexpectedly.

He was so upset by the encounter he failed to notice that Victor was not holding the cup of coffee he so passionately insisted he had stepped out to get, nor did he notice that the reason Maggie did not respond to him was because she *could not* respond. Her tongue had been removed and was being held prisoner on Victor's desk, sealed in a crystal jar, wiggling like a plump earthworm trying to squirm away into the darkness of the earth.

The Bumpy Wardrobe

While the tongueless Maggie was meeting her fate, Thelma was at home recording her endless list of frustrations with her father in her diary. First, he did not believe her about the strange nurse at the hospital, and now he had dismissed the events at the Christmas party.

During their heated discussion, Thelma had reluctantly admitted that it all could have been her imagination, a dream of some kind. Certainly—she could have seen Angelica's picture beforehand somewhere in the hospital and tucked the image away in her subconscious. Absolutely—the strange creature that had threatened her in the parking lot could have only been a feral dog of some kind. Yes, these could be the explanations, but wouldn't it then mean Thelma was insane?

She had been silent and kept to herself all morning, scribbling in her diary. She no longer wished to stay at the Peterson Estate with all of its wonder; it was now beginning to frighten her. She was ready to be at home, back in Indiana, where nothing was lurking in the shadows, waiting to grab her and take her away. It felt as if the entire transition to Raven Den had been nothing but a mistake.

Around noon, her father called and asked to talk to her, but she refused. She was midway through her latest diary entry titled "Reasons Why My Life Blows" when she noticed something odd. As she jotted her list onto the empty page, she thought she saw faint images, letters, and words other than her own appear on the paper. Reaching up, she turned on the lamp and held the book directly into the light to see nothing there but her own writing.

Mimi hung up the phone and suddenly insisted that she and Thelma take a quick shopping trip. Thus began what felt to Thelma like a never-ending bargain hunting adventure, endlessly traveling from one store to the other. Thelma's heart sank when she heard they were to meet Norma at the arts and craft store. A craft store…at Christmas time, nonetheless. *Not scrapbooking!* She knew once the women became lost in the plethora of scrapbooking accessories, they would be at the store for an eternity.

While in the store, Thelma spotted the girl with glasses from her neighborhood, the one that had been skating the day they had arrived in Raven Den. She, too, was being hauled through the aisles by her mother in search of crafts. She gave Thelma an exhausted glance as her mother dragged her away to the silk flowers. "Girl, I know how you feel," Thelma said to herself.

By the time the trip was over, her feet pounded and she was very ready to be home. On the drive back, Mimi would only ask short *yes* and *no* questions, completely avoiding the topics of the hospital or the party. Did Thelma like this? Was this frame pretty? Would Edwin like that for Christmas? Blah, blah, blah.

Thankfully, her grandmother was not one to pry and tended to allow her to address things when ready. Mimi never pushed or interfered. Thelma answered only when spoken to and did not say another word, even though there was a part of her that longed to talk to someone. The only thing she had to do now was figure out how to get home to Indiana. But, deep inside, she knew she would not be happy without her father, no matter how angry she was with him at the time.

As they pulled into the driveway, Thelma could see that her father was home early from work. Mimi parked and turned off the car.

"I'm not going in there," Thelma spat.

"Are you hungry?" Mimi asked, ignoring her statement. She opened the car door and began to get out.

"I'm not crazy," Thelma stated firmly.

"Oh, Lord," said Mimi, lifting her leg back into the car and shutting the door.

"Dad thinks I'm lying…or nuts."

Mimi sighed. "Honey, I don't think your daddy knows what to think at the moment. A few days ago you were in very bad shape. Your father thought he may lose you. Eddie has always been a practical boy, not like you and me. He

is more like your Grandpa. You got all of the imagination, and you got it from me—and don't let them tell you different."

"But, Mimi, you know I wasn't lying," Thelma continued.

Mimi looked at her. "Listen, I am certain something happened. Actually, I *know* something did; you know it did. And right now, we are the only ones who need to know. I don't know who or what visited you the other night or what was after you in that parking lot, but I know something took place. We just need to figure out what it is and why. That is all that matters right now. Let your father come around when he's ready. I'll talk to him…promise."

Thelma began to sniffle. "But, I'm scared," she said as a big tear fell down her cheek. It was obvious that she felt ashamed of her fear; she prided herself on being mature.

Mimi reached over and hugged her tightly, pulling Thelma over to her side of the car. Mimi knew Thelma must be afraid—anyone would be. Mimi was afraid for her. Mimi didn't understand what was going on or why, she only knew that for some special reason Thelma was becoming aware of things normal people could not sense.

"Honey, there is no shame in being afraid sometimes. You know, looking back on it, you remind me a lot of Anna. Oh, I thought she was so weird, but I loved her. She had the wildest imagination. She was all the time talking to something that wasn't there. One day it was an imaginary cat she had. Or, the wardrobe upstairs that Anna used to swear would take her anywhere she wanted to go. Or that old desk in the library she befriended. Who knows why she said the things she said? I wouldn't have been surprised if the toilet had been her best friend."

Thelma laughed. "You're just trying to stop me from crying."

"No, no, really," Mimi giggled as she began to get out of the car. Thelma got out as well and they both began walking toward the door. "Let's just try to remain open and see where the adventure takes us. As for now, your father has a *surprise* for you."

Mimi unlocked the large doors and pushed them both open. The house was completely decorated for the holiday season. Thelma lit up with joy. It was the most magnificent thing she had ever seen. Large rolls of garland and lights accented the banisters of the staircases. Wreaths hung in every window. And lights—there were lights as far as the eye could see—brilliant, white lights tucked into almost every corner.

Thelma ran from the front door to the sitting room. There, by the fireplace, was their old tree standing tall and proud. However, it only had lights on it. Her father knew that Thelma loved to decorate the tree, so he had left that for her to complete. All of the stockings were hanging on the chimney, just as she had pictured. It was simply splendid.

Mimi stepped beside Thelma and set down their shopping bags. "I know you thought I was flipping my lid, but I had to stay gone long enough for him to finish, honey. He wanted it all to be a surprise, with the exception of the tree, of course. He knew you'd have his hide if he finished the tree."

"It's amazing!" Thelma said.

"What's amazing is that I can stand upright after getting all of this unpacked and ready to go!" Mimi said falling into the chair.

Thelma laughed. She was so enamored with her surroundings that her anger for her father began to fade. Looking at the twinkling lights, she began to comprehend that her stories were difficult to believe…even for her. Why, then, should she be angry that her father had a difficult time understanding it? At the moment, it was of little importance, because her new home was decorated for the season.

After she had finished admiring the decorations, she called out for her father, but he didn't answer. She searched the whole lower level and could not find him hiding anywhere. Thinking he could be upstairs, she went to the second level and called again, but no reply. Then she noticed that her bedroom door was closed, which was unusual. She walked to the door and placed her ear against it. From inside she could hear the soft tinkering of a music box. She gently pushed the knob and the door opened with a snapping creak. It was then that she saw the decorations, which outshined everything else she had seen thus far.

Large wreaths decorated with elegant bows made of red velvet hung in her windows. There was a large white pillar candle on every surface one could imagine. Beside her bed was a small ceramic Christmas tree with little bows and lights. It slowly turned as it tinkled with musical Christmas carols.

On her pillow, there was a present wrapped in white and gold paper. Taking a seat on the bed, she sat down and unwrapped the gift to discover a small handmade wooden box. Carved into the lid was a very sophisticated tiny leaf, and under it were the words *Doctor Chen's Gifts of Nature*. Inside was a beautiful pair of silver earrings with teardrop-shaped amethyst stones hanging from small silver leaves that matched the leaf on the box. She began examining them, studying how special they were.

Bump!

Thelma was shaken by a rumble from the wardrobe beside her bed. *What was that? A rat?* Cautiously, she scooted backward onto the bed near the center, gauging the quickest route of escape.

"Dad?"

Bump!

Once again Thelma heard the noise, louder this time. Whatever was inside slightly shifted the wardrobe with its movement. She began to think that what she was hearing was neither her imagination, nor a rodent.

"Thelma…"

Thelma squealed, jumping behind the pillows.

Edwin laughed entering the room. "Oh! Did I scare you? I didn't mean to. Didn't you hear me coming down the hallway?"

"No!" Thelma said with a nervous giggle. "Now that you're here, I think there's something in the wardrobe. Get it!"

"I wouldn't doubt it," Edwin replied. He walked over and opened the door wide, rustling through the clothes. "Nope, nothing in here…unless he *ran into your shoes!*"

"Stop!" Thelma said lightly kicking her father in the back of the leg. "What are you doing home, anyway?"

"Oh, let's just say that Victor gave me a little present today," he replied. "*And thanks, Dad,* for all the hard work you did on the house and…"

Thelma ran from the bed and threw her arms around his neck. He hugged her back tightly.

"So, I'm forgiven, huh?"

"Well…I suppose. And, yes, thank you, Dad. I love it all. It's great."

"You're welcome, Pumpkin," Edwin replied. "I told Mimi I was coming home early and that she was going to have to keep you out for a long time. Did you like your earrings?"

Thelma smiled. "Eh, they're alright."

"Oh, that's all?"

Thelma laughed and picked up the box from the bed. "No, they're great."

Edwin smiled. "Good. I'm glad. I bet you're hungry after all that shopping Mimi put you through. Now, come on, let's eat."

After dinner, Thelma went upstairs to bed in her own room, which felt much safer and warmer with its decorations. Flopping onto the bed, she reached for the key to her diary, unlocked it, and began recording the day. There was a new entry to write titled "Reasons Why My Dad Rocks." Then once again, she noticed writing other than her own fading into view on the paper.

This time, the words and images grew darker and more distinct. She stopped writing and sat there watching the page. An anxious feeling crawled into her throat, scratching at her voice box. As she flipped through the pages, underneath the ink of her own writing, words and images now filled the once empty pages of the book. She turned to the first page, which now read:

The Beginner's Guide to the Neither Realm for the Incredibly Gifted

The Neither Realm! It began to rush back to her, like a wave of warm water rushing over her body. It was the name of the place she had visited during her accident, the place made of light. Through her scribbles she could read:

This instruction book will guide you through the wonders of the Neither Realm, because you are incredibly gifted. Only those who are remarkable and pure of heart can see what is written within these pages.

Turning the page, she saw a Table of Contents that contained entries like *Ghostly Bodies, Edenia & It's Wonders, Perditia—That Other Place, Rooms of Uncommon, The Boogey Men,* and even *Introduction by Beauregard Whittleton: Grand Director of the Neither Realm.*

Beauregard Whittleton…the little man in white. He had met her as the figures brought her soul through the gate. He told her he had something important to give her, something powerful. What was it? She turned to the introduction.

Dear Friend,

My name is Beauregard Whittleton and I would like to welcome you to the wonders of the Neither Realm, named so for it is neither here…nor there. I am certain you are quite bewildered by what you are seeing. Do not worry, this response is quite common. It is possible that you naturally possess a talent, a gift that allows you to see these pages. Then again, you may have experienced a great trauma that may have led us to meet in person. Rest assured that what you are seeing and/or hearing is real. You have been provided with an ability, a skill that allows you to experience worlds that are mostly hidden from the eyes of the living.

And this gift you must not fear. If you were supposed to fear it, it would not be called a "gift" now, would it?

Please note that in just a moment, your assigned Spirit Guide will arrive. In preparation, we ask that you DO NOT faint when they introduce themselves, for that is quite rude. DO NOT scream, for even the dead can have a headache. DO NOT throw things, for you cannot physically assault a ghost. You may end up breaking something valuable, and we of the Realm are not responsible for your damaged property. Naturally, the arrival of the dead may shock the living at first, but understand that your Guide is there to handle all of your customer service needs, and customer satisfaction is our number one priority.

After some brief introduction, your Guide will prepare you to meet with your Phantomite. It may shock you to learn that your Phantomite may be your favorite book, a cherished toy, or even a kitchen appliance. Again, please refrain from fainting. Your Phantomite will debrief you on your ability, what it means to you, and what you mean to us.

At that point, please feel free to share tea and biscuits as available, for the dead love tea and biscuits.

*By the way, your guide should be arriving…***now.***

Rattle…

Thelma came to full attention, looking to the wardrobe. The lamp beside her went dark, leaving only the glow of the scattered candles to illuminate the room. Her eyes opened wide, focusing through the shadows. The flickering shades moved along her walls making it hard to recognize things that did not belong.

Rattle, rattle…

The noise from the wardrobe came again. Thelma pulled the blankets tight around her neck and examined its doors. In her imagination, she could see them opening and a large demon-like monster crawling from the wardrobe, ready to devour her. Then, she heard something else, something strange, almost like someone was…*singing?*

The melody grew louder. The wardrobe began to rattle and bump and shake to and fro. Thelma jumped from her bed, taking her blanket with her. She ran to the adjacent wall and cowered down to the floor. She was far too afraid to dash past the wardrobe, suspecting whatever was within would reach out and snatch her. The singing grew louder and quite obnoxious. Thelma thought she may scream. The singing grew higher in key, as if the vocalist was building up to some extraordinary finale.

Boom!

The doors busted open and out jumped what appeared to be a girl, glowing translucent and iridescent. Thelma jumped to her feet and screamed at the top of her lungs. The figure opened its arms and smiled widely as its glow took on a more flesh-like appearance.

"*Ta-daaaaaa!*" she sang.

Then Thelma's eyes rolled into their sockets, and with a *flop*, she fell backwards to the floor unconscious.

"Well…*thrppp*," the ghost sputtered in disgust. "Guess you didn't read the introduction!"

Dead Anna

As Thelma began to find her way back to consciousness, she could feel that she was now on her bed. She would have thought it was all a terrible dream if not for hearing the dreadful singing again.

"*I know of a phantom who just eats for pleasure…his fanny is so big it cannot be measured…I offered him toast…But he preferred roast…and that's why I can't handle a finicky ghost…*"

Thelma jerked herself awake and frantically peered around the room. There was nothing but darkness.

"Who…who's there?" Thelma asked, her voice shaking.

"I'm not coming out until you promise you're not going to go all *heebie-jeebie* on me again." Thelma didn't answer at first. Maybe she wouldn't be able to keep from going all *heebie-jeebie*. "Weeelll?"

"Okay! Whatever, fine. I'll try not to," replied Thelma.

"Good. You already ruined my big entrance, so this is all you get now," it replied and with a slight *poof* it appeared at the foot of the bed. It was definitely a girl. She was a little older than Thelma, but not by many years. "There you go. That's all I got. Just *poof*…that's it."

The girl wore a simple dress with a red ribbon around her waist. The sleeves were short and slightly poufy. She had a ponytail tied with matching red ribbon. Her attire looked dated, like from the 1950's or 1960's.

Thelma cocked her head. "Uh….who *are* you?"

"Oh, for cryin' out loud," the girl replied slapping the palm of her hand over her eyes. She took on a more solid flesh-tone as she walked toward the bed and picked up the Guide. "Did you, like, even crack this thing at all? Because if you didn't read the intro, then I have to explain to you…and I gotta tell ya—you've already made me work too hard tonight, sister."

Then it came to Thelma. "Anna?"

"Bingo!" Anna said.

"Mimi told me about you," Thelma said.

Anna looked at her and smiled. "Aw! And how is she? She's a hoot, your grannie."

"She's…fine," Thelma said somewhat confused. "Are you the one Beauregard said would be visiting me?"

"Whew! He *did* tell you about me. Allow me to introduce myself. I am…or was…Anna Peterson. Now that I'm kinda deceased and all, they call me Dead Anna, and you are living in my house."

"*My* house," Thelma corrected.

"No…*my* house, sister. I let you guys stay because I kinda like you. Trust me, if I wanted ya out, you would be gone. But, that is neither here nor in the Neither Realm."

"Are you, like…a ghost?"

Anna laughed. "Oh yeah, I am so, *so* dead. You got that, right. I'm a ghost. 'Boo' and all that crap. I tried to introduce myself to you the first night you guys were here, but you didn't seem too friendly."

"Well, you could've done a better job!" Thelma said sitting up in the bed, rubbing her head. "I think I'm flipping out…hallucinating, or something. So far, I've spoken with some dead nurse, I've been chased by a demonic dog, and now here *you* are. I'm not all there. I'm losing it!"

Anna walked closer to the bed. "Well, I don't claim to be a psychoanalyst or anything, so you may be nutty as a fruitcake, but I can say that you are *not* hallucinating—I *am* here. I was supposed to be the first ghost you met, but Angelica came in to check on you since you ended up in the hospital. Of course, you wouldn't have even been there if you would've listened to me and stayed away from the pool, but hey…whatever rings your bell. Now the rabid dog thing? You're on your own with that one."

Thelma's eyes widened. "Really? So, that was your voice calling to me that night. I'm not crazy after all."

"Hey…I don't judge. But I'm hoping you're at least a little nuts, or you won't be any fun at all." Anna flopped down on the bed.

Thelma smiled—she didn't quite know why. Anna was intriguing. For a dead person, she definitely had a certain charm about her—outgoing—not at all like Thelma. "Have you always been inside that wardrobe?"

"Oh, no, no, no. That thing is what we call a Nexus, like a portal that you can use to get where you need to go really fast. It doesn't have to be a wardrobe. It can be, like, a car, a room, even a mirror."

"Can I use it?" asked Thelma.

"Well, I don't know about right now. I don't think you're strong enough. But one day, maybe." Anna stretched. "Alrighty then...I have to prep you," Anna said. "Let's see. I am what you call your *Spirit Guide*. I'm like your ghostly assistant ."

"Does everyone have a Spirit Guide?" asked Thelma.

"Yep...everybody. It's just that most people can't, like, see and talk to theirs, which leads us to our next lesson...your gift. Whittleton probably took you to this room, said some really important-sounding stuff, and asked you to touch this whirling, twirling, light thingy, right? Exactly. That thing is an energy source known as the Secret. When you touched it, it gave you your gift."

"And that's seeing dead things?"

"Well, what did you want for dropping dead? A car? You are really special, though. You're what is known as a *Conveyor*. You can talk to the dead and see them and all that jazz." Anna fumbled with her ponytail.

"So, there's other gifts?" Thelma questioned.

"Yeah, yeah...let's see. There's an *Auditor*. Those people can just hear the dead. There's also *Visionaries* who can only see the dead. That's what makes you rare—you can do both."

Thelma studied the ghost. In her flesh tone, she looked just like she was real. "Can I touch you?"

"Well, yeah, right now. When I *phase* you can't, though. That's when I get all glowy and everything."

Anna's skin felt just like the nurse's had felt. "Wild," Thelma smiled.

"Isn't it?" Anna said with a giggle.

Thelma looked at her, overflowing with questions. "Have you always been my Guide?"

"Naw. Your other one retired, and when you moved into this house I volunteered. Not to give you the big head, but I felt privileged. You're kinda special."

"Special? How?"

From downstairs, they could hear the chime of the grandfather clock. "Ah! Midnight. Okay, sister, I could sit here all night and go over this stuff with you, but that ain't my job. We have someone in that position, though. Just so happens you already have an appointment with Ernie." Anna stood up and walked toward the door.

Thelma began to climb off the bed to follow Anna. "Ernie?"

Phantomites & Other New Words

Anna led Thelma down the hallway to the stairs. Anna seemed to float effortlessly through the air without the need to stride as the living do. Once downstairs, they approached the library doors.

"Is Ernie in there? Is he my Phantomite?" Thelma asked.

"Very good! Yes, he's in there alright. He's *always* in there," Anna chuckled.

Without Anna touching them, the doors of the library opened. The fireplace was already ablaze, cutting through the darkness, making the area seem more majestic than in the glare of daylight. Anna floated into the room and Thelma followed. The ghost stopped in front of the large desk Thelma had sat at when she had arrived at the Peterson Estate. Thelma walked around and took a seat in the leather chair behind the desk.

Thelma whispered, "Okay…what is Ernie?"

With a swift kick, Anna knocked the leg of the writing desk twice. "Wake up, Ernie! Your twelve o'clock's here."

As the desk began to move, Thelma jumped backward in the seat. The shiny oak creaked and screeched as it was awakened. Thelma did not know what to think. She rolled the chair back and ran to the front of the desk. Though it was difficult to see, she began to notice the image of a face developing in the intricate woodwork designs of the old antique. Then the desk blinked its large eyes and yawned.

"What do you mean *lazy*? I heard you," yawned the desk. "It's the middle of the night. I don't see what is wrong with sleeping at…" The desk stopped and looked to Thelma. Its eyes grew wide and it smiled.

"Hello," said Thelma.

"Thelma Thimblewhistle!" the desk exclaimed. "I'll be. I can't believe I'm finally meeting you at last. We've been expecting you. Whittleton put the word out that you were coming."

"Um," Thelma muttered not knowing how to respond. "Nice to meet you, too."

"Good! Now, I trust you've read your introduction in the Guide?" began Ernest.

"Yes, I read it. You are my Phantomite."

"Precisely."

"So, what exactly is a Phantomite?" asked Thelma.

"All in due time, my dear, all in due time," answered Ernest. "I am to get you prepared, give you a run of the basics. Allow me to introduce myself. *Ernest Oakberry the Third*," said Ernie bowing to Thelma as much as a desk could manage. "My friends call me Ernest and those who have no manners call me *Ernie*."

"Nice to meet you, Ernest," replied Thelma politely.

"Likewise. Now, let's see…let's see. We need to take notes. Every important meeting has meeting notes and there is much to review," Ernest said.

Thelma was glad to oblige. She didn't mind taking notes. It seemed there was going to be a lot to remember. She walked around and took a seat behind Ernest and began searching the desktop for a pencil, but there was not one to be found. There was an inkwell on the desk, but no pen to partner with it.

"I don't see anything to write with," Thelma stated.

"Oh no—*you* don't have to write. We let Solomon do that. Solomon?" called Ernest.

Suddenly, the top middle drawer of Ernest, one of the same drawers that had been locked the day Thelma arrived, popped open. She was apprehensive to look inside it, but mustered up enough courage to lean forward. Something peeked out at her from the drawer, a small, thin object, with a shiny point. It appeared to be a pen, a beautifully elegant fountain pen. The pen rose slowly from the drawer and faced Thelma.

"Thelma, we would like for you to meet *Solomon J. Inkwell*," said Ernest. "He had quite a nasty time getting to us. He was stolen, you see. Luckily, he was able to escape and enjoy a return home in your father's briefcase."

The pen leapt from the drawer onto the desktop and took a bow. Thelma smiled in wonder. This was the shiny object she saw scurry across the floor the night her father's briefcase had fallen open. Thelma noticed that the pen was engraved with the same emblem as Ernest and the Guide.

"Hello, Solomon," Thelma said. "You were the thing I saw run out of Dad's briefcase the other night."

The pen glanced around the desk searching for something.

"Oh, sorry, dear fellow," Ernest said. The far right drawer unlocked and opened to reveal a large stack of stationary. "Would you be a dear, Thelma, and give our friend some parchment?"

Thelma took a few pieces of paper from the drawer and laid them on the desktop. Solomon popped open the inkwell, dipped his tip into it and wrote, "Yes, it was I. Greetings, Miss Thimblewhistle."

It was surreal. Thelma thought certainly it must be another dream.

"Ernest, what is this symbol with the star and moons, the one on you and Solomon?" Thelma asked.

"That, my dear, is the Seal of the Neither Realm." Ernest cleared his voice. "Now, let's begin. We'll start with a few definitions. To understand the world you are seeing, you naturally have to know what things are called, of course. If you didn't know a balloon was called a *balloon*, then what would you call it?"

"Well, I'm not sure," Thelma said.

"Precisely. We will start with the most important definitions. First and foremost, Solomon and I are what you would call *Phantomites*."

Solomon wrote the word *Phantomite* on a blank piece of paper and underlined it to indicate its importance.

Ernest continued. "A Phantomite is an inanimate object that is possessed, so to speak, by the life energy of someone who loved it very much, but has since passed on."

Solomon continued to quickly scratch down his words.

"So, the spirit of someone is inside you?" Thelma asked.

"Not actually," Ernest clarified. "We were just adored so much by our owners that when they passed on, a slice of their energy was left with us, and that gives us life. I was owned by Reginald Mistwater, a famous detective with Scotland Yard. He was a very smart man. Our friend Solomon here was owned by a gypsy fortune teller named Griselda."

Solomon wrote the name "Griselda" and drew a small heart next to it.

"Phantomites are part of the world of the dead and once an object becomes a Phantomite, it is branded with the Seal of the Neither Realm that you see on

Solomon and me. In the world of the dead there are Realms. First and foremost, there is the *Realm of Edenia*. It is known by many names, but you may know it as Heaven. Then there is the *Realm of Perditia*, also called *That Other Place*. Sitting in-between is the Neither Realm, named so for it is neither here nor there."

"That's where I went," Thelma said. "I saw the three gates."

"Yes, exactly. When you leave this life, the Neither Realm is where you go to get where you're going."

Anna leaned forward. "Think of it like a big train station for dead people."

"Uh…yes," added Ernest. "These entryways you observed—the one to the left goes down to That Other Place, and the one to the right goes to Edenia, and the one in the middle leads into the Neither Realm. The recently deceased are ushered into the Realm and sent to the *Room of Arbitration* where they are evaluated for placement."

"I think Mr. Whittleton took me to a place called *Arcanium*," Thelma said.

"Arcanum," Ernest corrected. "Yes, there are many rooms in the Realm," Ernest agreed. "The room you visited, the *Room of Arcanum*, is where the Secret, the most powerful energy source known, is guarded. Its door will only open for the gifted. There are different gifts."

Thelma perked up. "Yeah, Anna said I'm a Conveyor."

"And so much more," Ernest said.

With that comment, Thelma got up and took a seat in front of Ernest. "What do you mean, so much more?"

"Well, you see, the Emerald Moon has warned the Realms. It has provided us a sign," Ernest explained. "*A moon of emerald, bright and high, warns of wickedness nearby.* Something evil is brewing, and that, dear Thelma, is why we believe you are here. We are confident that you are the *Defender of the Dead*."

Thelma's eye grew wide. "The *what* of the dead? What kind of sign?"

Ernest sighed. "We realize this information can be very unsettling, but you must trust us on this matter. Know that in the spirit world, just as in the world of the living, some souls are not friendly. In the Earthly Realm, there are a select few who carry a dark, evil magic—wicked individuals known as *Mavens*. You may think of them as witches or warlocks, but very nasty ones indeed. They have corrupt powers bestowed upon them by *Nickolas*, the atrocious ruler of That Other Place."

Thelma raised her eyebrow. "You mean the Devil?"

"Yes," replied Ernest.

"Named Nickolas?"

"Yes."

"So, what's God's name?"

"George."

"*George?*" Thelma said in shock.

"You're getting off our agenda," warned Ernest. "We believe you will be a significant soldier in a battle that has been taking place for hundreds of years, a war between light and darkness. Long before you were even born, there was a malevolent Maven known to all as *Felix Payne*. In life, he was not much of a threat to anyone. But, in death, he became something much worse."

"What did he become?" Thelma asked.

Ernest gazed at her grimly. "The Boogey Man."

With those words, Solomon hopped behind a photo on Ernest's top, trembling.

"Wait," Thelma said with a smile. "The Boogey Man? Like, the *real* Boogey Man?"

"Absolutely," Ernest confirmed.

"Okay, what do *I* have to do with the Boogey Man?"

"Well…defeat him, of course," Ernest said.

"*Defeat* the Boogey Man?" Thelma said with shock.

"Boogey *Men*, actually," corrected Anna.

"There's more than one?!" gasped Thelma.

Anna patted Thelma's arm. "Don't worry, sister; they're in jail…at least for the moment."

"Oh, that makes it better," Thelma snapped. "Listen, I thought the Boogey Man was just something grown-ups created to scare kids."

Ernest raised a wooden eyebrow. "Boogeys are very real. Using a secret incantation of his own design, Felix sacrificed his life to transform into an apparition, a phantom far more powerful than any mere ghost or poltergeist— a paranormal leech that feeds off of the fear of the living, growing more and more powerful the more fright it consumes. As years went by, he desired more and more power. Wanting to rule over all Realms, he began enlisting other twisted souls and changing them into Boogey Men, creating an army of parasitic apparitions. Together, they broke into the Neither Realm and attempted to steal the Secret. Luckily the Realms were able to band together to defeat him and his henchmen, but not before Felix was able to enter the Room of Arcanum and absorb power from its energy source."

Thelma gulped, her mouth dry. "The Secret? What did he do with it?"

"He grew stronger. Thankfully, his army was captured, but Felix managed to escape with minimal injury. Though he had not stolen all of the power he had hoped, once back to the Earthly Realm he used his newfound energy to begin taking control of the living."

Anna walked over and hopped on top of Ernest, causing him to grumble. "Felix helped bring war and darkness to the living, it was one of the most horrible times the Earthly Realm had ever seen. He figured out how to possess things, even without their permission, even *dead* things, which I still can't figure out."

"So, where is he now?" questioned Thelma.

"Oracles," Ernest answered. "The Oracles took care of him. They were the most powerful of the gifted. Banding together, they tracked Felix down and took his power away, banishing him to imprisonment with his army. But it took all thirteen of them to do so. Unfortunately, the battle also drained their magic. So, over time the Oracles died away into extinction. That's why you are so important, Thelma. While you do not possess the powers of an Oracle, it was foretold that the Emerald Moon would bring the dead a champion. Something in the Earthly Realm is working to free the Boogey Men from their prison in Perditia."

Thelma shook her head. "How would you free something from…That Other Place?"

"That we don't know," Anna said. "The living can't get into the Realms while they're alive. There's no way."

Ernest agreed. "Correct, only the Oracles could travel freely between the Realms while alive. But still, a plan is in action. Whomever is the mastermind stole poor Solomon, attempting to use him in their evil plans."

"Great! Can't Solomon just *write* who it was?" Thelma asked.

"Sadly, no," Ernest answered solemnly. "He's been bewitched. Poor soul—every time he attempts to identify the culprit he gets a terrible case of *Nonsense*. Only goobley scribbles fall out."

Thelma stood. "Listen, how do you know I have anything to do with this? I can't be the Defender of the Dead. I don't know the first thing about killing Boogey Men or warlocks! I can't even defend myself!"

Ernest looked up to her. "It is written that a guardian would come forth from the land of Evermoore, the soil upon which this very house is built—a little girl. And this girl would save the lives of the dead. You took possession of this land the very evening that the Emerald Moon rose into the sky. It must be you."

"But you don't *know* it's me," Thelma pleaded.

"You are correct. We do not *know*. We only hope. I hope," Ernest specified. Then he could see the fear on Thelma's face. "The answers will all come in time, child. Do not worry. The ground this house is built on is powerful and pure, charmed by the Evermoore bloodline that lived here for hundreds of years. Rest assured that you are protected from the likes of the wicked while on this land and you cannot be harmed while in the shielding walls of this fortress."

Thelma rolled her eyes. "Well, great. I'm safe as long as I don't, like, go to school, or have a life, or anything."

"Hey, no school! That sounds to *die* for!" Anna chimed in. Thelma shot her an impatient glare.

Ernest yawned. "I think that is enough for one evening, Thelma. You get your rest. Everything else you'll need to know is written in the pages of the Guide, and there is much to study." Thelma and Anna prepared to leave. "And one more thing," added Ernest. "You must never tell the living the things you now know. You must guard these secrets."

"But what if the person is open?" asked Thelma thinking of Mimi.

Ernest's expression turned serious. "Out of the question. It would be undeniable evidence of life beyond death. There would no longer be a need for faith, and George declares faith to be of utmost importance."

Anna looked down to Ernest. "And could you imagine? We would have mediums and cheap-trick psychics everywhere wanting us to take messages to dead wives and husbands or dead dogs…"

"But my grandmother—she'd believe me. She and I have already…"

"Thelma, you mustn't involve the living," Ernest reiterated. "Especially during these gloomy times. Bringing your grandmother any further into our world will only place her in danger."

Thelma would never risk placing her family in harm's way. "Okay, I won't…promise."

"Good girl. Now, remember we are always with you. Do not fear. Should you ever need to speak to me, come anytime. Knock upon my wood. *Kicking* is discouraged," Ernest said with a wink.

Thelma and Anna bid Solomon and Ernest good night and left the library. Thelma had the Guide to study. Though she was tired, she wondered if she would be able to sleep. Learning that she could be part of something so fantastic, yet so dangerous, was very disconcerting, to say the least. Only hours before, her world consisted of being nothing more than Thelma. Now, she may need to become a hero.

She would have settled for simply remaining Thelma.

Once inside her bedroom, Thelma picked up the Guide from her bed and flipped through its pages. "Anna, am I really protected in the house?"

"Yep. You are. This place is like your personal shield. Pretty awesome, I think." Anna opened the door to the wardrobe. "Oh! There's one more thing, something that may not be in that Guide there."

"Please…no more. This is worse than school." Thelma moaned falling to the bed.

Anna bent down and began patting her leg, making clicking sounds with her mouth. "There you are!" She leaned into the wardrobe and then turned to Thelma holding what appeared to be a fat grey and white cat—a *poltergeist* pussycat! Thelma could hardly believe it. "This is Miss Pawpaw. She is what we call a *Spectre*."

Thelma nearly squealed with joy. "A Spectre?"

"Yep. Obviously, she's a *dead* cat. Spectres are the spirits of animals."

"Oh, man, is she mine?" Thelma said excitedly.

Anna pulled Pawpaw closer. "No, no, no, honey. She is *mine*. But! Well, you know, I stay pretty busy. I don't have a lot of time to take care of her and give her the attention she needs. And the other day I heard you talking to your dad about a cat—I put two and two together."

Thelma reached for the cat. "Oh…I love her."

Anna handed her over. Thelma could barely feel the animal that was like cotton in her hands. Pawpaw nearly had no consistency at all. If not for the loud purr, Thelma may have been able to overlook the animal altogether.

"She likes you," Anna said.

Thelma could only smile. "Thank you so much." She sat there a moment, admiring Pawpaw. "Anna?"

"Yeah."

"How did you…well…"

"Die?"

"Yeah. Mimi said you drowned." Thelma felt strange for asking, but after her conversation with Mimi she was very curious. After all, it was the first time she had met a ghost.

"Yeah…I drowned…I think, in the pool outside. I don't remember much. Once you pass, you start to forget things like that. Anyway, next thing I knew I went to the Neither Realm and began learning the things you're learning now."

"Oh," was the only thing Thelma replied. "I really like Pawpaw. Again, thank you very much."

"Ah, no problem." Anna replied. She stretched and yawned. "Okay, sister, enough. I've got to go and you've got to get some sleep. Oh, and another thing: don't wake me before dark. I'm grouchy in the daylight. Ghosts are pretty lazy. You know, *eternal rest* and all."

With that, Anna said good night and disappeared through the wardrobe portal. Thelma climbed into bed with Pawpaw. First, the cat went completely under the covers. Thelma could feel the cat's chilliness move alongside her body mingling with the warmth of the blankets. Once she got to Thelma's feet, she turned around and made her way back toward the top. She lay down halfway in and out of the blankets and purred loudly. Thelma fell completely in love. She now had a cat and the best part was that no one would ever know. Pawpaw was her little secret, just like the worlds she now knew. She began to drift, to fall gently to sleep, lulled by the purring vibration.

What wondrous dreams awaited her?

The Beginner's Guide to the Neither Realm for the Incredibly Gifted

"Wake up, sleepyhead," said Edwin.

Thelma smiled and began to stir. She could feel her father sitting on the edge of her bed. But where was Pawpaw? Thelma sprang awake with a sudden jerk. "Good morning," she said, trying to appear tranquil.

Edwin jumped back and put his hands in the air. "Whoa, wait a minute there. School's not started yet. Calm down."

All of a sudden, she saw Pawpaw jump onto the bed, announcing her presence with a slight coo. Edwin turned to see what it was, obviously feeling Pawpaw's presence. He dismissed it after he saw nothing. "So, what are you and Mimi going to do today?" he said, paying no attention to the ghostly cat.

"Uh, I don't know yet. I'm sure Mimi will think of something," Thelma said.

"Well, you may want to think about putting away some more of your things," Edwin suggested as he rose from the bed. "I noticed that there were some of your toy boxes in the spare room down the hall. Maybe…may…may…*Aaachooo!*" Edwin exhaled a huge sneeze into the sleeve of his shirt. Thelma was stunned. Could her father actually be allergic to a cat that *did not exist?*

"Bless you," Thelma said.

"Thank you. Anyway, you need to get at least a couple of, uh, uhhh… *Aaachooo!*" he sneezed once again. "Gosh, I don't know what is wrong with me. Have you been around a cat?" Edwin rubbed his eyes.

"No," Thelma said nervously. "Where would I find a cat?" Thelma got out of the bed. Pawpaw was trying to swat at the necktie Edwin held in his hand. Of course, he had no idea the cause for his allergic convulsion was right next to him, trying to play with his clothes.

"Good. Well, I should be home early today. I have to go in and have a little chat with Victor. He may not be too pleased about it."

Thelma paid no attention to the comment because she was watching Pawpaw follow Edwin around the room as he made his way to the door. The cat seemed to be extremely fascinated with him. It was true—cats seek out those who want nothing to do with them.

The doorbell sounded with a loud *ding-dong.*

Edwin moved quickly. "That's Mimi. Okay, I've got to run." Edwin kissed Thelma on the forehead and then walked out the door to prepare to resign from his new job. He let out another loud sneeze as he made his way down the hall. "Have a good da…*Aaah-chooo!*"

Thelma laughed. "I will!" She stroked Pawpaw for a few moments and then put her robe on to shake the chilliness in the air. She could hear Mimi talking downstairs and hoped breakfast would soon be on its way. All of the adventure from last night had made her hungry! Pawpaw lay down on the bed.

"Thelma," Mimi sang. "Get moving, honey. I'm going to whip up some breakfast and then after we get things straightened up, we're going to go *Christmas* shopping!"

"Fun!" called Thelma. *Oh, not more shopping.*

Mimi laughed and made her way into the kitchen. Thelma sat down on the bed and scooted closer to Pawpaw, taking a deep sigh. She wished she could talk to Anna, but she didn't want to disturb her too early. The dead could probably be crabby. There were so many questions. Maybe answers were somewhere in the pages of the Guide.

Thelma opened the book and stretched across the bed. Pawpaw resituated herself, lying against the curve of Thelma's side. Thelma looked at the front page of the guide. She glanced at the Table of Contents and decided to visit the

section called *Defender of the Dead* first. Yes, that passage seemed very important. It read:

DEFENDER OF THE DEAD

A moon of emerald, bright and high, warns of wickedness nearby.

Beware the Emerald Moon that rises in the sky for to thee it shall signify the return of an evil that will be released from imprisonment to threaten all Realms. Be cautious, but do not fear. For unto the Realms from the land of Evermoore, a great and powerful champion shall be given—a Defender of the Dead—a...

The bottom of the page was torn. Turning it, she could see that a new section began. A piece of the page had been ripped and with it the remainder of the passage had been lost. "Figures!" she groaned. She turned back to the Contents and then to the section called *Boogey Men: Do Not Be Afraid.*

BOOGEY MEN: DO NOT BE AFRAID

Knowing Your Boogey

Boogey Men (A.K.A. Boogeys)—evil apparitions capable of infecting the living with nightmares and fright. The main staple of the Boogey is terror. Able to sense what frightens their prey, a Boogey may employ a *Direct-Boo* method or *Night Terror* techniques to shock their victim and harvest the victim's fear. Being easily frightened, Boogeys typically prey on children. Usually, once a child is selected, a Boogey remains with them until such a time that they are no longer afraid.

Boogey Categories

- *Category I Boogey:* Standard spook. Direct-Boo method only. Closet lurker.
- *Category II Boogey:* Intermediate scare factor. Posseses some Night Terror capability.
- *Category III Boogey:* Medium-high scare factor. Shape shifting. Fear probing abilities.

- *Category IV Boogey* [Rare]: High scare factor. Can inflict physical harm. Extreme caution is suggested.

Fear is a potent emotion that carries incredibly strong power. The more fear a Boogey consumes over time, the stronger it becomes. Therefore, it is imperative that you learn how to handle your Boogey.

Handling Your Boogey

- Do NOT be afraid—only a Category IV Boogey (rare) presents any physical danger to the living.
- Light—Boogeys cannot tolerate bright light, especially sunlight.
- Weaknesses—Boogeys inherit the weakness of the form they take. For example, should your Boogey transform into a vampire to frighten you, a stake to the heart should severely weaken them.
- Laughing—the most deplorable thing to do to a Boogey is to laugh at it. Not only does this steal their power, it hurts their feelings.
- Vanquishing—Regretfully, Boogeys cannot be destroyed. They can, however, be drained of energy. Each defeat a Boogey experiences greatly reduces their fear capacity.

Thelma sat there wondering how she would go about defeating a Boogey Man. How would she even begin? How would she know what category she was dealing with? It was all very confusing…and frightening. Since being dead was an important part of the Neither Realm, she thought it best to take a look into the chapter about the Grimm Reaper.

BEING DEAD: THE GRIMM REAPER—HE'S NOT SO GRIMM

The Grimm Reaper (A.K.A. The Ferryman, Death)—he is the usher to the newly dead. His primary responsibility is to ensure that new souls enter into the Realms unharmed and intact so that they can await their evaluation. Also called the *Keeper*

of the Candles, he maintains and protects each mortal's Flame of Existence until their thread of life is severed by the Fates. He enjoys long walks on the beach, pudding, and playing a spirited game of chess. Should you be fortunate enough to beat him (currently undefeated), he will grant you one desire.

Thelma now understood that it had been the Reaper who had saved her soul from the serpent who tried to devour it the night she had died in the pool. She wondered what it would be like to play chess with Death. Her father lost to her on a regular basis. If she knew how to call upon the Reaper, she would challenge him to a game that very second. Maybe if she beat him, she could wish herself out of danger.

She turned to *Mages & Mavens.*

MAGES & MAVENS: THE GOOD, THE BAD, AND THE MAGICAL

Magical folk divide into two categories—*nice* and *naughty.* Nice magic is known to be performed by Mages. Naughty magic is a Maven's specialty.

- *Mage*—a worker of WHITE magic. Power and strength can vary. Mages can be *Casters* or *Chemists.* Casters can perform incantations, while Chemists work primarily in potions.

- *Maven*—a worker of BLACK magic. Power and strength can vary. They, too, can either be a Caster or Chemist. Often harboring hidden self-esteem issues, they will employ the aid of a henchman whom they can abuse. The most popular underling is the treasured shape-shifting Ghoul.

"Hey, kiddo…breakfast," Mimi called.

Thelma closed and locked the guide and put it in her nightstand drawer for safe keeping. She turned to Pawpaw and patted her head. "Well, I guess you can come. Not like you're going to be seen or anything."

The cat jumped from the bed and the two made their way down the steps to the kitchen, where Mimi had provided French toast, jams, jellies, bacon, sausage, and eggs. Thelma could hardly wait. She made her plate and took a seat at the counter. Pawpaw patiently sat beside Thelma as if she were asking for a plate of her own.

Did phantom pussycats eat?

"We're going to have so much fun today, I tell you," Mimi said, finishing up the last of the bacon. "We're going to get these dishes washed up and then go shopping. Lord, I love Christmas. We have to go by Welman's. They have a great big sale going on today. Fifty percent off! I'm going to get your father that coat he was eyeing the other day. Ooh, he will just *spit!*"

Mimi scooped the last few pieces of bacon out of the pan and placed them on the plate beside her. In a flash, Pawpaw appeared on the kitchen counter next to her. Thelma's eyes widened. Knowing that Mimi couldn't see Pawpaw, Thelma tried to remain calm. The sneaky phantom hunched down and began shaking its hindquarters from side to side, preparing to attack. Then, it slowly reached out for a piece of bacon. With one quick swat, Pawpaw knocked the meat onto the floor, leapt down, and gobbled it up.

"Oh, my goodness. I just dropped…" But when Mimi looked down, there was nothing on the floor at all. "I could've sworn I just heard a piece of bacon hit the floor. Did I drop a piece?"

"Uh…I don't know. I don't think so," Thelma replied trying not to laugh.

Pawpaw appeared on the other side of the counter where the sausage was displayed. Once again, the cat shifted and lurked, stalking the sausage. She slowly stretched out a paw and knocked a piece to the floor.

"Look at that!" Mimi said. Mimi walked over to the sink and got a paper towel, but when she returned, the sausage was gone. "What the…young lady, are you up to something?"

"No, no. I've been sitting here the whole time," Thelma laughed.

She continued to chuckle, which only heightened Mimi's suspicions. As Pawpaw scurried around Mimi's ankles totally undetected, Thelma suddenly found herself being thankful for living at the Peterson Estate. She had wanted to go back to Indiana just days before. But now, with her newfound friends and the wonders she had discovered, she could not imagine being anywhere else in the whole world. The "gift" Mr. Whittleton had given her was the best present she had ever received.

"You're sneaky. Teasing an old lady like that," Mimi said with a smile.

Now with a full tummy, Pawpaw jumped back beside Thelma and began licking her paws, congratulating herself for a job well done. Mimi sat down at the table and began to eat, still going on about the day she and Thelma were

going to have, but Thelma hardly heard a word. She only smiled and stroked her spectral cat, completely unobserved.

Lillian's End

Edwin entered his office unnoticed and was surprised to see the voicemail indicator on his phone glowing. Could it be Maggie? He still needed to inform her of Lillian's alleged hospitalization. Knowing how upset Maggie had been, she was probably still beside herself with anxiety over the matter. He dialed his voicemail and picked up his pen to take notes, if necessary. The automated announcement informed him that he only had one message.

"Edwin, this is Victor," Victor's voice said in a surprisingly humble tone. "I would appreciate it if you would come by my office as soon as you get in. That is, *if* you come in. I acted absolutely dreadful to you yesterday and I feel that we need to discuss it. If you do come in today, please come by at your earliest convenience."

As he hung up the line, Edwin took a deep breath, stood up from his desk, and started to Victor's office. Whatever explanation Victor had was of little importance; Edwin's mind was made up to leave. As he neared Victor's door, he was amazed to see it stood wide open with Victor sitting at his desk...*working*. He appeared to be focusing on something substantial, wearing his reading glasses and typing away. Edwin gently rapped on the open door.

"Oh, Edwin, come in, come in," Victor said.

Edwin walked into the room as Victor continued typing, looking down through his spectacles at the computer screen. The normalcy that was in the room made Edwin want to laugh. "Good morning, Victor."

Victor pushed his glasses up his pointed nose. "Good morning, yes. Before we begin could you come around here and look at this for me?" Edwin walked around and saw a report for the Merchant Division displayed on Victor's screen. "The revenue of these accounts is not making sense. These numbers should be higher."

Edwin quickly studied the figures then reached around Victor. By adding only a few simple calculations, all the figures magically balanced.

Victor smiled. "See, I knew there was a reason I hired you."

"And that's what I need to speak with you about," Edwin said, walking to the chair on the opposite side of Victor's desk. "Mister Von Hallow…"

"See, too formal. This can't be good. Call me Victor," Victor interjected.

"Okay…Victor," Edwin returned. He realized that Victor was trying to be personable with him. "I appreciate you giving me this opportunity. However, I feel that my employment here is not a good fit, on a personal level. So, I would like to offer my two week notice."

Victor took of his glasses and stood up slowly. "I see." He walked around to Edwin and leaned on the desk. "Edwin, I chose you because you are smart, very smart. Since you are so intelligent, you know that I am aware of why you are leaving, correct?"

Edwin looked down. "Yes, I would imagine you are."

"Edwin, *please* accept my apology. I had no right at all to speak to you the way I did, especially in front of a former subordinate."

"I am not used to being spoken to in that way, Victor."

"Completely understood," Victor replied.

Then, Victor's words sank into Edwin's mind. "What do you mean by 'former' subordinate?"

Victor shook his head. "Well, that is what had rattled me so. You have seen firsthand what a predicament the Facilities Department is in, Edwin. There are important files that no one can locate, sensitive information. Maggie has continuously ignored expense and in doing so she's allowed our supply costs to skyrocket. We just lost our vendor account with Cooper Supply because she didn't send in the contract."

"So you've let her go, then?"

"Yes…regretfully, I had to. The Board was not pleased with those gaps."

Edwin sat quietly, thinking to himself. Maggie had admitted her lack of attention to her job. Maybe it was true. "Victor…what exactly happened to Lillian?"

Victor stopped and looked uncomfortably at Edwin. Then he sighed. "Fine, if you must know. Understand that I am not proud of the fact that Lillian and I carried on a personal relationship for over a year. Unprofessional, I know.

Nevertheless, we were two lonely people who found an attraction to one another. Regretfully, she could not maintain discretion. How would it have looked for the Board to realize that we were involved? Well, eventually, she befriended Maggie and not only began to tell her our secrets, but also confidential information."

"What type of information? Was it really that sensitive?" Edwin asked.

"Well, that depends. You see, Maggie used to work for a competing bank in the region. She was hired against my better judgment, but due to her experience, I had tried to overlook it. I suspected that Maggie was taking our information and giving it to her previous employer, pilfering files from the vault. Of course, she was questioned immediately. I wanted her gone, but Lillian would not have it. So, I gave Maggie a warning that if she ever tampered with internal information, she would be terminated immediately."

Edwin sat forward. "So, Lillian was upset?"

Victor shook his head. "Of course. I knew they spoke, but I did not realize they had grown so close. Lillian was angered by my correction of Maggie. It was a terrible argument, one that severed our relationship, regretfully. Over the next several weeks, working together became unbearable. Rumors of our affair spread throughout the company, even to the members of the Board. So, I secluded myself to this floor and never again ventured to the lower levels of the building. I was certain, at least at that time, that if the Board could have, they would have elected to move me out of my chair altogether. Lillian and Maggie had made me out to be a chauvinistic monster, and it was simply not true. What *was* true was that I loved Lillian. I did. I do. Unlike I have loved anyone. She's just not a healthy person…*mentally*, you understand."

Edwin was quite surprised by this display of emotion. "I…I'm sorry, Victor."

"Oh," Victor sighed, wiping the wetness from an eye. "It is fine. It was some time ago. I have never told anyone the whole story, you understand."

"Yes, I understand."

Victor stood up. "That is why my emotions were so high, Edwin. That is why I was so upset. You were unfortunately in the line of fire, and you have my sincerest apologies. I assure you it will not happen again."

Edwin did not know how to respond. Did these facts make him trust Victor more? No. But, it helped him understand. There would always be a small, hidden quality about Victor that Edwin would never be able to pinpoint. Nevertheless, he only had two choices: believe Victor, or disbelieve him.

"Okay…I accept your apology, Victor," Edwin said rising.

"Wonderful, dear boy. May I trade that for your partnership?" Victor said with humor, another shocking trait that had suddenly surfaced.

Edwin thought for a moment and then said, "Yes, you can."

"Good man, good man!" Victor said rounding the desk with a smile. "I am very glad to hear it."

Victor shook Edwin's hand and patted his back. They both began walking to the door.

"Well, let's get to work. If you need anything today, just let me know," Edwin added.

"I will be certain to. Tell me, how is little Thelma doing? I must say I have to apologize for the party. I've no idea what kind of mangy animal was lurking in the parking area. She seemed very frightened."

Edwin smiled. "Oh, she's doing fine. I'm certain it was just an old dog. It probably looked much meaner in the dark. Hopefully the holidays will help her forget. She'll start school afterward, so that will help keep her occupied, too."

"Yes! What school and grade?" Victor asked.

"Wilson Middle. She will be finishing out the sixth grade. Big step!"

"Certainly! Wilson Middle School, you say?"

"Yes," replied Edwin.

"My niece just moved here two weeks ago and is starting Wilson Middle in the same grade. What a small world."

"Is that so?" Edwin replied.

"Yes. Maybe they can help one another get acclimated to the new environment."

"That would be great. What's her name? I'll have Thelma look her up."

"*Igraine*. Igraine Von Hallow."

Edwin thought that to be a fairly odd name. "Good. I'll have Thelma keep an eye out."

"Splendid. Let me know if you need anything," Victor said.

Victor closed the door behind Edwin. It was all so easy, much easier than Victor had imagined. Poor bleeding-heart Edwin, Victor knew that a love story was the path to success. Now, he felt sure that Edwin had no idea what was in store.

As Victor walked back through the room toward his desk, he could hear a small sound, like sniffling, coming from a dark corner of the room. Someone was *crying*. "Oh, for the love of cheese and rice, Iggy, stop blubbering!"

"It…it was so *beautiful*. I didn't know that you were in love," said the weeping Iggy as he faded in from the shadows. "You could've talked to Iggy about it, you know. You didn't have to keep it bottled up inside."

"Oh, shut up, you loathsome ghoul!" Victor growled. "It was all a lie. I had to keep him from walking out, not when we are so close. If only he would not have come outside looking for the girl during the party, I would have had her. Now more than ever, I have to keep an eye on him, keep him out of the way."

Iggy hopped into a chair. "So, what's next, Master?"

"It is simple, my dear Iggy. Last evening while taking my bubbly bath— you know how I love my bubbly baths—I began thinking about transforming into a Boogey, about freeing that foul creature Felix and his army, and it occurred to me that I am worth more than that! I deserve more than becoming some fear-sucking phantom for handing my life over to Felix. So I think I have found a way to have the power I desire without having to trade my flesh to get it."

"Oh…" said Iggy with subtle disappointment. "I mean, yippie!"

"Yes…I thought you'd be *pleased,*" Victor sarcastically said. "So, as the old proverb goes, keep your friends close and your enemies closer. Since I have nothing *but* enemies that should be fairly simple. What I plan to do is use Edwin's daughter. I will capture her, make her do my bidding. On the Eve of the Great Feast, she will be the one to give her life…for *me*. She knows the exact location of the Room of Arcanum and her gifts will allow her to open it freely. She will snatch the Secret, bring it back to me, and after I have that power I will release Felix and his army. Felix Payne will bow before me and I will be the ruler of the Boogey Men! If they do not submit, I will drain every ounce of their power. Oh, it is so lovely! I have chills. I do…look!"

Iggy rocked back and forth in the chair, holding his little feet. "And, how will you do all that? You will be busy—the holidays coming up. You have done no shopping. Then, your little niece starting school. How will you find the time?"

Victor chuckled and grabbed Iggy's plump cheeks. "*You* are my niece, dear man."

"Bu…Ith not a gurrl," Iggy muttered through Victor's grasp.

"Ah, you can be a girl, Iggy. With your shape-shifting talent, you should have no problem passing as my little niece Igraine. I mean, it was you who was able to fool Lillian's old landlady by taking on Lillian's form to close her lease, was it not?"

"Yes…but…but Iggy was teased in school," Iggy uttered.

"Aww," Victor said rounding the desk and giving Iggy a big hug. "Would Iggy rather be teased or *dead?*"

Of course, Iggy didn't want to be dead. Teased seemed much better than dead. "May I have a pink backpack?"

Victor cuddled Iggy and cooed, "Of course, you may have you a *whittle pink backpack*, and crayons, and glitter! Have we missed tax-free weekend?"

A Very Phantomite Christmas

Edwin wiped his mouth and leaned back from the table. "Now," he smiled. "It's time to open presents!"

"Well, I'm ready!" Norma said jokingly. "I want to see that diamond ring I got!"

"Woo hoo!" Thelma and Mimi squealed simultaneously with delight.

Thelma scooted her chair back and ran into the living room where all the presents were nestled under the tree. Not only was she excited to open her own presents, she was excited to give gifts to others, including Anna, Ernest and Solomon. But, she would have to wait to see her ghostly friends in secrecy later that evening.

"Eddie," Norma said. "The place has really turned out nice! Your mother did such a good job decorating." Mimi smiled.

"Well, Mom's got a knack for it. What can I say?" Edwin replied slyly. "Now, who's going to play Santa? I guess it will be me. Let's see. To…Mom from Norma."

The group opened presents and the pile of wrapping paper grew larger and larger. Thelma got a gift card, three beautiful sweaters, a curling iron, earrings, and a new pair of shoes. Last but not least, her father had a final surprise for her—a brand new game console of her very own that had a game in 3D!

"But, Dad, you forgot your last present," Thelma said noticing her father's special gift still sitting on the tree skirt.

Edwin looked at Mimi and smiled. "Oh, what is this? I wonder who this is from?"

"You'll just have to see," Thelma said with a smile.

He carefully unwrapped the package, pulling and tearing at the bright foil paper. It was definitely the back of a large picture frame. He looked at Thelma and smiled.

"Well, this is…wow! This is great."

"Turn it around, goofus!" Thelma laughed.

He turned the frame around to see a collage of pictures carefully placed in a large picture frame. They were black and white photos of Edwin, Thelma…and Juliana. In the center was his wedding picture with Juliana, one he often tried to avoid in fear of the memories it held.

Naturally, Thelma expected a smile of joy from her father, and he did smile, but through the smile his eyes began to glisten. His bottom lip somewhat quivered. Large tears fell from his eyes as he stared at the frame. Norma's eyes were also beginning to tear. She stood up and walked behind Edwin, placing her hands on his shoulders in comfort.

Thelma had not wanted to hurt her father's feelings. Confused, she looked to Mimi who had been moved to tears as well. Then Thelma, too, began to cry. Yes, she felt bad about her present, but mostly the tears came because she missed her mother, on their first Christmas without Juliana's presence.

"Honey," said Mimi reaching out for Thelma.

"Oh, Pumpkin," said Edwin wiping his eyes. "No, no, no. You didn't do anything wrong. You didn't do anything wrong at all. I *love* it. I really do. It is the perfect present. It is."

He took Thelma gently by the arm and hugged her, but she only cried harder. With the sudden outpour of memories, she found it impossible to stop. The grief of losing her mother was completely on the surface now. The dam which had opened could not be closed. She needed to get away from everyone, so she ran into the kitchen. Edwin soon followed. As he entered, he saw her sitting at the counter sobbing gently. He smiled and walked to her, gently taking her hands into his.

"It was a wonderful present," he said.

"No it wasn't."

"Yes…yes it was."

"Really?" Thelma replied.

"Oh, yes. The best present I ever got in my life. Well, with the exception of you, that is." He rubbed her hand. "You know, Pumpkin, I miss your momma, and I know you miss her, too."

"I do…I miss her," cried Thelma, tears welling in her eyes again. "She knew I wanted cake…it's my fault!"

"Oh, no, no, no," Edwin said as he hugged her tightly. "You didn't do anything at all. It's just…well, I think we need to finally accept that it's okay to want her back." Thelma leaned up and looked at Edwin. Her wet, red eyes were swollen. "Sometimes, I used to sit at our other house for hours, waiting on your mom to get back from the store. As a matter of fact, that's the main reason I wanted us to come down here with Mimi, so we could get a fresh start. And, I think we've tried so hard to pretend that everything is normal, that we sort of forgot to *miss* your mom. You know?"

Thelma wiped the tears from her cheeks. "Yeah, I think so."

He sat with her another moment, allowing her to calm down. Then he smiled and said, "Good. Now, let's get back in there. We have some games to play."

Thelma smiled. "In 3D!"

"Yes," Edwin giggled. "In 3D."

They went back into the living room, set up her new gaming system, and began a video game adventure. They played and played. Edwin wasn't doing a very good job, mostly because he refused to wear the 3D goggles that came with the game.

"Dad!" chuckled Thelma. "You have to wear the goggles."

"But, they make me look like a goofus."

"So! You can't see the clues if you're not wearing the glasses!"

Edwin finally put them on and the entire room flew into hysterics. He did look absolutely foolish. It was all so much fun, and Thelma had additional gift-giving ahead of her. After the festivities had come to an end and Edwin had tucked Thelma in for the night, Pawpaw jumped onto the bed with an announcing purr.

"Well, hello, you," Thelma said with a smile. "I didn't forget you." Thelma had managed to sneak a portion of ham in a napkin and bring it to her room. The cat ate and purred while Thelma stroked her back.

Suddenly, Anna *poofed* into existence at the foot of the bed. "Merry Christmas, woman!"

"Ahh!" screamed Thelma. "Listen, you need to find a better way of entering a room."

"Yeah, yeah, yeah. So what did you get?" Anna asked as she phased into a more solid form.

Thelma proceeded to tell Anna of all the presents she had gotten that evening. "In spite of Mom being gone, I had a very good Christmas."

"It sounds like it. I miss Christmas sometimes," Anna said as she played with some trinkets from Thelma's nightstand.

Thelma grinned. "Well, now that you mention it, I got you something."

Anna looked at her and held out her hand. "You did? Well, lemme have it, girl!"

Thelma got up from the bed, reached behind the wardrobe, and retrieved a bag with wrapped gifts inside. She searched for a moment and handed Anna a small package with red and gold paper. Anna smiled and eagerly unwrapped the gift. It was a picture frame containing a photo of Anna and Mimi from many years ago. Thelma had found the picture as she was constructing her father's gift.

Anna smiled at the thoughtful gesture.

"Do you like it?" Thelma asked.

Anna touched the photo and remembered what *alive* felt like. "Oh, yeah, I really do." Anna began to think back to the ways of the living, which she did not often do. Having grown accustomed to the spiritual world in which she now existed, Anna didn't think of the past. "You know, you may not believe this, but I actually thought to get you something, too."

"You did? You didn't have to, though. You already gave me one of the best presents," Thelma replied, petting Pawpaw.

Anna got up and held out her palm. "Yes, but you may wind up *needing* this someday." Her hand began to phase into its ghostly shape as she leaned down and gently blew across the surface of it. There was a soft glow that soon took the shape of a small crystal egg. It was detailed with various designs of leaves and vines. It was just smaller than a robin's egg. Anna cupped her other hand over the object and when she lifted it, it was magically attached to a shiny silver chain. She reached out and handed it to Thelma. It was very lovely.

"How cool. Thank you." Thelma said as she put it on.

"You are welcome. It's called a Beckon. It's like a *cell phone for ghosts*. Ha! Let's call it *Boo-tooth*…get it? You can contact just about anyone from the Neither Realm you want with this thing." Anna said.

Thelma was impressed. "Oooh, really?" She held it up and looked at it more closely.

"Sure. Come here and I'll show you how to use it." Thelma stood up and followed Anna to the center of the room. "Take it off and hold it in front of you." Thelma did so. "Now, say, *Hello, this is Thelma Thimblewhistle. I need to place a collect call to Dead Anna. I'll accept the charges.*"

Thelma laughed. "Are you serious? Geez, how much is a long distant call to the other side?"

Anna laughed and walked back to the bed. "Really, you just have to think of who you want to talk to and there you have it."

Thelma's laugh began to fade as she held the charm. "Could I…could I call my mom?"

Anna looked down with regret. "No…no, see…your mom's not in the Neither Realm, Thelma. She's gone on…all the way."

"All the way?"

"Well, some souls are given, like, jobs," Anna explained. "I was given the chance to remain here and help out the living, and I thought *cool.*" Anna ran her hand down Pawpaw's back. "And it's not for a spirit to decide where they go. Sometimes, you have a job you have to remain behind and do. Maybe it's one job, maybe it's a lot. You never know. Once a soul is in their new home, they are there to stay. You're not allowed to cross Realms. They say it confuses the living. I think continuously searching for a loved one who has passed kinda keeps the living from moving forward with their lives."

Thelma's eyes began to tear ever so slightly, but still she smiled. "Well, that's okay. Just wanted to ask is all. It's a great gift. I love it. Thank you, Anna."

Anna smiled at her and gently touched her shoulder. "You're welcome, sister." Anna looked in the bag. "Okay, who are these for?"

"Oh, yeah. We have to go see Ernest and Solomon. I got them some stuff, too."

Anna and Thelma made their way to the library and once inside, Thelma gently knocked on Ernest's wood to wake him. Solomon leapt from his drawer, excited to hear Thelma's voice. Anna took the same seat by the fireplace as she had before.

"Merry Christmas!" exclaimed Ernest as he roused.

Solomon had actually sketched Thelma a Christmas card with the message *Merry Christmas and Happy New Year, Thelma Thimblewhistle.*

"Merry Christmas," Thelma replied. "I got you *both* presents."

"Really?" said Ernest, somewhat surprised.

Solomon was apparently surprised, too. What were a desk and a pen to use? What would be a gift? Thelma reached into her bag and set a present in front of Ernest.

"Um, would you help me, dear fellow?" Ernest said to Solomon, who jumped down to the floor and used his tip to rip open the package. It was a beautiful wooden desk clock with brass fittings.

Thelma leaned down. "Do you like it?"

"It is wonderful," Ernest said gratefully.

Solomon opened his gift, which was a set of inks of various colors for him to use. He bounced to Thelma's ankle and leaned against it affectionately.

"Ah, you're welcome, sweetie" Thelma said to Solomon.

It was a delightful night for Thelma, one of discovery and bonding, of giving and receiving, and she was thankful. Though there were things she had lost in her short lifetime, she began to realize that she had so much more than most. Even though she did not have her mother physically with her, she still had a family, on earth *and* in the spirit world. It was for this reason she knew that her mother was out there somewhere, watching from a Christmas star.

And Thelma felt as if she was the luckiest girl in the world.

The Recollection

Thelma bid them good night and began up the stairs to her room. The excitement of the holiday had drained her to the point of exhaustion and she was very much ready for sleep. As she neared her room, she noticed something unusual. Smoke was seeping from under the door next to her bedroom. She sniffed into the air, but didn't smell the burning of fire. Warily, she approached the door, her senses heightened. From inside she could hear clatter, voices, and shouting, like a busy intersection in the city. She glanced back down the hallway toward the steps. "Anna?" There was no reply.

She took hold of the doorknob and slowly turned it. A horse and buggy nearly clipped her arm as she stumbled onto a cobblestone street. It was nighttime, dark, and crowded. The foggy streets were humming with life. She began to walk down the sidewalk in disbelief of what she was seeing. It appeared that she was somehow in London, England, but not in the present day. It was London from long ago, with horse-drawn carriages and gas-lit street lamps, just like she had seen on television. Passing the dark window of a dress shop, she could see her reflection. Her dress was very lovely, red velvet, with a white bow around her waist. In her hat was a large plume. She touched the reflection with her white glove.

"The Slasher strikes again! Read it here!" called a man on the corner standing beside a stack of newspapers.

Thelma walked to where he stood waving copies of the tabloid he was attempting to sell to the people. Reaching down, she took one and read the headline:

London Tribune

August 19th, 1888

Slasher Claims 5th Victim! Citizens of London Beware!

"Hey, kid! Buy it or bloody drop it!" the salesman called, his black teeth snarling at her through the smoke of his cigar.

She swiftly put the paper back and rushed away down the opposite street. The roadway she found herself on was much darker than the main city street. The thick fog rolled around her feet as she tried to see in front of her. She walked forward into the darkness, slowly and carefully, listening intently to the pops and creaks of her surroundings. "Hello?" she called.

A woman's hysterical screams in the distance sliced through the air, sending chills of panic down her flesh. She turned and began to run back to the busy city street where she had once been. Suddenly, she tripped, but before she could fall to the ground, someone grabbed her. Thelma screamed as loudly as she could.

"Hey, hey! Little girl! What are you doing out here at this time of night," said the heavy policeman. "You can't be out here all alone with a madman running about." Thelma broke away from him. His eerie glass eye oogled her as she backed away. "What? You scared of this?" He chuckled to himself as she kept backing away. Then he wiggled his fingers at her saying, "Boooo! Ha! How's that for scary!"

She turned and ran into a small store behind her where the safety of light appeared to be. Closing the door, she could hear voices behind her. As she looked down, she realized she was no longer wearing the elegant velvet dress she had once donned. This dress was torn and gray. Her hands were dirty and cold. From the opposite side of the door she no longer heard the busy London streets, but the sounds of gunfire, screams, and explosions. The sounds of war.

Boom!

The sound of a distant blast made her back away from the door. She turned to see a group of strange people. They were huddled together in the small dark

room, waiting. The atmosphere was tense, anxious. One woman, who paced nervously back and forth, began to speak to the group.

"Mary is still missing." She was wringing her hands, rubbing them together, her small frame shaking. "She said she would be here, Mark, she *promised*."

The man called Mark sternly sat in the middle of the room in front of a massive mirror, thinking, planning their moves one step at a time. His broad shoulders in his torn uniform overshadowed the room. "She'll be here, Adria," he said with a slightly southern drawl. "I know it. Calm down. We've got to remain focused. We'll win—I've seen it."

"I hope you're right," said a figure from the back of the room. The tall woman walked to a small window of the safe house and peered out.

"I *am* right, Helga," Mark said flatly.

"Yes, we hope you're right. The plan is going to take all of us," the nervous Adria added. "All of us must be involved, or it will not work. Our efforts will be in vain. Then what will we do? It was so difficult for us to find one another."

"Stop this!" said a man with a thick African accent stepping forward. "We must not be negative."

Boom!

Another explosion sounded. This one was closer.

"She'll make it through the Nexus. I know it," Mark said. "The Mage is keeping us hidden. We can't afford to be found yet, not when we're so close. If Felix remains in power, he'll rule everything."

Thelma wondered if they could be waiting for her. Why was she there? Just as she was about to step from the shadows, the tall mirror began to glow. The light illuminated the room, shining on twelve anxious faces. A very beautiful, dark haired woman stepped through the mirror's light into the room, covered in sweat, clearly out of breath. Exhausted, she fell into Mark's arms.

"Mary!" Mark exclaimed. "Get me water…a towel!" he called to the others.

One of the people in the background poured liquid from a canteen onto a torn cloth and handed it to Mark. He took it and wiped Mary's forehead. The others crowded around them, observing intently. Thelma hid behind a wooden support beam in the back of the room away from their eyes.

"I…I'm fine. I'm ok," Mary said. She looked to Mark and smiled, then gently caressed his face with her palm.

Mark smiled back. "You, my dear, are late."

"Well, am I ever on time?" Mary asked.

Mark continued to wipe sweat from her forehead. "Where's Marilyn?"

"She's safe…with your mother." With assistance from Mark, Mary stood and regained her composure. "Ok. Now, everyone, let's introduce each other. I have the list here." She took out a piece of paper with names written on it and then took a sip of water from Mark's glass. "Let's begin on this side. First names only and country; let's keep it simple."

The first person stepped up, a man in his early twenties. "Edvard, Sweden."

The woman beside him looked forward. "Yara, Brazil."

"Chandu, Ethiopia."

"Helga, Hungary."

"Qua-li, China."

"Jacque, France."

"Gerardo, Italy."

"Claudia, Chile."

"Theresa, Canada."

"Laura, Ireland."

"Adria, England."

Mary took Mark's hand. "Mary, United States."

"Mark, United States," he said as he looked into her eyes. "We appreciate everyone coming. We've been able to brief most of you on why we're here. For those of you who aren't clear, several months ago after being wounded in the field, I was placed in an Army hospital. While there, I met a soldier from Poland named *Paul Perlmutter*, an Oracle." Mark held up a tattered envelope for the group to see. "Learning that I was an Oracle, too, he gave me vital information in this letter telling the story of a creature we all know, Felix Payne, the Boogey Man who no longer scares just children, but the world."

Helga stepped forward. "How did he get here?"

"We aren't really sure," Mary said. "After the battle in the Realms, Felix fell from sight for years. Some thought he was gone for good. Maybe that's what Felix wanted…to be forgotten. But Paul believed Felix wanted to become a leader, influence the world, start wars. With his army of Boogey Men locked away in the Underworld, he needed to find others who also desired to conquer the world."

"Yes," said Mark. "*War* was the game Felix really wanted to play. I imagine he spent years and years hopping from body to body. Paul thought maybe he was studying methods of conquest, war, or even politics. Maybe he was looking for the perfect host—we don't know. What we do know is that he finally found his next home in the man we know today as *Reich Leader Rudolf Hildenburg* of the Nazi Army."

"So," Mary said. "We're dealing with a monster hundreds of years old. He's smart and cunning. He knows what scares us."

Mark stood up. "Exactly. This thing has killed hundreds, thousands of people—innocent people. This is our chance, our *one* chance to take care of him once and for all, all of us together."

"If Felix desires ultimate power, why hide in Rudolf? Why not just go on and take control of the Führer himself?" Jacque asked.

"And be the primary target?" questioned Chandu.

"That's right," added Mark. "Think of it like a chess board. The King is the piece that all the others are after. Rarely is he the piece that wins the game."

Qua-li leaned forward with confidence. "There have never been so many Oracles in one place."

"I didn't even know there were others," replied Jacque.

"We knew there were others," said Mark." "We just didn't know where to find you. That's why my encounter with Paul was so important. He gave us the precise location for each of you. He planned this for over a decade. Paul saw the Emerald Moon in the sky and knew what was coming."

"Have we found the Defender? The moon indicates their arrival. Let's allow them to take care of Felix," said Adria nervously.

"There isn't time for that," Mary said. "It's been twelve years since the coming of the moon. We can't wait for the Defender. We don't even know if they exist. We have to act now. This is our time."

"Yes, there is no time to waste. I wish Paul could have been here for this moment," Gerardo said.

Sadness appeared on Mark's face. "Yes, so do we. I was finally able to leave the hospital, but Paul wasn't able to pull through."

"Do we have the Mage?" Jacque asked.

A woman in a nurse's uniform walked to the middle of the room and faced Mark and Mary. "Yes, I'm here."

"This is Angelica Miller, from the United States," said Mark. "She saved my life."

Thelma's mouth hung open as she realized she was seeing the nurse from the hospital, the same one that had come to see her.

Mary took Angelica's hand. "Angelica, we need you to locate Felix. He doesn't stay anywhere that doesn't have a Nexus available for quick escape, but we don't know where to begin. Since he has closed all contact to the Neither Realm, no one else can help us."

Angelica smiled kindly and walked to the middle of the room where she sat down on the floor and crossed her legs. She removed the pencil that held back her hair to allow it to fall loose. Then she tilted her head and focused her eyes forward.

Mary bent down to her and said, "I never got a chance to thank you for saving the life of my husband, Angelica."

Angelica caressed Mary's hand and Mary walked away. Placing both hands ahead of her, Angelica said, "Felix Payne, evil soul, with your heart of stone. Come out of your secret darkness—make your presence known."

A glistening mist began to emit from her hands. The fog grew thicker and thicker as it began to slowly turn clockwise. It increased in speed with more force and power as a wind circulated about the room. A bright light began to shine from Angelica's hands. Then the group gathered and joined hands as the nurse began to levitate from the ground, her eyes fading, becoming glowing orbs in their sockets, her hair blowing wildly about. The smoke took the shape of the entire city of Berlin, a three dimensional map.

"The gardens in Reichskanzlei at 77 Wilhelmstraße," called Mark loudly, his voice cutting through the wind. "It's where most government buildings are located. There!" Mark pointed to a bright red point on the map. "There he is!"

Angelica began to grow weary, her powers fading. As the map disappeared, she fell to the floor. Mary ran to tend to her.

"Are we ready?" said Mark.

Everyone gathered together and joined hands. Mark looked toward the mirror in the center of the room and extended his hand. With a simple snap of his fingers, the gateway opened in a burst of light. Mary and Angelica waved goodbye to one another. Then, the Oracles were gone, the mirror-Nexus closing behind them.

Breathing heavily, Angelica rested on the floor. Thelma still could not believe what she was seeing. As she tried to step closer and get a better look at Angelica, her foot slipped giving away her presence.

"Who's there?" Angelica called.

Thelma barely stepped into the light. "Um…hi, I don't think you know me but…"

"Thelma?"

"Yes…how did you…" Thelma said as she walked into the room.

"Thelma, listen to me," Angelica said urgently. "You must come see me at the hospital. There are important matters to discuss."

"What? Just tell me now," Thelma said.

The sound of a plane flying low overhead caused Angelica to cautiously look upward. "There's not time. Now, Thelma, you have to wake up. Wake up…now!"

"But…"

The Nurse & the Soldier

*B*oom!

"Wake up!" Anna said, shaking Thelma.

Thelma sprang from her dream. In her mind, she could still see the underground safe house and feel the heat from the fireplace. The scent of destruction was thick in the air. Those people—they were the Oracles, the ones Ernest had told her about. What was Angelica doing there? Sweat saturated Thelma's wavy hair.

She was confused. "What happened? Where was I?"

"It was a dream. You were just having a dream," Anna said.

"No, no…it wasn't a dream," Thelma said. Her heart was still racing, beating against her ribcage.

"Trust me, you're fine," Anna replied. "What in the world were you dreaming about? Who are Mary and Mark?"

Thelma got out of the bed and began pacing the floor. "We have to see the nurse…Angelica. She said she had something to tell me." Thelma walked over to the wardrobe and opened the doors. Her clothes hung neatly in a row, shoes underneath. She reached through the layers of fabric and touched the back of the closet. "Okay, how do we get through this?"

"Get through what? The wardrobe?"

"Yeah, you said it's a Nexus, right?"

"Well…yeah, but I don't think you're strong enough to do the Nexus thing, Thelma. Why?"

"I don't have time to explain. We have to go. Now! Tonight!"

"Alright…calm down, sister," Anna said. "I'll lead, but you're not gonna like it."

"I don't care, let's go," Thelma said as she examined the closet.

Anna rose from the bed. "Listen, you're gonna have to calm down before we do this because you *have* to concentrate." Thelma looked at Anna and began to breathe slower. "Okay, typically, we would prefer to practice first." Anna phased and floated over to hover beside Thelma. "Okay…first time Nexus transportation for those who have *skin*. Let's see. This can be kind of tricky. It's not like being teleported, like on *Star Trek*. The place you want to arrive at has to have a Nexus, too. If it doesn't, then you can't go there. I'm not totally sure there's one at the hospital. As you can guess, it's been a while since I've needed a doctor."

"How do we find out?" Thelma asked.

"Well…like this." Anna held her hand out and closed her eyes. A vapor flowed from her fingertips, swirling like a magical whirlpool, glowing, pulsating. Pawpaw scurried under the bed. The spinning smoke went faster and faster as it began to change shape. Anna had created a three-dimensional map of the entire city, made of bluish, translucent fog, just like the one Angelica had created in Thelma's dream.

Anna stood back. "Okie doke. Here is a map of the city."

Thelma rolled her eyes. "Right. So, where are the Nexuses?"

"Right here." Anna snapped her fingers and small glowing dots appeared throughout the city on the map. "These are all the Nexuses in the city. You see here? This is where we are." Anna pointed to a dot that was reddish in color. Thelma could then make out their house almost perfectly. Then she noticed Mimi's house also had a red point.

"Mimi has a Nexus?" grinned Thelma.

Anna shrugged. "Well…yeah—the big, tacky mirror in the corner of her bedroom. Just like she told you, she and I were pretty close friends, *best* friends. Don't you think I pop in to check on her from time to time? I always try to leave the smell of violets around; they're my favorite flower. I think they remind her of me. Dead people like to be remembered." Anna continued to search. "Ah! There's the hospital and it has a Nexus. I thought it might with Angelica being there, but better safe than in Limbo, I always say." Anna waved her hand and the map dissipated.

Thelma coughed, waving the smoke from her face. "Okay, let's go."

Anna sighed. "Alright, follow me. You asked for it. I hope you're not prone to motion sickness!" They both stepped to the doors of the wardrobe and

Thelma opened both sides. Then, Anna took her by the hand. "*Think* of where we're wanting to go."

Thelma began thinking of the hospital room in which she had stayed, how it smelled and looked, and how she felt while there. Suddenly, she could feel a slight tremble in the floor. The hair on her arms began to stand on end, like she was close to electricity. It was weak at first, but air soon began to circulate through the clothes in the wardrobe. A light appeared.

Thelma felt as if the light was drawing her to it. Before she realized it, she and Anna were being pulled in its direction. Sparks began to spit from the wardrobe doors like small fireworks. Thelma was no longer certain she was prepared to travel in this manner. What happened if she got lost? What if she didn't arrive at the hospital? What if she and Anna were separated?

But, it was too late.

The light swirled faster and faster as Thelma tried to calm her fear and focus on their destination. She yelled, "Hey, um…are you sure this is supposed to happen? It wasn't like this when you came through."

"Yeah…*but I'm dead*," Anna yelled back.

Whoosh!

With that, they were sucked into the wardrobe, doors slamming shut behind them. Thelma had never experienced a sensation like this one. She soared through the air into nothingness, holding tight to Anna's hand. The Beckon around her neck was like a guiding light, shining brightly, completely unlocked in the dimension through which they were traveling. Thelma's body felt like it was ten feet long, her legs flapping behind her as they soared through the wormhole.

To avoid feeling nauseous, Thelma tightly closed her eyes. Then, as quickly as it had begun, the two of them began to slow down and stop. It was not a sudden stop, like the brakes of the car, but rather like the stop of an elevator.

Anna took a deep breath. "Okie dokie, here we are."

Thelma slowly opened her eyes in the blackness. It felt like she was in a small space, locked inside, like a coffin. "Uh…where are we?"

"Who knows? Maybe we're in the morgue."

"Oh, shut up," Thelma barked. "Get me out of here!"

Thelma felt a door handle and popped it open. The area was dimly lit. The smell of formaldehyde burned her nose. She could see rows of small numbered doors aligning the walls. Thelma glared at Anna.

Anna floated to the floor. "I swear I was joking about the morgue."

"Ewww!" said Thelma in disgust. "Get me out of here!"

Anna grabbed Thelma's hand as she began to squirm and wiggle her way out of the cabinet. Losing her balance, she fell to the floor and then stood up quickly. Obviously, there were no other *living* people in the room besides Thelma. Two cadavers were hidden under stark white sheets. Having never been in a morgue before, Thelma did not find it the least bit pleasing.

"Whoooooooooh," Anna moaned.

Thelma swatted at her. "If you don't stop, I'm calling the Ghostbusters!"

Anna snickered as the two of them made their way out of the room. Finally, they were in the brightness of the main hallway. They searched the walls hoping to find a sign that would lead them to the correct area of the hospital, the wing where Thelma had stayed. A set of doors to their right suddenly opened. They hid in a breezeway while an orderly walked by them, pushing a new body into the morgue. They managed to slip through the doors before they closed completely.

"Excuse me!" called a voice from behind them.

Poof! Anna phased and evaporated as Thelma spun around to see a nurse who worked on the floor.

"I…I…," began Thelma.

"Are you lost?" the nurse said.

"Uh, yeah. Very lost. I am visiting my…sister. She had…her tonsils removed," Thelma lied.

The nurse obviously sensed Thelma's dishonesty. "Really? What room number is she in?"

"231. Her nurse's name is Eunice," Thelma said. "I was trying to find a cafeteria or a vending machine or something. I'm starved."

This seemed to appease the nurse. "Well, you're a long ways away. Follow me." Thelma followed her to a set of elevator doors. "You'll take these up to the fourth floor. Get off and turn left. You need to head towards the Miller wing. Once you get to the double doors, you will see the name 'Angelica Miller' above them. The nurse's station is right inside. You should pass a few vending machines on the way."

Thelma smiled at her. "Thank you." She got on the elevator and pushed the fourth floor button.

"Oh, you are so good," said Anna fading back into view.

"No thanks to you," Thelma commented. "Where did you go? It's not like she can see you."

"Listen, ghosts have to be careful in a hospital. No telling who can sense us."

The elevator opened and Thelma and Anna made their way to the wing of the hospital where Angelica roamed. They finally found an empty room and entered.

"So, how do we find her?" Thelma asked.

Anna fell onto the empty hospital bed and rolled her eyes. "You *never* listen to me. Use your Beckon and call for her. Just hold it out there and ask for her."

Thelma reached into her shirt and pulled out the small egg. "Oh…yeah…Beckon, right." She took a deep breath and held it in her hand. She closed her eyes. "Angelica Miller. I need to…"

"I thought that was you," interrupted a figure from the corner.

Thelma jumped. "Hello?"

Angelica phased to flesh and stepped into the light of the room, still wearing the same uniform she had worn during their initial meeting. "I thought it was you, but I couldn't be sure." Angelica noticed the Beckon. "And where did you get such a lovely necklace?"

"She got it from me," Anna replied.

Angelica turned to Anna. "Goodness…girl! How are you?"

"Hey, honey, just fine. You?" Anna said.

"I'm good, good. *Dead.* But good." said Angelica, obviously more comfortable now that Anna had made herself known.

"I had a dream tonight," began Thelma. "You were in it. First I found myself in London, England in the year 1888. I ducked into a store to get away from some creepy policeman. Then, suddenly it was nearly sixty years later during the middle of World War II!"

"Actually, you experienced something called *Recollection.* Some sensitives can remember a past that is not their own," Angelica said. "When we first met I didn't know if you were gifted enough to have one. I figured if you were who I thought you were, you'd come to find me sooner or later."

Thelma walked to her. "Were all of the people in that room Oracles?"

"Of course," answered Angelica. "With the exception of myself."

"And Mark and Mary?"

"Markus and Maria Evermoore—two of the most powerful Oracles ever."

The graveyard rushed into Thelma's mind. She could see their tombstones. "Listen, you told me that you had something to tell me. What was it?"

Angelica moved towards the door, shutting it completely. "There's only so much I can tell you, girls. Much of it I don't remember, the details and all. Dead people sometimes lose memories of life."

"That's okay…anything will help," Thelma said.

Angelica took a seat in a small chair in front of them. "It was World War II. The fight was still raging against the Germans. I volunteered to go overseas, because there was a shortage of medical staff and the Allies were in desperate need of help. I'd been on duty for about two months, I think, when a wounded private from Tennessee was placed under my care. His name was Markus Evermoore. With my abilities as a Mage, I could sense that he was an Oracle. At that point, I'd never met one, but I'd heard about them. I had started to think they were just a myth. Soon Markus and I knew of one another's abilities.

"Well, about a week after Markus arrived, a Polish soldier by the name of Paul Perlmutter was admitted. He was badly injured, but alive. I couldn't believe it—I had never seen an Oracle, and now in the span of one week, I was taking care of two of them! Anyway, Paul began to bring us into this plan, a plan he had been working on for years. You could imagine the surprise when Paul told us that we had to defeat the Boogey Man, Felix Payne, who just happened to be residing in the body of one of the highest ranking officers in Hitler's army—Rudolf Hildenburg. No one had even thought about Felix in decades. He had just vanished. But somehow Felix had used Hildenburg's body to rise as one of the most ruthless commanders of the Nazi Army—evil, pure and simple. Paul's plan was completely insane…so, naturally, Markus and I were immediately on board.

"Paul provided Markus with the location of all the living Oracles in the world. Markus' job was to gather the group together and attack Felix at the same time, working as one. Together, they would use their power to drain his energy, rip him from Hildenburg's body, and then banish him to Perditia to be caged along with the other Boogey Men. The small group of us, infiltrating hidden bunkers of the Nazi Army—it was insane! We were all to use the closest Nexus to travel toward a secret location. He told us to just enter our Nexus and he would use his powers to guide us through.

"One by one, Markus helped guide me and all of the Oracles from around the world to this small, abandoned flat he had discovered during his service in Berlin. But Maria got lost in her Nexus. We thought she had been captured, but Markus was able to pull her through. Then it came time for me to locate Felix. Using my magic, I was able to pinpoint his location—a buried bunker about eight meters beneath the garden at Reich Chancellery. Markus activated our Nexus, and then the Oracles stepped through to take Felix down. I was so weak I could barely move. Then, of course, that's when I saw your image there with me."

"What happened to you, Angelica?" questioned Thelma.

"Felix had discovered our hiding place and sent bombers to destroy it. Fortunately, the Oracles had already made it through. Unfortunately, I hadn't."

Thelma looked down. "I'm sorry."

Angelica just smiled. "It was a small price for me to pay."

"There was something else in the Recollection." Thelma said. "When I first stepped into it, I was in London, in the past."

"How far in the past?" Angelica asked.

"I picked up a newspaper that said August 1888."

Angelica looked at them blankly. "That doesn't ring any bells for me."

Thelma stood up and began pacing the floor, thinking, trying to piece her puzzle together. "Do you know anything about the Defender of the Dead?"

Angelica thought. "What most of the dead know, I guess. The Defender would be sent to the dead to save them from the Boogey Man."

Anna chimed in. "Do you think it's her?"

"Listen, no one knows who the Defender could be, but since I heard that you took over the old Evermoore grounds the night the Emerald Moon appeared, I can make an educated guess," Angelica said looking to Thelma.

"Okay, so let's just say I'm the Defender. What do I have to do?" Thelma moaned. "I don't have, like, superpowers. I can't shoot heat rays from my eyes or leap tall buildings and stuff! I just talk to dead people!"

"Hey!" Anna said, taking exception.

Thelma rolled her eyes. "In the Guide, there's this passage. It says something like, *from the land of Evermoore you shall be sent a champion, the Defender of the Dead who will...*do something-or-other, but the page is ripped. I don't know what it says."

Angelica shook her head. "Honey, I just know what most of the dead know, which isn't much."

Sensing Thelma's disappointment, Anna spoke up. "We can try something else, Thelma. Maybe there's someone in the Neither Realm who knows what the page says. There's got to be another copy. I can ask Whittleton."

"There is someone who may be able to help," Angelica suggested.

Excitement filled Thelma's stomach. "Who? Where?"

"Allister, the Evermoore's Phantomite," Angelica said.

"Allister?" Anna said. "No one's heard from him in forever, Angelica."

"But if you could find him, he would know everything. He's been around since before Felix became a monster."

"Where do we start?" Thelma asked.

Angelica looked at them. "He belonged to the Evermoores, so he is somewhere on the grounds."

"Oh…that's great!" Thelma laughed petulantly. "That only gives us about ten acres of ground to cover. Allister could be anything."

Angelica phased and floated over to Thelma with an understanding expression on her face. "Listen, honey, I know this is hard for you. What is being asked of you is more than anyone should ask of a girl your age. Why save the dead? They're dead, right? But if this is the path destiny is giving to you, then I guarantee it will not leave you empty handed. I would bet that Allister is right under your nose. Just open your eyes…"

Allister the Storyteller

The sun had begun to rise into the sky before Thelma stopped searching for the Phantomite called Allister. When she finally closed her eyes to sleep, it was from absolute fatigue. Not long after she lay down, her father stepped into the room to kiss her goodbye before leaving for work. Mimi even tried to rouse her, tempting her with various treats, but she remained in bed saying she was not feeling well. That seemed like a much more logical explanation than the ghost hunt adventure she had been on all night.

Pawpaw remained curled up beside her. Every now and again, when images in dreams would begin to wake her, the cat would purr loudly and press against her, letting her know that she was safe in bed. How long she would remain safe was yet to be answered.

Forcing one eye open, she could see the clock read three in the afternoon. If she wanted to search the grounds for Allister, then she had to utilize the daylight at her disposal. She felt heavy all over, but a shower helped revive her. After eating, she felt even more energized, but still she felt the sticky film of weariness on her skin.

Throughout the day, she had managed to cover most of the grounds. She searched every object, every rock, and every blade of grass for the Seal of the Neither Realm, but nothing bore it. She even checked the headstone of Markus and Maria, which at one point she was certain must be Allister. It was hopeless.

Volunteering to unpack the rest of her belongings, she managed to search the entire left hallway of the second level. She looked in every room, even the vacant ones, but found nothing. The right hallway had nothing to offer either, though in the closet of one of the spare rooms she did manage to find an old toy, one of the aluminum puppets with a lever to animate it. She sat in the floor talking to the metal monkey like an imbecile, making it speak back to her as if it were Allister. On the positive side, she did manage to unpack the rest of her belongings.

After nighttime came and everyone was fast asleep, Thelma ventured to the library with Anna. Thelma knocked upon Ernest's top to rouse him and Solomon soon joined. She sat listlessly behind Ernest in the leather chair, which she had even spoken to several times hoping it could be Allister.

"He could be one of these books," Anna said.

Thelma scoffed. "Uh…there's just ten thousand of them. Be my guest."

Solomon hopped over to Thelma and started to scratch something on a piece of parchment. It was a picture of Anna with very over exaggerated features, bugged eyes, huge lips, and wild hair. Under it he wrote: *Dead people think they know everything!* Thelma laughed.

"What? What are you laughing at?" Anna asked walking over. But Solomon quickly scratched out the drawing. "Yeah…you keep on. I'll pour that ink in the toilet. Then what'll ya do?"

Thelma sighed. "Ernest, are you sure you don't know anything about Allister?"

"My apologies, madam, I only know that he exists…or did at one time. He is very, very old. As a matter of fact, he could possibly be the first Phantomite in existence."

"That's it…we're looking for a stone wheel that was chiseled by dead cavemen," Anna spat.

Thelma leaned back in the chair. "Oh, this is just hopeless. I'm never going to figure any of this out."

And it did appear to be hopeless. For the next while, Thelma and Anna began checking books in the library for the seal. On a lighter note, there was some wonderful reading contained on the old shelves: *The Adventures of Sherlock Holmes, Scary Stories to Tell in the Dark,* and some books about a boy wizard that Thelma wanted to read…as long as he was a good wizard. She had enough Mavens on her plate at the moment, she was afraid.

By two in the morning, Thelma was nearly fast asleep sitting behind Ernest. Solomon continued to scribble and draw. Anna sat over by the fireplace, staring into it, watching her own hand phase in and out again.

"Would you stop doing that? You look like a strobe light!" Thelma moaned. This, of course, prompted Anna to begin humming a tune and blinking on rhythm. Thelma leaned back and stared at the walls. It was time to give up and go to bed. She was achieving nothing with Solomon's doodles and Anna blinking.

Then something caught her eye. Around the border of the old wallpaper in the library, she thought she could see it, barely, but it appeared to be there. Getting up from Ernest, she walked over to the wall and looked closer.

"Watch this! I can get really bright…" Anna glowed. "…or really dim…" She faded to flesh. "Bright. Dim. Bright! Dim." She noticed Thelma was captivated by something on the wall. "Sister, what are you looking at?"

Thelma reached over and attempted to turn on the main light of the library, but the light bulb was broken. "Wonderful, yes, you can blink. How cool. Come here." Anna phased and floated over to Thelma who climbed the rolling library ladder to the very top shelf. She motioned for Anna to join her. "Now, glow."

As Anna lit up brightly, there it was, the Seal of the Neither Realm, faded and worn, but printed into the border of the wallpaper of the library.

"Is that the seal?" Anna asked.

"You've got to be kidding me." Thelma stepped from the ladder and started for the door. Again she could see the seal cleverly carved into the framing of the library doors. She traced the seal with her fingers, feeling it in the wood. Then she smiled and ran into the foyer.

"Where are you going?" Anna called.

She could see it—it was practically everywhere, etched into the wood of the staircase railings, around the crown molding at the ceilings. She looked down to the marble floor and could see from under the area rug that there was a triangle-like shape in the tile.

"Help me!" she called to Anna. Together they moved the huge, heavy area rug that rested on the foyer floor. Thelma dashed up the steps to the second level and looked down to see that there, made into the marble floor tiles, was the Seal of the Neither Realm.

Anna was in shock. She looked down at the floor and then up to Thelma. "Do it."

Thelma closed her eyes and took a deep breath. Then she knocked on the wood of the railing three times and said, "Allister, I need to speak with you. Please come forward."

Then, the most amazing thing began to happen.

It started small, a tremble, a flutter of air throughout the room. Then the floor actually began to move, in a roll, like a subtle wave of the ocean. A low voice that sounded almost like a *grunt*, reverberated throughout the room, like a grizzly bear was awakening from hibernation. Thelma could feel the floor moving under her feet and ran back down the steps to where Anna was floating. She braced herself against the front door.

The two staircases and their banisters began to move on their own appearing to take the shape of what could have only been a *mouth*! The whole house began to creak and pop, to yawn and *come to life*. The two great windows that sat at the top of the staircases *blinked*—like eyes. The elegant chandeliers that hung in front of them now looked like pupils and the curtains were eyebrows and hair.

The colossal windows stared down to Thelma, who was holding onto anything stable and was amazed that her father hadn't rushed from his room to see what the matter was. As the house completed its transformation, it took a deep breath and exhaled. The foyer of the old mansion had transformed into the face of an *old man*.

The staircases that formed his mouth stretched wide in a smile and his window-eyes blinked as they examined his surroundings. He looked curiously at Thelma and wiggled his wooden nose. Completely alive, the house was breathing with power.

It was then clear that Allister was none other than the Peterson Estate itself!

"And…who…are…you?" groaned the house.

"My name is Thelmawhistle," Thelma fumbled. "Uh…*Thelma Thimblewhistle*."

"Well, Thelmawhistle, I am Allister Wisenguard," Allister said.

"Nice to meet you, Mister House…*Allister*, sir."

The wood and drywall around Allister's face creaked as he spoke. "A pleasure to make your acquaintance, Thelma Thimblewhistle."

"I'm glad I found you," said Thelma.

"Asleep, but never gone," Allister explained.

Thelma stepped forward. "If you don't mind my asking, how did you become part of this house?"

"I am not part of this house," said Allister. "It is part of me. I've served the Evermoore family for generations. I am made of every blade of grass, every tree—I am the very soil this house rests upon. Once the construction of this house was complete, it became part of my energy."

Thelma then understood that Allister was not a desk, a book, or a pen, it was the land itself, the same land the Evermoore family had lived on for generations. "Allister, I need your help. I just moved into this house…*you*…recently. On my first night here, there was a green moon in the…"

"I know you, Thelma Thimblewhistle," Allister confirmed. "I have always known you, even before you knew yourself. You have come to save us. You are the Defender of the Dead."

"So it is me?" Thelma asked. "Save you from what?"

"Centuries ago, there was an insignificant sorcerer named Felix Payne. He lived in a village called Laraboleuse where he would make his living performing magic and selling potions to villagers in the town square during each full moon. Most found him amusing at best. During his last performance, a group of callous children bumbled his act making him the laughing stock of the village. Felix was humiliated and was determined to have revenge. So he used all of his remaining power in a ritual that transformed him into a phantom, an eternal spirit of corruption. Felix was no longer Felix, but a vile poltergeist that haunted nightmares, feeding from the fright of the living, growing more powerful with every scream.

"No one cared that Felix was gone. That was, until the children began to disappear. The ones who had pranked him were the first to go. Then hauntings spread to the other children. They cried and complained of monsters and shadows lurking under their beds. Children were the easiest to frighten, you see, so Felix plagued them like a sickness spreading to all the children of the village, and eventually the world. As the years passed, people began calling the entity the *Boogey Man*.

"Felix grew hungry for more than fear…he wanted *power*. He needed a source, something incredibly potent. There are some immensely powerful objects protected in the Earthly Realm that could have been used: the Golden Fleece, Pandora's Box, or the sword Excalibur. But, being a Boogey Man is not without its limitations. In being only a spirit, Felix could not access these items. Therefore, the only other source he could capture was the Secret protected in the Neither Realm. He began recruiting other vile souls, allowing them to give over their lives to be transformed into Boogey Men. He entered into the Realm with his army and tried to take the Secret's power. But Edenia and Perditia would not allow this and sent their own armies to fight. All the Boogey Men were captured, with the exception of Felix, who had managed to steal just enough of the Secret's power to have the ability to possess and command the living."

"In my Recollection, I saw London, an old London, from the 1800's," Thelma said.

"The Slasher," said Allister.

"Yes, yes, that's what the paper in the vision said."

Allister breathed deeply. "Felix spent years going from body to body, mastering the art of physical domination. One day, he happened upon a man in London named Dr. Charles Carpenter and took control of him. While in his body, Felix went on a murderous rampage. The papers called him the *Slasher*. He used the doctor's sterling reputation in the city to commit murders without the risk of being suspected. It was just the practice Felix needed to go on to his greatest achievement. *War*."

Thelma looked up. "Hildenburg."

"Yes. Years later, Felix found his final home in an insolent young boy named Rudolf Hildenburg. Rudolph was the perfect specimen. He was young, very strong, and his father was influential in the German Army. His body was the perfect home for Felix, who used him to become one of the most prominent officers of the Nazi army. If not for the Oracles, Felix would have eventually ruled the Earthly Realm. Together, they used all of their energy to weaken Felix, pull him from the body of Rudolph, and banish him to imprisonment."

"What happened to the Oracles? To Markus and Maria?" asked Thelma.

"Sadly, Markus died in battle with Felix. Maria and the others found they had little magic remaining. Their weakened bodies could no longer fight off sickness and one by one the poor Oracles faded away to be no more."

Thelma walked up and laid her hand on the staircase banister. "But, how do I fit into this, Allister? What am I supposed to do?"

"The Emerald Moon has warned us that there is an evil creature with plans to free Felix and his army from their prison in Perditia. This creature is keeping himself well hidden. The Defender of the Dead is the only one who can stop him."

"In the Guide, there is a passage, but the page is torn. It says…" Thelma began.

Allister looked to her with deep sadness reflecting in his window-eyes. "Beware the Emerald Moon that rises in the sky for to thee it shall signify the return of evil that will be released from imprisonment to threaten all Realms. Be cautious, but do not fear. For unto the Realms from the land of Evermoore a great and powerful champion shall be given—a Defender of the Dead—a girl, young and pure, who shall give forth her own life to save the dead from dying."

Meeting Igraine

And there it was—the painful truth that in order to save her ghostly friends, and possibly even the world, Thelma had to sacrifice her life. It was unbelievable. Anna was completely beside herself, as were Ernest and Solomon. Everyone had suspected that Thelma was to be their hero, but no one had imagined that she would have to die to save them. This changed things.

Ernest had demanded that Thelma run away from the Peterson Estate and leave the dead to fend for themselves. Anna had denied that Thelma had to give her life at all, suggesting that Thelma had already died to save the dead the evening she drowned in the pool. That logic seemed sound enough. So they all agreed to believe just that; it made it easier to accept. Although, Thelma knew this was not the case. She could feel it in her bones. No, death awaited her, like an old friend waiting to see her once again. And should the time actually arrive when she must offer herself to save her friends, she imagined she would do so.

A fate Thelma felt was worse than death still awaited her: the first day at Wilson Middle School. Since Edwin had to work early on her first day, he asked Mimi to drive her. Her father mentioned that his supervisor's niece was also starting at Wilson Middle School, but Thelma did not care. Her mind was elsewhere, trapped in places where fate, destiny and death were things which could not be avoided.

It was still dark outside when Mimi woke Thelma for school. She so dreaded the first day; she was certain she was not going to make any friends. Middle school had been a huge adjustment for her. Now, she had to introduce herself all over again and become acclimated to yet another new place. The house was frigid, an unwelcome change from Thelma's warm blankets. Pawpaw didn't budge from underneath them. Reluctantly, Thelma got dressed and made her way down the stairs.

"Now, don't forget—I may be a bit late getting you this afternoon. Me and Norma have a scrapbooking class after lunch." Mimi noticed Thelma's unresponsiveness. "Honey, do you feel well?"

"Yeah, but if I say no can I stay home?"

Mimi gave her a sympathetic look. "Oh, Thelma, I know you don't want to go, but you have to. I promise it won't be that bad. You'll make some friends."

"I bet," was all Thelma could manage.

Obviously, it had been a while since Mimi had been in school. Things were different now. Sensing her awkwardness, children did not seem to gravitate toward her. Sure, she had a few acquaintances at her other school in Indiana, but very few. In many ways, she was too mature to relate to most of her peers, and the loss of her mother had made her even more so.

After breakfast, she finished getting ready, patted Pawpaw goodbye, and she and Mimi started on their way. The wind cut through her coat, even though it was very thick. It took Mimi's car so long to warm up. Thelma thought they may make it to the school before it would be a suitable temperature. What would be the point then?

"You'll make new friends," said Mimi cutting into the silence.

"I don't make a lot of friends."

"Oh, you will this time. I know it. Southerners are nicer people. It's a fact." They drove a few moments longer in silence. "Thelma…honey, how have you been? I mean, we haven't really spoken about the things that happened…"

"I've been okay," interrupted Thelma. She had to find a way to direct Mimi's conversation elsewhere, even though she so wanted to tell her the things she knew. "Things have been great."

"Well, I just wanted to ask, because you've not said another word about the night of the party, the nurse, or anything."

Thelma looked down. The truth was right on the tip of her tongue. All she had to do was say it aloud, but to do so would put her grandmother in danger, and she could not allow that to happen. "You know, I think I may have just been scared, being in a new place and all."

Mimi found Thelma's sudden change of heart strange. "Well, you have been through a lot the past year, honey."

"Yeah," agreed Thelma. "But I think it's going to get better." She looked out of her car window, tears glistening in her eyes.

"I know it will, Baby. You'll see."

They pulled into the long line of cars at Wilson Middle School. Children exited vehicles and made their way into the large front doors. Thelma knew that she was to go into the main doors next to the *big tree*. It was one of the largest old trees she had even seen in her life, so large that a person could almost live inside it. Once through the doors, she was to make her way to the office which was located on the right. After Mimi completed Thelma's registration, Thelma would be taken to Ms. Pennyworth's sixth grade homeroom.

As they made their way into the school, Thelma could see the building was very old and in the process of being renovated, especially the auditorium, which was being completely remodeled. Thelma made a conscious effort not to gaze directly into anyone's eyes. It was best not to make eye contact, not immediately. They entered the office and Mimi began completing paperwork while Thelma sat down in the chairs where other new students were seated. There was a strange looking little girl who was studying Thelma, apparently trying to get her attention. Thelma tried to refrain from meeting her eyes. However, no matter how much she tried to ignore her, the little girl persisted. Finally, the girl got up and walked over to Thelma.

"Ah-hem," said the odd little girl clearing her throat. Thelma looked up at her. "I am Igraine."

Igraine? That was the name. This had to be the girl her father had mentioned, his boss's niece. Immediately, there was something about Igraine she simply did not like. She couldn't quite put her finger on it. Maybe it was her attitude. Igraine seemed a little overly confident and a bit conceited and she did not care for those sorts of attitudes, not at all. Nevertheless, Thelma didn't want to be rude.

"Hey. I'm Thelma."

"I like your shirt."

"Thank you," Thelma replied.

It wasn't long before a beautiful young woman entered the office and approached them. She stopped, looking at the group. "Ms. Pennyworth's homeroom?" she asked. Thelma, Igraine, and two other boys gathered together. "I am Ms. Pennyworth. If you'll follow me we'll get to class. I'm so glad you'll be joining us!"

"Me, too!" Igraine said with obvious excitement.

Mimi waved goodbye to Thelma as she and the other new students followed the teacher to what would be their homeroom class. They walked out of the office and made their way straight past the auditorium where contractors were busy at work. They entered the classroom and began to take their seats.

"Could my new students come up here, please?" Ms. Pennyworth asked. Thelma and the others followed her to the front of the room. "Class. Everyone settle down. Now, I trust everyone had a refreshing holiday break. It seems that we have a few new students with us. Here we have Thelma Thimblewhistle, Igraine Von Hallow, Robbie Rosenburg, and Steven Stallswert." Ms. Pennyworth bent down to Thelma and smiled sweetly. "Hey, Thelma."

"Hello," Thelma replied.

"Can you tell me a little about yourself? Where are you from?"

"Indiana."

"Oh, that's a very pretty state. I like it a lot. How did you end up coming here to Raven Den?"

Ms. Pennyworth asked Thelma the questions loud enough for the class to hear, but kept the conversation between the two of them. She appreciated that Ms. Pennyworth didn't make her announce the answers to the whole room on her first day.

"My dad got a job here."

"Really? What does your father do?"

Thelma cleared her throat. "He works at a bank, Hallow Savings and Loan."

"Oh, and where do you guys live?" Ms. Pennyworth asked, smiling.

"We live in the big house on Willowford Lane."

"Ooh, the haunted house," said a stocky boy from the back of the room.

"Timothy, I hope we don't have the same trouble this semester as we did last semester," Ms. Pennyworth warned, causing the boy to go silent. She turned back to Thelma. "You may take your seat, Thelma," said the sweet teacher. "Hello, Igraine," she said turning to the strange little girl.

"Hello to you. You're pretty," said Igraine.

"Well, thanks," Ms. Pennyworth said, laughing.

"My uncle owns the bank that her daddy works at. He's her daddy's boss," said the obnoxious Igraine, pointing at Thelma.

Thelma felt her cheeks turn red with embarrassment. This was all she needed. She didn't care what her father said; Igraine was rude and she wanted no part of her. She had no intention of being her friend, no matter whose niece she was.

"Blah, blah, blah," said a voice from behind Thelma.

Thelma turned around to see it was the girl with glasses she had waved at when arriving in Raven Den, the same one she had seen in the craft store during the holidays. The two exchanged smiles as Igraine stuck out her tongue at them.

"Now, Igraine. It's not polite to boast or to stick out your tongue. It may fall out. Then what would you do?" said Ms. Pennyworth. "And Patty, work with me this year, okay?"

With that, the teacher permitted Igraine to take her seat while she finished introducing the other two students. The class was allowed to tell everyone about their holiday break. Surprisingly, most of the children seemed nice, especially Patty.

Learning where her new classes were located was challenging for Thelma. Through the day, she encountered Igraine in the hallways on several occasions. She could not help but notice that most students seemed to not care for Igraine at all. Some laughed about how strange she looked. She could tell that even though Igraine tried to have a superior attitude, some comments and snickers from the students hurt her feelings. Thelma understood—many times in the past, it was she who had the bruised feelings.

Before Thelma knew it, it was time for lunch. They were having pizza and corn that day. She loved school pizza. There was something about it, something special, much more special than regular pizza. She took her tray and made her way to a small table in the corner and began to eat.

"The name's Patty, Patty Franklin," said a voice that startled Thelma.

She turned to see Patty standing there with her hand extended. "Well, hey, Patty."

"Don't you just *dig* pizza?" Patty said sitting down with her.

Thelma smiled. "It's my favorite."

"Uh! Mine, too!" said Patty excitedly. Thelma giggled. Patty showed Thelma a container of something chocolate. "I also like chocolate pudding."

"Yeah, me, too."

"Chocolate pie?"

"Uh-huh."

"Uh! Me, too!" said the ecstatic Patty once again. "What else do you like? I like the band *Harmony*. The lead singer, Justin, is *so* cute."

Thelma shook her head. "Um, I don't know them, but I do think the lead singer of *Boys 4 Real* is cute," Thelma said.

"Uh!" Patty said slapping the table. "I can't believe it. *Me. Too!*" She handed Thelma a piece of paper with a phone number scribbled on it. "You're my new best friend. Here's my number—call me all the time."

As they laughed, Thelma looked over and saw Igraine sitting alone. She was being taunted by the mean boy from homeroom. No matter how much she and Patty laughed, Thelma couldn't help but notice Igraine and how hurt she looked, sitting in silence, absorbing the boy's insults. Suddenly, Patty stood up and turned like she was going to walk to where Igraine was seated.

"No, no," began Thelma.

Patty put her hand in the air. "Girlfriend…I got this."

Then Patty shook her head confidently, and winked. She walked over to Igraine's table. The boy, Timothy, was teasing Igraine about her nose, which was, in truth, a little *big*, but it was still hurtful to point it out.

Timothy laughed and pointed. "I bet if I squeeze your nose, it'll honk."

Patty stepped in-between them. "I bet if I pop yours it'll bleed."

"Oh yeah, *Pa-tri-cia*?" said Timothy standing up.

"Yeah…wanna see? Come on. I'll do it right now. Pow!" said Patty meeting him face to face. A teacher sitting at the main lunch table tapped her glass loudly against the table. "Sorry, Mrs. Meekly," said Patty. She looked back to Timothy. "Boy, you better be glad," she muttered. Patty took Igraine by the hand and led her to where she and Thelma were sitting. Thelma was astounded at Patty's courage.

"Thank you," said Igraine, obviously surprised by Patty's defense.

Patty curled her nose. "Ah, you're welcome. This is Thelma. She's my best friend."

"Yes, I remember from class," Igraine replied.

"Hey, there," said Thelma to Igraine. She turned to Patty. "That was really cool. Weren't you afraid he'd slug you?"

"Girl, please. Timmy ain't nothing but hot air. I whooped him three times last summer. He picks his nose when he thinks no one's looking. I mean, digs in it!"

Thelma and Patty laughed while Igraine giggled uncomfortably. Thelma kept attempting to engage Igraine in their conversations, but surprisingly, now Igraine had little to say about herself. It was as if she had no past. She stumbled around the simplest of questions. Maybe there was something about Igraine's family of which she was embarrassed. Igraine told them that she was staying with her Uncle Victor for a period of time. She didn't elaborate as to why, and neither Thelma nor Patty asked. Originally, Igraine had seemed to be a very

proud girl. Thelma believed that someone who was that obnoxiously prideful had much of which to be ashamed. Still it made Thelma feel sorry for her.

The three of them laughed, especially at Patty's wonderful, hard-to-believe stories. Finally, the lunch period was over and the three girls emptied their trays and began walking to their classes. It was turning out to not be such a bad day after all. Thelma was surprised at how well it had turned out, actually. She felt more confident, less strange and peculiar. Maybe Anna was right. Maybe her death in the pool was the death foretold.

"You know, you guys ought to come over to my house tonight," Thelma said as they walked. "We could play the game I got for Christmas."

"What game?" asked Patty.

"Mystery Manor. It's in 3D with special glasses and everything. So cool!"

"Uh!" exclaimed Patty, dramatically grabbing her chest and taking a deep breath. "I *love* 3D!"

Thelma looked at Igraine. "So, what about it, Igraine? Can you come? Will your uncle let you?"

Igraine smiled widely, almost slyly. "Oh, yes. I am certain he wouldn't mind at all."

Lillian's Letter

Edwin wanted to go home. It was one of those days where he did not want to be at work or have responsibilities. He felt like a child wishing for a snow day from school. So, feeling as if he had worked hard and earned some relaxation, he decided to leave early for the day. Thelma would be at school until the afternoon.

Checking his calendar, he saw that he had no appointments for the remainder of the day. With his network access, he could check email when he got home; he'd never be missed at all. He smiled to himself, got up, and put on his coat. Then he shut down his computer and piled everything into his briefcase. The plan was simple: he would slip out quietly and undetected.

He stood there waiting on the elevator to reach the thirteenth floor hoping that he would not be spotted by Iggy, or even worse, Victor. Departing early was something he felt he deserved after all the hard work he had done. He had worked extra hours on several occasions—he was certain to have time owed to him.

The elevator was so sluggish that he thought he may go insane waiting on it. Finally, the ding of the bell sounded and the doors slid open. He boarded and pressed the button to the ground floor. There was much he could do at home. He could fix the squeaking hinges, call the landscaping company and schedule an estimate, or fix the light in the library. Maybe he could sneak home and play *Mystery Manor* to practice without Thelma knowing and then beat her later on. Without anyone there to laugh at him, he could even wear the goggles. He had looked so silly wearing them, but you simply could not play the game without them.

With a *snap*, his briefcase popped open spilling the contents to the elevator floor. "Man! The first thing I'm gonna do when I leave here is stop and buy another briefcase!" He bent down and began scooping up his files and papers when he noticed the strange note from Lillian that Maggie had handed him on the evening of the party.

Your assistance is needed. In order to see, one must first look…

He rolled his eyes and stuffed the letter back into his case, closing the latch hard. There was no doubt in his mind that Lillian was a tortured soul. He wondered what it was that could have driven her to the point where she needed to be hospitalized. But…what if she was not in a hospital? What if Maggie had been right all along? *Dad…you have to wear the goggles. You can't see the clues if you're not wearing the glasses!"* Those glasses—those odd reading glasses that had been in the desk drawer. Was there a chance they held the key to Lillian's note?

Edwin immediately hit the button to the third floor and headed to the Facilities Department. He had to find the box he had tossed the glasses into. He only knew the box was orange. It took some time, but the Facilities assistant was nice enough to help search the thirty-three orange boxes they found. Of course, they finally located the glasses in the very last box they searched. He hurried back to his office, locked the door behind him, and pulled the letter from his briefcase. Holding the letter in front of him, he slowly slid the glasses onto his nose.

"And here we are," Edwin said. Words appeared on the blank page. To verify his eyes weren't playing tricks on him, he lifted the glasses above his brow and the words were gone. Somehow, Lillian had written this letter with ink that couldn't be seen without using her glasses. "You may not be so crazy after all, Lillian." He placed the glasses back on and began to read.

Your assistance is needed. In order to see, one must first look…

I apologize for the puzzle, Maggie. But coming to you directly would've put you in danger. If all has worked out the way I planned, you have received this note in the office mail right after I've disappeared. I only hope that when you cleaned out my office, you found my glasses and put two and two together.

But Edwin knew that Maggie had not been permitted to go into Lillian's office after she was gone. He read on.

At this point, it's too late for me. With any luck you've found this letter before it's too late for the family who has moved into the Peterson house. I don't have much time. Victor has me trapped in this office and he'll be back any second. I'm certain that lately everyone has been thinking that I've gone crazy. Please believe me when I tell you that what you are about to read is real.

I came into the office several weeks ago to get caught up on the Peterson Estate deal. It was late, I think, around ten PM. When I got off the elevator, I heard Victor in his office talking to a guy named Felix. The two of them were making some kind of deal, something where Victor would sacrifice himself and Felix would turn him into some kind of immortal monster. They kept talking about a girl, a kid who was supposed to be some kind of protector, with some tie to the Peterson Estate. Victor was to get the house and have it demolished before the girl could arrive.

I was completely overcome with terror. As I tried to sneak away from the door, Iggy caught me and notified Victor. He threatened to hurt me and others I love unless I continued to help him. He did something to me then, I don't know what it was. But it prevented me from telling anyone about his plans. Every time I try my mind gets fuzzy.

Edwin could not believe what he was reading. Could any of it actually be real? His insides quivered as he continued Lillian's story.

As unbelievable as it sounds, Victor has this pen on his desk that writes by itself. It tells him about the future—I've seen it! It told him that this girl would lead to his downfall. You could imagine how worried I was when the Peterson's called and told me that another bid had been entered for the house by a man named Thimblewhistle, who just happened to have a young daughter. I thought if this girl was going to be the key to Victor's ruin, I wasn't going to stand in her way. So, I didn't counter the offer and the contract was awarded to Thimblewhistle.

Victor was furious when he found out tonight. I'm sure you're wondering about the phone call you got. I tried to warn you, but I couldn't. So that I wouldn't be able to tell anyone, he removed my tongue and placed it in a jar like a trophy. He says my eyes are the next to go.

Maggie, you have to get yourself away, far away. You also have to get to the family at the Peterson Estate. You have to warn them to be careful. I get the feeling that girl is our only hope against Victor and what he plans to become. This letter is my only chance...

The letter ended there.

"Hello, Edwin."

Edwin spun around to see Victor lurking behind him. "Victor! Um, I was just looking…"

"Oh, shush, shush, shush," Victor said as he placed one of his sharp claws against Edwin's lips. "It is perfectly alright, Edwin. Perfectly alright."

Edwin sat there trying to think of a way to escape. The office had only one door, one way out, and Edwin was certain Victor would beat him to it before he could leave. "Victor, listen, I don't know what you're planning, but you're going to leave Thelma alone. I will *kill* you if you hurt her. You can't hold me here. I promise you, I'll be missed."

Victor laughed. "Ah, I am certain you will missed, dear boy, especially by that pretty daughter of yours. You will be *missed*…but…the question is will you be *found?*"

Then darkness consumed the light from Edwin's office.

Revelations

"What kind of tea is this?"

"Oak Bark tea. It's good for my psoriasis," replied Norma making her way to the love seat.

Mimi looked at her skeptically. "Woman, you don't have psoriasis."

Norma took another sip of tea and put her scrapbook on the table. "See, it works."

"Ah…too bad it doesn't cure silly. You could use that remedy. Hand me those scissors," Mimi replied.

They laughed. The two of them had much in common: they were lonely, widowed, full of fun, and adored scrapbooking. Norma brought out Mimi's adventurous side, as if she needed any assistance in that area. They sat together with the entire room full of photos and scrapbooking materials.

"So, when do you have to pick up the little one?"

Mimi put more sugar in her tea. "Actually, we're off the hook. Mrs. Franklin called and said she was going to drop them at the house today to play that game Thelma got for Christmas, so we have all the time we need to finish."

"Patty Franklin's mother? Lord, that child has the biggest mouth."

"Now, Norma…be nice."

"I am being nice. So, I have to ask," Norma said curiously, "how have the *ghosts* been?"

Mimi leaned in. "I've left Thelma alone about all that stuff. You know how I am. I don't like to pry." Norma rolled her eyes. "But this morning I asked her, well, in a roundabout way. It occurred to me that, all of a sudden, she just quit mentioning any of it, like she had forgotten about it all."

"What did she say when you asked? Hand me the glue."

"She said she felt like she had imagined the whole thing, that she was just nervous about being in a big old house," Mimi said as she handed over the glue sticks. "I mean, Edwin's old house was small and cozy, you know. I'm sure it was a change moving to the Peterson's."

Norma sighed in agreement, opened her scrapbook, and inserted a page. "Well, that could be true. Of course, all those stories you've told over the years probably didn't help anything. You and your stories, Mimi. You're worse than the kids in the neighborhood!"

Mimi leaned back. "Oh, now wait a minute. I told Thelma scary stories about that old mansion for fun. I wouldn't have told those tales if I had thought for a second she and Eddie would someday live there!"

Norma laughed. "Honey, you would have told those old tales regardless. You live for it. I'm just glad that you didn't tell her the truth about poor Anna. She's too young to know things like that. I'll never forget the day my daddy came in the door, white as a sheet, telling us that old Coy had drowned poor Anna in the pool. I mean…it still boggles my mind to this day! Why would that old man have killed her? There was no cause to it. Said that someone had put him up to it."

"Yes, can we talk about something else, please?" interrupted Mimi.

"Sorry, honey," apologized Norma. "Well, I'm still glad that Eddie got that place. Aren't you?"

"Couldn't be more tickled. Hand me that die cut."

"If old Mrs. Evermoore was still alive, I bet she wouldn't know what to think seeing that big old house where her little shack used to be."

"Whatever happened to her, Norma," Mimi asked reluctantly taking a sip of the bitter tea.

"Well, after her daughter-in-law passed of pneumonia, there was no one left to take care of her or that grandbaby. The baby was put up for adoption and Mrs. Evermoore had to be hospitalized out at Sunnydale. Could you imagine? Losing your son and then being put into a home less than two years later? It's a tragedy, I tell you."

"Pass me those pictures…the ones from Eddie's Christmas party." Mimi watched Norma fumble around trying to locate them. "Right there. To the left! Put on your glasses, woman!"

As Norma handed over the pictures, she dropped them in the floor scattering them about. Mimi looked at her impatiently. "Don't you say a word. Not a word!" Norma began picking up the photos and happened across the photo of Mimi, Edwin, Thelma, and Victor.

Mimi noticed the expression on her face. "What?"

"Who is this?"

"Who is who?"

"This man…right here…with you guys?"

Mimi looked at the photo. "Oh, that's Victor Von-Whosy-Whats-It. He's Eddie's boss." Mimi took the rest of the pictures. She looked over and saw Norma examining the picture. "What?"

"Are you sure his name isn't Percival?"

"Percival? No, why do you ask," Mimi replied with a giggle.

"Percival. That was his name. I am telling you, Mimi, this is him."

"Are you sure there isn't something else in this tea?"

Norma stood up and walked over to the lamp to get a better look. "Mimi, this is him. He's a little older, not half as old as he should be. If I didn't know better, I would say this here is the man that came and tried to talk Henry out of the Evermoore land."

Mimi looked at her in disbelief. "Norma, you're not serious."

Norma looked at her with a somber expression. "I'd bet our friendship on it."

Mimi knew if Norma wanted to be taken seriously, she would swear on their friendship. "Honey, that can't be him. He'd be older than we are!"

"I'm telling you. It's him. I don't know how he's done it; he's hardly aged at all. My daddy said he was really strange. The boy wouldn't even step on the grass, let alone come in the house. He told Peterson he would triple what he had paid for the property. Henry finally had to call the police on him."

It was curious indeed. Mimi subtly changed the subject, trying to act as if Norma was just mistaken, suffering from "old-timer's" disease. But all of a sudden, she felt the need to get back to the estate. She had to be there when Thelma returned home from school. There was a feeling, a scratching at her heart telling her that her granddaughter was in danger.

After parting with Norma, Mimi immediately made her way to the mansion, trying to beat the children home and conduct research. She wasn't certain what she was looking for, but she was certain that somewhere in that house was confirmation that Thelma's stories were true. Deep within her soul, Mimi had always believed in the things Thelma had told them, those strange, magical things. The stories themselves were so amazing—the ghost nurse, the monster in the parking lot—it would have been difficult for Thelma to make up those stories in such detail.

Arriving at the house with time to spare, Mimi hurriedly made her way to the library and threw open the large doors, pushing her way into the gloominess. She began to carefully and cautiously search the room, but there was nothing to be found. Then she went to Thelma's room and began searching in Thelma's dresser, in her chest, under her bed, but there was nothing except Thelma's diary in the middle drawer of the nightstand.

True, she felt simply awful breaking into her granddaughter's diary, but if it contained answers, then it had to be done. Using a fingernail file, she was finally able to pry the lock open. With the exception of the first few entries, Thelma had recorded no other entries, no clues or evidence. All the other pages were blank.

Then, Mimi began to see writing steadily appear.

The Beginner's Guide to the Neither Realm for the Incredibly Gifted

This instruction book will guide you through the wonders of the Neither Realm, because you are incredibly gifted. Only those who are remarkable and pure of heart can see what is written within these pages.

Mimi placed her hand to her mouth in awe. Again, she flipped through the book and began glancing at the now fully illustrated pages. It appeared to be a guide with maps and pictures of all types of marvelous beings and worlds, written in elaborate detail.

"My God," Mimi said to herself.

Rattle!

Mimi turned her attention to Thelma's wardrobe. There were noises coming from inside, like something was hiding in there. The door handle wiggled and turned with a slight shift. Was it the wind? Mimi tried not to pay it mind, but then the door cracked opened with a creak.

Rattle…rattle…thump!

"*Mimi*," she heard a whisper say. "*Mimi, run away.*"

The voice was low, barely audible. Mimi couldn't clearly hear it, but she knew it was there. If only she could have seen Anna hovering in front of her with a frantic expression on her face. Though Mimi did not realize it, she was

an Auditor—gifted, like her granddaughter. Mimi rose from the bed and walked to the wardrobe door as it opened even wider.

"Mimi! Mimi! Run away!" Anna called.

Mimi jerked with fright. She had heard the voice very clearly that time and it caused her to shiver deep inside. *"Anna?"*

Two great monstrous hands of mist reached through the wardrobe and snatched poor Mimi inside. The scream was brief, and she was gone. Before she knew it, Mimi found herself in a strange place she had never seen before. It was the den of a grand home. The only light was from a roaring fireplace. She tried to move, but her hands were bound. In front of her, in the middle of the room, was what looked like a cemetery gate made of iron. She could see a name worked into its metal…*Evermoore.* The letters were woven into the iron around the top of the entrance archway. Undoubtedly, it was the gate from what used to be the Evermoore's family graveyard.

But what was it doing there?

"Do you recognize it?" asked a figure from the shadows. "It is an antique…just like you."

Mimi's eyes began to focus through the gloom to see the figure of a large, nicely dressed man, dark in appearance, with a moustache. He raised a cigar to his mouth and lit it, allowing the small flame to shine on his long, thin fingers tipped with claws, like a feline. His eyes were like that of a snake.

"Who's there?" Mimi said with a tremble.

Victor stepping into the firelight. "Aw…I am hurt. Don't you remember me?"

Mimi could now plainly see the man she knew to be Edwin's boss in front of her. "Yes, from the party. My son works for you."

"Not anymore," Victor said walking over to her.

"What do you mean?" Mimi asked. He knelt down to her, placed a hand on her knee, and then smiled politely. Mimi could see that his appearance seemed to grow more ghastly by the minute. "What have you done with my son?"

"Well, let's just say Edwin is…*being detained.* At least until I can take care of some business. He has been an obstacle, you see."

"What do you want with us?"

Victor stood up and waved her fears away. "Oh now, calm down, calm down. You will be fine, both of you. What I want, actually, is for the two of you to be out of my way for a short time, and to be my bargaining tool. I only need your granddaughter."

Mimi's eyes widened. "Thelma?"

"Correct."

"What do you want with Thelma?"

Victor laughed and began to pace. "Well, let's just say that your granddaughter is *special* to me. She is a gifted young woman. She has a power that is quite amazing. There is something I need for her to retrieve for me, and she will use her gifts to do so."

"What?" asked Mimi. "I'll go get it. Where's it at?"

"Oh, I am sorry," Victor said shaking his head. "It doesn't quite work that way. Only Thelma knows where this object is. It is the most powerful object ever known, stronger than anything on earth or in the heavens. It is so powerful that it will make me invincible, *immortal*. It will make me…a *Boogey Man*."

Mimi burst into laughter.

"Well, I know it sounds droll, but you need not be rude about it," Victor scoffed.

"Oh, I am sorry, honey, go on."

"Thank you," he said crouching beside her. "*Boogey Man* is merely a label, a name people created to define it. Really, it has no description. It is only power, the power to live forever. The downside is that you aren't really *alive*. Oh, but with your granddaughter's help I am going to make it much more than that…much more."

Mimi was growing weary of Victor's ramblings. They were making no sense to her. "Where are Edwin and Thelma? What have you done with them?"

"Oh, now, let's be still. All will be explained in due time. As a matter of fact, your granddaughter will be arriving any minute. My, um, *niece* will be sending her here."

Mimi said, "I have to say, you don't seem to be fit to be around children."

"Oh, dear woman," Victor began to laugh. "I had to have someone bring Thelma to me. You were to be disposed of by now. However, having you as bait will prove more beneficial, I think."

"Why involve your niece? Why didn't you go get Thelma yourself?" Mimi asked.

"You know, that would have been the smoothest solution. Unfortunately, there are certain boundaries that the Evermoore land possesses. So, I have to rely on more subtle forms of capture," Victor said.

"Do they call you Percival?"

Victor looked at her astonished. "I have not heard that name in years, decades actually. I think I look quite well for someone over seventy years old, don't you? Magic does have its advantages."

"So you *are* the one who wanted to buy the land from Peterson," Mimi said.

"Of course! The old fool. I offered almost four times what he paid for it. No matter what deal I offered, he always declined. The property is quite special to me, as I'm sure you've realized. The Evermoores were a powerful family. Yes, Markus and Maria Evermoore. Do you know of them?"

"No, I am afraid I don't," Mimi replied.

Victor smiled widely and leaned down to Mimi's face. "You should, madam. After all, they were your *parents!*"

Iggy's New Teddy Bear

Patty's mother gathered the girls from school and left them at Thelma's house. Igraine was finally beginning to be more at ease and comfortable, which made Thelma feel good. The bad thing was, apparently Igraine was not very bright. Thelma thought Igraine would never decipher how to use the video game controller. It was like she had never seen one before. What child had never seen a video game controller?

"When's your grannie supposed to be back?" Patty asked.

"Soon, I'm sure. She's probably still scrapbooking with her friend," Thelma replied.

After they had played for a while, Igraine leaned forward and set down the game controller. "Could I use your restroom?"

"Well…yeah. It's upstairs to the left," said Thelma.

Igraine excused herself and started up the stairs.

Patty shook her head as she watched Igraine walk away. "Strange gal. I mean, freaky strange."

Igraine locked the door, pulled Thelma's stepstool over to the bathroom sink, and climbed up to the mirror. She began running water into the basin as she reached into her pocket and pulled out a vial containing oil. Once the sink was filled halfway, she turned off the water and opened the vial, placing one drop of the oil into the water. Then she stretched both hands in front of her, closing her eyes. She began to speak in her natural voice, a much *Iggier* voice.

"Master," Iggy began. "Master, it is I who call you. Come forth and guide me to do your bidding."

The surface of the water began to glow and move, swirling around like a tiny whirlpool. Faster and faster it went until the center of the pool began to rise and take shape. There, in front of Iggy, was Victor's likeness shaped into the water. Iggy grinned with fascination. He slowly reached out and touched the tip of Victor's watery nose. Victor shook his head quickly and swatted Iggy's hand away.

"I hate it when you do that!" said the wet Victor.

"Hee, hee. But it's just so very interesting," replied the girlish-looking Iggy.

"Oh, please! Is the girl there?"

"Yes, and another, named Patty," Iggy said scratching his wig. "I don't know what I think about her yet, that Patty girl. Oh, but Thelma is *very* nice. We're playing a game on Thelma's television called *Mystery*-something. It's the neatest thing! It's in 3D. You can almost touch it! You have a character that you control…and, and you search all through the—"

"Iggy!" boomed Victor.

"Yes?"

"Please, get on with it. You're killing me. You really are."

Iggy shuffled nervously. "Oh, sorry. Yes, we're here. But where is the old lady? I thought once Thelma was captured, I was to do away with her?"

"I already have her. She fell right into my living room, you could say," Victor said, pleased.

"Good. I didn't like the thought of *offing* old ladies," Iggy said, twirling his curly hair.

A watery hand snatched Iggy. "Listen…to…me. You had better get used to doing what needs to be done, ghoul. I can't afford your mistakes or your bleeding heart."

"Y…yes, Master."

"Now, find a way to get rid of that Patty girl and get Thelma up to her room. I have to have her near that wardrobe. I cannot control the destination of a Nexus very long. Get her near the doors—push her into it if you have to. I will do the rest."

"Yes, Master."

Knock, knock, knock…

Thelma called from the other side of the door. "Are you okay in there?"

Victor and Iggy looked at the door panicked. The watery image splashed back into the sink. Iggy reached in and unplugged the drain, letting the ghostly liquid flow from sight.

"Um, um…yes," Iggy said in Igraine's raspy voice. "I'm coming. It was those…um…*burritos*."

"Okay. Patty has to leave, so it's just the two of us until your uncle picks you up."

That was good news. Now Iggy wouldn't have to contend with getting rid of Patty. The girls were a little surprised to see that Igraine was soaked with water, her face flushed, and hair a mess.

"Girl…maybe you shouldn't be eating burritos anymore," said Patty who was standing at the door ready to leave. Iggy looked down at himself, unaware of how he looked. He laughed nervously. Patty cocked her eyebrow. "Well, I am going to scoot, girlfriends. I'll see you both at school tomorrow."

"Bye," said both Thelma and Iggy.

Thelma shut the door. She looked at the clock. "I wish I knew where Mimi was. This isn't like her. If she's not here in the next few minutes, I'm going to call Norma. I hope they didn't go to the scrapbook store. We may never see them again."

"Maybe she's in your room," Iggy said.

Thelma looked at Iggy in surprise and smiled. "Uh…why would she be in my room?"

Iggy sat there smiling, thinking. "Maybe she's cleaning it?"

Thelma walked into the sitting room to sit down. "You are strange, Igraine." Thelma picked up a carrot stick and munched.

"Yeah," said Iggy sadly. "I know. That's what they tell me."

Thelma sat up. "Oh no, I didn't mean that bad or anything. Strange can be good, too. People call me strange…they do it all the time."

"Really?" said Iggy surprised. He had always thought *strange* meant bad, unnatural.

"Really. I think strange is the best way to go. I've always been strange. People tell me that all the time."

"They do not," Iggy said smiling. He thought Thelma to be quite normal and very pretty.

"Seriously. I mean, I don't really get into *girl* stuff much, or toys. Dad says I am a little 'tomboyish' but I don't really think so. I just like different things, I guess." Igraine seemed to be comforted by her comments. "You don't talk about your family much, Igraine."

"Well, there's not much to tell, really."

"I bet there is. I bet there's a lot. What about your mom and dad?"

"I never really knew them. All I have known is Mast…my Uncle Victor," replied Iggy. "What is it like having parents?"

Thelma picked up her drink. "Oh, well. Sometimes it's a pain. But, most of the time, it's pretty cool. My mom, she died over a year ago in a car accident."

"Oh, that's awful," Iggy said.

"Yeah, it was bad. I miss her. But my dad is great, though. He is so much fun. You know, when I was really little, he used to always take me shopping with him. Every time we would go, he would get me a milkshake. I love ice cream."

"Ooh me, too!"

Thelma smiled. "Really? Yeah, it's my favorite. So, he would get me a milkshake every time I would go places with him. Does your uncle do anything like that for you?"

Iggy looked down. "No, not really."

"Well, what kind of nice things does he do?"

"He's not that much fun. We really don't play games or anything, or go places."

"You don't? Then what do you do?"

"I don't know," Iggy continued. "I do some chores for him. He's always got a list for me to get done."

"Well…does he tell you jokes or anything?" Thelma asked.

"No."

"Does he buy you stuff?"

"Nope."

"Does he, like, take you to amusement parks or anything?"

"Nope." The more Iggy thought, the more he reasoned that Victor didn't appreciate him at all. Not in the least.

"Really?" Thelma replied. "Well, I hope I don't make you mad by saying this, but your uncle doesn't sound like a nice guy at all."

And Victor wasn't nice to him. As a matter of fact, Victor was very mean. Did Iggy have anyone at all to *care* for him? No. He had no parents, no siblings. He hadn't seen his ghoulish friends in the forest in what seemed to be an eternity. Realizing the lack of compassion in his life caused him to cry.

"I know. He isn't nice to me. Not at all." Iggy sniffled and wiped his plump nose. "It's all the time, 'Iggy, do this,' and, 'Iggy, do that.' He never says thank you or anything. Oh, and if I make a mistake, he always yells at me. He didn't even get me anything for Christmas!" Thelma leaned over and gently hugged him. He felt a warm sensation run over his body. He had never had a hug

before. It was nice. "All I wanted was a toy…or a little stuffed animal, something, because…because…*because I am all alone*! I don't have a momma or a daddy. Nobody likes Iggy!"

To be honest, Thelma regretted opening Igraine's floodgates of emotion, but she knew what it was like to need someone. "Well, um…I like you, Igraine. I think you're pretty cool. As a matter of fact, come on."

Thelma took Iggy by the arm and they went to her room. She left him standing in front of her bed and walked around to the bedside. With her hands behind her back, Thelma returned to where Iggy was standing.

"Now, close your eyes."

Iggy did so and Thelma placed something fuzzy in his hands. He opened his eyes and looked down to see that he held a brilliant white teddy bear with the curliest white fluff fur and a big red bowtie. "Is…is he mine?"

"Yeah, you can have him. His name is Bartholomew Bear, but you can call him Bart. My grandmother got him for me when I moved here."

Iggy looked at the little bear, sniffed, and wiped his eyes. No one—not one other soul—had given Iggy anything in his life. He didn't quite know how to act. He threw his arms around Thelma and hugged her tightly. Thelma laughed and hugged him back.

Unfortunately, Iggy had led her into the jaws of the trap without even realizing it. As they embraced, Iggy looked behind Thelma to see the wardrobe door begin to open. Creeping from the darkness within was Victor's hideous, ghostly arms reaching out to snare Thelma at last.

"No!" Iggy yelled pushing Thelma behind him.

"What? What?!" Thelma said.

"We have to go, little Thelma," said Iggy, taking her by the hand. "We need to get out of here, right now!" He took her by the hand and began leading her downstairs towards the library.

"Why? What's the matter?" Thelma asked. Thelma could not understand what was happening. Iggy ran into the library with Thelma and slammed the doors behind them.

"Is your wardrobe the only Nexus in the house?" Iggy asked.

Thelma was shocked that Igraine even knew what a Nexus was. "Wait…who are you?"

"There's no time. I'll explain later, I promise."

Thelma noticed that Igraine's voice was completely different now, not at all like it had been. Solomon, who was slumbering peacefully in Ernest's drawer, heard the familiar voice he had listened to for so long while trapped with Victor. He sprung to life and wiggled his way out of his drawer. There, in the library was Iggy, holding poor Thelma hostage. Solomon jumped to action. He bounced across the floor and in one swoop, impaled his tip deep into Iggy's foot. Iggy howled with pain.

"Solomon!" cried Thelma. "What are you doing?" Solomon quickly hopped away and began scribbling on the floor. "Igraine…what is going on?"

Then Thelma looked over to see that Solomon had written the same word repeatedly, all over the floor around them: *Enemy*.

"No, no, I am not, I promise! I am no enemy," cried Iggy.

"You!" yelled Thelma. "You are the one who wants to be the Boogey Man!"

"No, no!" Iggy pleaded.

Thelma broke free from Iggy's grasp and escaped through the library doors. She ran through the foyer with Iggy trailing behind, pleading for her to stop and listen. But she would not slow down for a second. She bolted toward the front door.

"No! You mustn't leave the house! He can get you if you leave!" Iggy called.

But it was no use. Thelma was already outside. Iggy ran after her. Thelma had to get to Mimi's house. Maybe Mimi was there somewhere, being held prisoner. Iggy ran after her as fast as his small legs could run, holding his little teddy bear with all his might.

"Get away from me!" Thelma screamed.

"No, no…Miss Thelma, please!"

Thelma took the key from under Mimi's welcome mat, opened the door, and ran inside. She managed to shut Iggy out before he could follow her into the house. Then, she ran upstairs to Mimi's bedroom.

"Mimi! Are you here? Are you okay? Mimi, help!" yelled Thelma, but there was no reply.

Thelma ran into the bedroom and ducked behind Mimi's bed. She had to find somewhere to hide, somewhere safe. Outside, she could still hear Iggy calling for her, pleading with her to come back to the Peterson Estate, but Thelma was going nowhere with that imposter. She was so frightened she had forgotten about the large, full-length mirror in the room, the Nexus that Anna used to visit Mimi. Mist began to pour from the reflection, taking shape, preparing to attack.

Iggy finally managed to gain entry into the house and ran upstairs after Thelma, but by the time he reached Mimi's room, the only thing left of Thelma

was her broken watch on the floor. Iggy could see the torn carpet from where Thelma had desperately tried to hang on.

But it was over.

Victor had her.

Oh, if she had only listened.

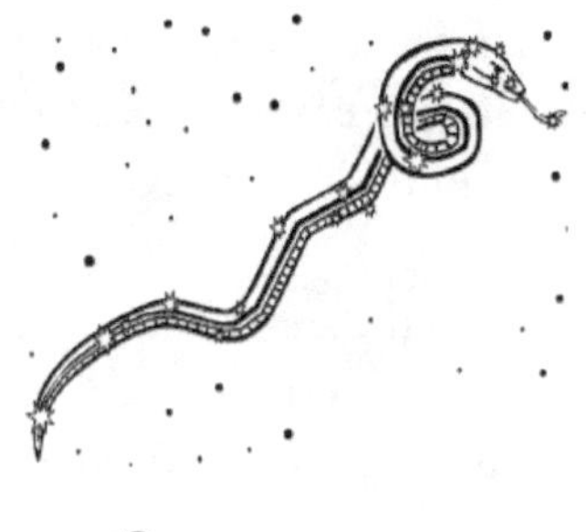

Slithers

"Hello?" Edwin called into the emptiness. "Is anyone there?" He could hear the crackling of a fireplace. The familiar scent of incense let him know that he was in Victor's office, his hands bound, his eyes blindfolded. "Hello!"

Still, there was no reply. He kept trying to move his wrists, attempting to loosen his binds, but he could not. He had to break free. He had to stop Victor from reaching Thelma. She was in danger. Victor had provided no detail to Edwin. It had all happened so quickly. Edwin knew that if Victor would have had the time, he would have killed Edwin immediately. Obviously, Victor had not counted on Edwin's discovery.

Crack! Pop! Hissssss…

Edwin could hear movement. Something was happening. He was not alone. He couldn't see it, but could feel it was there, coming for him. The sound of cracking stone continued—something was coming *alive*.

Ratttttle!

Edwin heard the rattle, like that of a snake. Immediately, he began rocking the chair to which he was bound. He pulled and pushed, rocking back and forth, finally tipping over the chair. He fell hard, nearly knocking the wind from his lungs. As he hit the floor, he heard the wood of the chair break. The back of it had come loose allowing his hands to be free. Quickly, he reached down and untied his legs. Then he felt something fall with a *thud* to the floor, something that was alive and in the room with him. Edwin kicked away from the chair, freeing himself from the ropes. He jerked the blindfold from his eyes.

There it was, the enormous stone serpent that once hung over the fireplace of Victor's office—*alive*—watching Edwin's movements. Slowly, Edwin stood upright, holding his hands in front of him. He didn't want to make any sudden movements that would cause the creature to attack. His pulse quickened. The snake stretched its long, ivory body high over Edwin, hissing, gently weaving back and forth, analyzing him.

Edwin flexed his hand and the snake's large eyes focused on it immediately, the pupils dilating as it prepared to strike. He had no idea how to fight such a thing. As it slowly approached, its tongue flicked, taking in Edwin's scent. He began to examine the room. The only weapon to be found was behind the snake, at the fireplace.

Edwin had to send its attention elsewhere. With a quick motion, he threw the blindfold forward, catching the snake's attention. He leapt for the fireplace, grabbing the poker from the stand beside it. The thing turned to him, more alert after seeing that Edwin was now armed.

It struck.

Edwin dodged the thing, rolling under its head. It struck again, impaling its stony fangs into the floor just inches away from Edwin's back. He flipped over and swung the poker at the beast, hitting its neck and breaking a large chip from it. It slung its head backward in pain, shaking to and fro. It glared at him again as he rose to his feet.

Like a strike of lightning, the snake had Edwin's arm in its jaws, its fangs barely missing his skin. It threw him high into the air, smashing him against the ceiling, dazing him. The poker fell to the floor as Edwin landed hard on his back, pieces of broken plaster falling on his face. He struggled to catch his breath. He scurried backward, searching for the poker and finding it on the floor, approximately five feet from him.

Thinking victory was inevitable, the serpent gathered in front of him and reared back, opening its jaws and exposing its dripping fangs. Edwin looked to the poker again. In a flash, the snake lunged at him as he rolled toward his weapon, taking it into his hand.

He swung, catching the thing across its face with the poker, shattering its snout.

The beast writhed in agony, whipping wildly back and forth. Pieces of it flew all around the room. Then, it tumbled to the ground, busting into millions of pieces. Edwin shielded his eyes with his arm. He stared at the shards before him, in awe of what had just taken place.

With the snake defeated, he laid back onto the floor, panting, trying to catch his breath. He had no idea what had just happened or how it could have

been possible, but he feared that this was the first of many unbelievable events that were to take place this day.

Looking for a way out, Edwin couldn't help but notice there were no longer doors or windows in Victor's office. It was as if they had completely vanished. He moved from wall to wall, feeling with his hands to see if he could find any crack, any indication of an exit, but there was nothing. He feared he might already be too late to save Thelma. For that matter, he was not certain he *could* save her. He knew nothing of magic or the supernatural.

Edwin began searching the desk drawers, desperate to find something that would free him from his predicament. In the top middle drawer he found a key, like a *skeleton* key. He didn't think it would do him much good, of course. There were no key holes to be found, no windows to leap from, nowhere to run. But then, he recalled his first view of Victor's office and the lifeless snake that had hung above the fireplace. There, perched on the fireplace mantle, was the eloquent apothecary chest with the golden keyhole in its center.

Edwin stood up and walked to the box. He looked at the key, and then the keyhole. It looked as if it might fit. He inserted the key, turned the lock, and heard the snap of the hinges. There were several creaks and pops, and then the doors slowly opened. Lined throughout the whole chest were small bottles in sets of two. Edwin looked closer, trying to make out what they contained. He could barely see movement, a gentle wiggling in many of the jars. Warily, he reached in and took one of the vials, pulling it closer to his face to see what it was. Inside the bottle was a *human tongue*. It wiggled and waved around inside the glass like a gooey worm.

"Oh, gross!" Edwin shouted, dropping the bottle, sending it crashing to the floor.

He took several paces back and looked down at the thing, wondering if he had killed it. It began to frantically wiggle like an inchworm toward the base of the fireplace, slithering through the grate, disappearing from view. He stood there, frozen, wondering if he would ever be able to process what he had just seen. He looked into the chest again, this time without removing any of the bottles. He could see that *eyeballs* were in some of the other bottles, moving in unison, gazing about the room.

"Help!"

Edwin was suddenly startled by the sound of a woman screaming. He backed up and began looking around the room, wondering where it was coming from. "Hello! Hello! Can you hear me?" Edwin yelled.

"Yes," the voice called.

"Where are you?" Edwin asked.

"Down here…down here. We're under the fireplace."

"We?" Edwin said to himself. "How do I get to you? I can't see a way to get behind the fireplace."

"There's a knob…under the grate in the front…under the fireplace."

Edwin began feeling around the floor. In the exact spot where the tongue had slipped through the crack was a knob that could be turned. He took hold and turned it to the right. When he did so, he heard a *boom* as the fireplace sank nearly twelve inches into the floor and slid backwards to reveal a small set of steps that led into darkness.

Though he was afraid, Edwin began to make his way to the area below. Small torches were hanging from the stone walls of the mysterious room under the fireplace. He could barely see around him. He could hear odd noises, noises he couldn't decipher, murmurs and mumblings and rattling chains.

"Hello?" Edwin called again.

"Hurry! You have to hurry."

Edwin ran into the room, not knowing if he was making a mistake. "Hello?"

"I'm over here. Go back and open the rest of the bottles. Bring something to light the rest of the torches. Go!" she instructed.

Edwin ran back to the chest and began carefully opening the rest of the bottles. The slimy eyeballs and tongues inside them excitedly hopped out and scurried across the floor, some slithering and rolling down Edwin's hands as he tried to contain his disgust. Tongues ran erratically around the floor before locating the stairway to the hidden room. The eyes rolled and bumped into each other like a grotesque traffic jam before bouncing down the steps. Little by little, Edwin began to hear many voices. He took a box of matches sitting near the fireplace and walked back down the steps into the blackness.

Edwin began lighting every torch he could find. As the light began to grow brighter, he could see that there were people, around twenty or so, distributed about the room. Each of them were chained to the wall. The eyeballs and tongues were wiggling their way into the mouths and eye sockets from which they had been viciously ripped.

Truly, it was not a pleasant sight to behold.

Once in possession of their missing organs, the people wiggled their tongues and moved their eyes about, trying to focus and regain control. The men's faces were all in dire need of shaving, the women appeared tired and drained. It was obvious they had been in this place for some time. Edwin simply

could not believe it. At the front of the line was a beautiful woman, blonde hair with scattered gray.

Edwin cleared his throat. "Who are you?"

"I'm Lillian Carlton," she replied.

"Oh, my God. *You're* Lillian?" Edwin said running to her aid.

"Yes, that's me," Lillian answered.

"Edwin, meet your Board of Directors," said a voice Edwin immediately recognized. Maggie Jordan smiled at him.

"Maggie! Is that you?" Edwin said.

"Yes," Maggie confirmed. "Listen, can you help us out here? That key, the one that opens the chest on the mantle, it should unlock these chains."

Edwin took the key from his pocket and began releasing them. "You are the Board of Directors of Hallow Savings and Loan?"

"Well, we *were* the Board," said a bulky, gray-haired gentleman. Edwin unlocked his restraints. "I don't know what we are now."

"Lucky to be alive," added another gentleman.

Lillian rubbed her wrists. "So, you're the one who bought the Peterson house, right?"

"Yes, that's right," Edwin replied.

"You have a little girl?"

"Yes…Thelma."

"What time is it?" Lillian asked.

"I don't know," Edwin anwered. "Late. And I need to find a way to get to my daughter right now," Edwin said.

"Listen Edwin, there's not a lot of time for explanation. You're just going to have to trust me. We've got to get you out of here, now. It's almost time and your little girl has a big responsibility ahead of her. Nothing can happen to her. She has to save us all. If she fails, then Victor will release a monster who will take over our world…and a few others, too, I imagine."

"What do I do?" Edwin asked. "I mean, I don't know how to fight something like this!"

"If your little girl is who Victor thinks she is, then she'll know exactly what to do." Lillian pointed to a wall. "Now, listen to me closely…beyond that far wall is a security pad. Use my code. It is *071733*. That exit leads to the lower level of the parking garage. Our cars are there. You can take mine. My keys are in the security booth on the right; they're the ones with the big silver keychain with a raven on it."

"Which car is yours?"

"The black Mercedes. Just press the unlock button on my keychain. The horn will beep and the lights will turn on. Take the tunnel to the left. It'll take you straight to a hidden entrance to Victor's house. You can't miss it. You'll see a walkway there…stay on it! Do not touch the water no matter what you do. You'll see a large door at the end of the walkway. There will be a riddle you'll have to solve to get inside. Remember…the answer is *silence*."

The Lonely Doorknocker

Silence?

Edwin was thankful he would not have to waste time solving riddles. The gears of his mind were turning so quickly there was little on which he could concentrate. He located the security pad at the door and used the code that Lillian had given him. Once inside the parking area, immediately to his right he saw the booth with keys on hooks lining the wall. The silver raven was easy to spot. Pressing the unlock button on the keychain, the horn beeped on a flawless black Mercedes at the far end of the corridor.

Edwin wasted no time. He jumped into Lillian's car and was on his way. He did as Lillian had instructed and took the tunnel to the left. He sped through the cave, his mind nearly whirling out of control. He had no idea what the entryway to Victor's was supposed to look like, or how he would identify it. The deeper he drove into the cavern, the darker it grew. He finally happened upon an enormous entryway, dark and sinister. He screeched to a stop and slowly exited the car, certain that this had to be his destination.

In front of him was a great lake filled with black water. At the other side of this lake was a door fitted with a large doorknocker: a face with a long beard and a pointed nose. Its eyes shined a bright crimson. From where he stood was a small, narrow walkway leading to the door. The foul water surrounded it on either side. Edwin carefully began making his way to the door. He was being followed by something, something hidden, lurking deep under the surface of the water around him. What it was, exactly, he did not know. He could feel that it was waiting for him, hoping he would lose his balance and fall into the sludge.

Edwin lost his balance only once, and as he did, the thing hurried to the edge to claim its prize. Regaining his footing, he backed away slowly watching bubbles rise to the surface. In his mind's eye, he could see tentacles thrusting out of the water to snare him, or a great squid rising from the depths to devour him, but the thing did not surface from the beneath water. It remained submerged, hidden, waiting. He slowly continued on his way.

Edwin breathed a sigh of relief once he had finally made it to the door. He searched for a handle, some way in which to open it. Out of nowhere, he heard what sounded like someone clearing their throat. He turned to look behind him, but there was no one there.

"Are you ready?" asked a voice.

Edwin turned back to see the doorknocker staring at him, waiting for an answer.

"Uh…what?" Edwin asked.

The knocker lifted its brow. "I said, are you ready? For the riddle and all."

"Um…yes, yes I am." After everything he had seen, a talking doorknocker was the least of his concerns.

The knocker cleared its throat. "I am greater than *George* and more evil than *Nickolas*. The poor have all of me; the rich need none of me. Should you eat me, you'll die. What am I?"

"Silence?" Edwin said.

The doorknocker looked at him oddly. "Silence? Seriously. Come on, how do you get 'silence' from that? You're not even trying!"

"But I was told that was the answer."

The doorknocker smiled. "Oh! No, no. You're thinking of the one that goes, 'Say my name and I disappear. What am I?' That was a good one, though. I liked it."

Edwin grew impatient. He had precious little time for games. "Oh, for crying out loud. Are you serious?"

"Indubitably," replied the doorknocker. "Now again—I am greater than George and more evil than Nickolas. The poor have all of me; the rich need none of me. Should you eat me, you'll die. What am I?"

"Well, how am I supposed to know? I don't even know who George is!"

"Guess!"

"Listen. I don't have time to fool around with you." Edwin began searching the area. "There's got to be another way into this place," he said to himself. He turned to leave, hoping that maybe there was another entry somewhere in the caverns.

"No! Wait…wait!" said the doorknocker. "Where are you going? We were just getting started."

"I have to find another door. I don't have time for questions. Nice to have met you."

The doorknocker smiled proudly. "But there isn't another door. I am all you have, sir. So, I suggest you try again. But you only get one more attempt. So, answer the riddle."

Edwin rolled his eyes and sighed. "Money."

"You are incorrect, sir!" said the doorknocker with glee. "The poor have all of me; the rich need none of me? Money? Come on…think! I'll give you one more chance."

"Time," said Edwin.

"Nope."

"Hope."

"No, sir."

"Love?"

"Definitely not."

"I give up!" shouted Edwin.

"Oh, come on," pleaded the doorknocker. "You *can't* give up!"

"Listen, you said I only had one more chance to answer, anyway."

"Well, okay. I will give you a hint, and *then* you will have one more chance to answer."

Edwin turned. "I think I'm going to go."

"Oh, please!" the doorknocker howled. "Wait. I never get to talk to anyone. I get so dreadfully lonely down here. All I hear is Enid, that idiotic water monster. It is so nice to actually talk to someone."

"Okay, listen. I have to get in there to save my daughter. *The Master* has her and is holding her captive. I have to get inside. So, you need to help me out, okay?" said Edwin.

"Agreed. But, I cannot simply give you the answer. I will give you a hint. To fill a glass with it leaves it empty," the doorknocker replied.

Edwin began to pace. He simply had to get inside immediately; he could already be too late. *To fill a glass with it leaves it empty.* What could fill a glass and leave it empty? *The poor have all of me. Poor. The poor have no money. Some have no hope.* Edwin continued to pace.

"How are you doing?" asked the knocker.

"Shhh!"

"Okay, okay…"

The rich. Now the rich have everything they could ever want. They need…nothing. Nothing. The poor have nothing. The rich need nothing. If you eat nothing at all, you'll starve to death. Yes, that had to be it!

"Nothing! It's nothing," Edwin said.

"Yes! And the crowd goes wild!" cheered the doorknocker.

"Woo hoo!" Edwin and the doorknocker cheered and laughed.

"Nothing is greater than George in the Heavens, and there is nothing more evil than Nickolas down below. The poor have all the nothing they could hope for, and the rich have nothing more they need. To eat only nothing will eventually kill you. Very good, sir!"

"Thanks!"

"Now…I will let you inside, sir. But, I must warn you—and I am only telling you this because I *like* you—inside you can get lost quite easily. There have been a few who have entered and never been seen or heard from again. Take some of those stones below your feet. They mark like chalk. Mark your path; find your way. And please…do not tell anyone I provided you with the suggestion."

"Of course, not. Thank you," said Edwin gratefully.

"You are welcome, sir." The big door unlocked and slowly swung open. "Best wishes on finding your daughter. If everything comes to a successful conclusion, don't be a stranger."

Edwin picked up a handful of the rocks, placed them in his pocket, and walked inside. The door shut behind him. He could plainly see that there were only two ways to begin—either left, or right. He turned to ask the doorknocker the best direction, but when he did, there was no longer a door behind him. Only a stone wall remained; nothing more. This was his only opportunity to locate Thelma. He could not fail. Moving to the tunnel on the right, he began on his way through the dark, twisting maze.

Prophecy 3

Thelma's stomach hurt and she felt nauseated. It was the same feeling she had experienced when traveling through the wardrobe with Anna. How had she been pulled through a Nexus? Had she been trapped by the evil little elf who had disguised himself as Igraine?

As she stood upright, she noticed the air around her was hot, bitter, and humid. The room danced with shadows and she could hear the crying of the wind which howled outside. Though she knew it was important for her to not be afraid, a strong feeling that she needed to escape overcame her. She wasn't certain where she could go without being consumed by the shadows.

"Thelma!" called a familiar voice in a hushed whisper. "Thelma, over here."

Thelma turned. It took a moment for her eyes to focus, but then she could see her grandmother, bound to a chair in the middle of the room. Thelma immediately ran to her.

"Mimi! Mimi, what are you doing here?"

"Honey, run! You need to get out of here. You need to get far, far away from this place. It's the man from the bank, your father's…"

"Hello again, Thelma," Victor uttered as he emerged from the shadows. "So glad to see you are doing well. Did you have a good nap? I was about to have to wake you. It is nearly midnight on the Eve of the Great Feast. We are growing short on time…and like any great villain, I have a *considerable* amount of monologue to get through in advance."

"You? What are you doing here?" Thelma turned to face him, standing protectively in front of Mimi. "You better let her go right now!" Thelma was in shock. It had been Victor the entire time. Why had she not she felt it? She felt so foolish.

"Or, what?" Victor cooed.

"Or…or," Thelma fumbled. She then took hold of the Beckon around her neck. It began to glow. She closed her eyes. "Anna…Anna, I need you!"

Victor smiled. "Perfect!"

With that, an opening of light appeared from the corner of the room and within seconds, Anna appeared.

"Anna help us!" cried Thelma.

"Thelma?" Anna began to float toward Thelma and Mimi.

With a snap of his fingers, Victor brought the potted tree sitting beside the fireplace to life. It shot forth at Anna with vines and branches that wrapped around her spirit like ropes, holding her in place.

"Let me go!" Anna shouted.

"Anna?" said Mimi to the emptiness. "Anna Peterson, is that you?" Mimi did not see the light that had entered the room when Thelma called out, but she could see that whatever the leafy vines were holding captive was struggling, trying to break free.

"Yes, Mimi, it's Anna. I'm here," Anna said.

"My God," Mimi said in disbelief. She could hear the familiar voice from her childhood, her best friend

"How touching," Victor said coldly. He snapped his fingers again causing a chair to slide across the room scooping up Thelma, bringing her to him. He placed one of his claws under her chin and smiled widely, revealing his stained fangs. "You won't need this anymore." He ripped the Beckon from around Thelma's neck and tossed it across the room.

Vines wrapped around Thelma, tying her to the chair.

"What do you want?" Thelma demanded.

"You know, I am glad you asked." Victor walked to the far side of the room, and began gently pacing the floor as he spoke. "Let me tell you a tale…most of which you already know, I'm quite certain. You may not realize it by looking at me because I've aged well, but in my younger days, I was quite awkward."

Anna snorted. "Ya think?"

Victor cast a look towards Anna, cleared his throat, and then continued. "As a child, I always knew that something was…*missing* from my life. I grew up with my grandmother, poor, in a rural part of the city. We were always looking for work, chores, something that could keep food on the table. We had to get money somehow, of course. Personally, I would have *stolen* the money. But Grandmama was determined that we be honest people and *earn* a living."

"Yeah? And how did that work out for you?" shot Thelma.

"Not too well, actually," Victor admitted. "Honesty has never been my strength. At any rate, I was searching my grandmother's desk one day for something to steal when I noticed a beautiful silver fountain pen in one of the drawers. I knew I could trade it for money, so I swiped it to sell in the market. Later that evening, the pen showed me something marvelous—it could write on its own—and not only write, but *tell the future*. Naturally, the pen was reluctant to tell me everything at first, but after threatening to break it into pieces, it began to agree with me. It wrote a spectacular story for me telling of my past and my future.

"I believe my mother always knew that I was destined for great things. Mother dear had been lucky enough to trap a wealthy man into marriage, a sap whom she accused of being my father. It was all a lie, of course, a plan to get his money. Being the superstitious bird she was, before I was born she went to see a fortune teller one late fall evening just to ensure that all was going to proceed according to her plan.

"Alas, instead of being told that she would marry money and live a fairy tale existence, Mother learned her future would be anything but blessed. The gypsy wrote a prophecy consisting of *three* events, occurrences so horrific that my mother could hardly believe them. First, her plan to marry would be ruined and she would be turned out into the streets. Secondly, her son would grow to be one of the most powerful, most evil creatures the world had ever known. Lastly, he would be the death of her...*literally*. Of course, she was so distraught by the reading that she murdered the gypsy and stole her mystical pen."

"Solomon," Thelma said.

"Yes, yes! Have you met him? Where is he? I have missed him so," Victor said.

"He's safe."

Victor smiled. "Well, we'll see about that." He stared into the fireplace. "Mother tried to ignore the gypsy's predictions. But then, her fiancé discovered her deceit and turned her out into the night, pregnant and penniless, just as it was foretold. Naturally, once the first prediction had come to pass, Mother knew she had to destroy me before I could kill her, but she went into labor. It was during my untimely birth that she died. It was my first murder."

"Congratulations," hissed Thelma.

Victor rushed Thelma, angered, grabbing her neck. Thelma yelped as she fought for air while Victor's grip tightened around her neck. She could feel his claws dig into her flesh. "I have had enough of your tone, child." He backed away, brushed back his hair with his hands, and calmly continued. "So, that leads us to the last piece of the prophecy puzzle, the one that is of interest to *you*. True, I did grow to be very powerful, and very, very evil. Dark magic led me to a dark entity named Felix, the King of the Boogey Men, who promised to grant me unlimited power in exchange for my sacrifice and his freedom. But, there would be one small catch: a child, a little girl, who would be the key to our undoing. The Emerald Moon would signify her arrival. She would come from the land of Evermoore to defend the dead. Not only that…she would be an heir to the Evermoore power."

Thelma looked up in surprise. "What do you mean?"

"Yes, dear. Haven't you figured it out? Maria and Markus Evermoore were your *great grandparents*," Victor cheered. "Isn't that lovely?"

Thelma could not believe what she was hearing. She looked into Mimi's eyes.

Mimi shook her head. "I didn't know, honey. I had no idea."

"Oh, yes. Maria's daughter," Victor continued. "After Felix and his army were conquered, his followers vowed to avenge him. Maria knew that she could not take the chance of one of them getting to her daughter, her precious *Marilyn*. The baby would never be safe with the name Evermoore. So after she passed, her frail mother-in-law gave the child to her neighbors, a young couple she deeply trusted, named Nerryweather. They could not have children of their own and the old crow knew they would provide a wonderful home for her grandchild. Isn't that touching?"

Thelma again looked to Mimi, wanting the truth, needing confirmation. "Mimi, what is he saying?"

"Tell her!" screamed Victor.

"Nerryweather was my maiden name, Thelma. Before I met your Grandpa Thimblewhistle," Mimi confessed.

"You're lying! You're a liar!" Thelma yelled to Victor.

"Oh, I assure you, I am not. At first, I thought that a different little girl was my nemesis, this one, as a matter of fact." Victor ran his hand along Anna's ghostly head. She fought against his touch as the vines tightened their grip. "The Evermoore land has never agreed with me, so I arranged for one of the groundskeepers to take care of her on my behalf."

"You mean, I was killed?" asked Anna in shock.

"Absolutely! I promised that old, sad geezer that I would resurrect his dead wife if he would do away with you. Sadly, raising the dead isn't within my power."

"You! Get me out of this!" Anna screamed as she reached for Victor.

Victor smiled. "The old fool was torn with guilt. He nearly turned us in…before I took care of him. After Peterson's daughter was taken out of the picture, I thought I was safe, but then Solomon told me that *you* were coming. I tried my best to buy the house from under your father, but that didn't happen. Then, when you took possession of the house on the very night of the Emerald Moon, I decided I had to remove you from the picture. After those attempts failed, I arrived at a new approach, a way to take advantage of the situation, get some use out of you!"

Thelma was so furious she could barely see. "You're going to lose! You'll never free Felix without sacrificing yourself."

Victor laughed at Thelma's comments. "No, no. I don't have to die…*you* have to die. Felix still believes that at the stroke of midnight, I am foolish enough to give my life to release him and his army. I finally had to ask myself why I would make such a sacrifice just to become a pawn in Felix's game? Well, I have no plans of dying only to live like a ghostly rat hunting for the fear of children. I plan to be much, much more. The Secret is the only thing that can grant that type of power to the living, and I will rip it directly from the Realm to use here, on earth. I will become the *ultimate* Boogey Man. Then I will release Felix and his army to serve me! And *you* are the one who will bring the Secret to me."

"No, I won't help you!" Thelma said.

"Oh, you will. In a just a moment, you will enter into the Neither Realm through this Nexus here," he said pointing to the Evermoore cemetery gates in the middle of the room. "The Room of Arcanum will open at your touch and you will enter it and steal the Secret for me."

"I won't!" Thelma shouted. "What are you going to do—kill me? Going to the Realm will kill me, anyway."

Victor bent down to Thelma's face and looked into her eyes. "No, I will not kill you, Thelma. But, I will kill all of those around you—your precious grandmother—and your father…"

"What have you done to my dad?" demanded Thelma.

"Let's just say that he is taken care of!" Victor walked toward the fireplace. "Who knows, he could still be alive. It all depends upon you. Dying is part of your destiny, child—your death has been foretold just like your arrival. And, as my mother learned, there's nothing you can do to change your destiny. If you defy me, child, I will rip the life from everyone you love. I will steal your tongue, your eyes, and leave you to rot in a dungeon with the others who have resisted

me. Or…you can be a willing sacrifice for your daddy and your dear old *mamaw*. It is your choice." Victor began to sink into the shadows. "Choose *wisely*."

Thelma began to cry. How could there be any other choice? Was her father alive or had Victor already killed him? Thelma couldn't go on if her father was gone. She wanted to take action, to do something, but what? What a champion she was turning out to be. If she did what Victor commanded, it would mean the end for so many, but if she did not, then it would mean the end for her family. She wanted to destroy Victor, to avenge her father, to save them all.

But how?

The Knight & the Dragon

Edwin wandered through the maze for what felt like days. He passed at least three corpses while on his path, unfortunate adventurers who had become lost within the walls. It appeared hopeless. He was beginning to feel like he would never find his way out. The maze kept changing, it seemed, as if it were purposely attempting to confuse him. Occasionally, the scurry of rats caught his attention. Other times, the shadows played tricks with his eyes. When the passageways narrowed he had to squeeze through the tight crevices—those were the worst.

Then in the distance, Edwin thought he could hear what sounded like crying. Could it be Thelma? He began to move feverishly, picturing the tears of his daughter. Could she be injured? He moved effortlessly around the maze, marking his way with the rocks as the doorknocker had advised. However, the closer he was to the sobs, the more he knew they did not belong to his daughter.

As he rounded a large corridor, Edwin found the source of the weeping. While it was not his daughter, it did appear to be another little girl, crying, sitting on a bench made of stone. She was seated next to a weary skeleton, clutching a teddy bear in her fist.

Edwin crept closer to her. "Little girl, are you lost?"

"Who is that?" shouted the voice, a male voice, a familiar voice. It sounded just like Iggy.

"Iggy?" Edwin said.

"Edwin Thimblewhistle?" Iggy said to the dark.

When Edwin neared, he could clearly make out Iggy's characteristics through the little girl façade. "Iggy! Yes, it's me, Edwin."

Iggy looked into Edwin's eyes, and then began to cry harder. "Oh…oh, please don't look at me. I'm ashamed. I have betrayed Thelma." It was then Edwin noticed that Iggy clung to Bartholomew Bear.

"What? What about Thelma? Where did you get this?" Edwin said as he jerked Iggy from the bench. "What have you done to her?"

"Please, she gave it to me! I didn't mean to! Well, yes, actually, when it all began I meant to, but I changed my mind. But it was too late, far too late." Iggy cried and hung his head.

"What's going on? What has Victor done with her?"

"Nothing!" shouted Iggy out of fear that Edwin was going to pummel him. "Nothing… not yet. But the Eve of the Great Feast is nearly here. He will make her do it then. Oh, poor, poor Thelma."

Edwin grew anxious. "Make her do *what* then? What will Victor make her do?"

Iggy sniffled and wiped his swollen eyes. "Victor is about to send your daughter to her death so she can retrieve an object for him, one of great power. If we are going to stop Victor and save Thelma and your mother, we must hurry. We have only minutes to spare and time is of the essence."

"He has my mom, too?" This was Edwin's worst nightmare. What would he do if he lost them both?

"Yes, yes…please, come. Come with me. I will lead you out."

While Edwin and Iggy were desperately trying to reach her, Thelma's mind was in pieces trying to find a way out of her predicament and save her loved ones. She refused to believe that her father was gone. In her heart, she knew it wasn't so. Then a large grandfather clock in the corner of the dark room began to chime.

Midnight.

A dense fog entered the room. "It is time," Victor said as he appeared through the haze by the fireplace. "What is your choice, Thelma?"

"Don't do it, Thelma!" shouted Mimi as she struggled against her restraints. With a snap of Victor's fingers, her chair slid toward the open fire.

"Stop it! Stop it!" Thelma cried.

"Well, what will it be?" Victor asked.

"Thelma, don't be afraid. It'll be…" Anna began. Anna's words were stopped short by the vines that wrapped their leaves around her mouth.

"Well?" Victor growled. His eyes transformed into red orbs, fangs glistening; he appeared to be changing, becoming something else, something hideously inhuman. He snapped his fingers once again and with a loud *crash* a glowing, shimmering light appeared in the middle of the Evermoore cemetery gate. Thelma could feel the pull of it tugging at her chair.

"Okay!" Thelma screamed. "Okay, I'll do it."

"Outstanding," Victor hissed.

Slowly, the vines began to loosen from around Thelma, allowing her to stand. She wiped the tears from her eyes and walked toward the gates. She stood there for a moment, knowing that this would be the end for her. Would she go on to Edenia? It would be nice to see her mother again, and now she would be greeting her father, too. Or, would she do more good by remaining in the spirit world to help defeat whatever Victor was to become?

With a trembling hand Thelma reached out and touched the flowing translucent energy of the gateway. It felt cool to the touch, much like the Secret had felt. Surprisingly, dying no longer frightened her. She knew what awaited her. It was so hard to see through the tears that kept falling from her eyes. However, it was either her life or the lives of others she loved, and she would rather be out of this world than in it without them.

"Go!" Victor shouted.

But Thelma did not move. She couldn't. She was frozen in place.

"Thelma, get away!" called a familiar voice.

She turned to see her father, beaten, tired, but still alive. And with him was none other Iggy, who smiled at Thelma hopefully. Thelma smiled back. "Dad!"

Victor was completely enraged at the sight. "*Enough!*" He grabbed Thelma by her neck and leaned to her ear. "You have five minutes to bring me back the Secret or he'll die!" With that, he shoved her through the Nexus. Her lifeless body dropped to the floor before them as her soul fell through the portal.

"No!" cried Edwin as he charged at Victor.

"You!" A bolt of energy flew from Victor's hand knocking Edwin to the ground. Then all the light drained from the room. The only illumination was the swirling glow from the open Nexus. A low rumble sounded throughout the room, like an earthquake. The fireplace behind where Victor was standing exploded with flames. Through the fire, there no longer stood the figure of a man, but something worse, something changing, becoming massive and wicked.

A terrible smell permeated the area, like rotting flesh. Victor's shape began to grow and pulsate; his massive shoulders grew larger and larger; horns splintered from the top of his head. Edwin ran to where Mimi was bound and began to untie her. Victor watched them with his glowing eyes as a rattling hiss reverberated along the walls. His bones began popping and cracking while rolls of thick fur covered his flesh, his clothes ripping against his increasing size. Thick tentacles extended from his back. Victor was no longer Victor, but a demon-like creature that turned to face them. It lifted its large arms into the air displaying its claws and then glared down at them.

Edwin and Mimi moved just in time as the beast crashed its claws into the wooden flooring where they had been standing. Iggy ran through the room, making certain to stay clear of the creature.

"Stay away from him, everyone!" warned Iggy. "He can't hold this form forever."

The creature slithered after Edwin, snapping at his heels. He had to find something to use as a weapon. He couldn't fight with his bare hands. On the far wall of the room, he could see a glimmer, something made of metal. Mounted on the wall were an antique sword and shield. Ripping the weapons from their post, he centered on the creature like a knight squaring off with a dragon. As the beast attempted to snare him in its fearsome jaws, its snake-like tentacles grabbed at his legs. With one great swing, he severed one of the beast's tentacles causing it to yowl with pain.

Edwin swung the sword violently with all his strength, but the creature dodged with agility. Suddenly, it became apparent that the monster's power was beginning to subside; its form was beginning to return to a more human shape. Iggy was right—Victor wasn't going to be able to hold this monstrous state indefinitely. The beast took Edwin and slammed him to the ground, throwing the sword from his hand. It bit at him, but he used the shield to hold its teeth at bay. It had him pinned to the ground behind the shield, fighting to keep the thing from biting into him. Edwin was bloody and beaten.

"It's over, *fool*!" the monstrous Victor screeched. "I should have killed you while I had the chance. Now, I *will* kill you. You have not won *anything*." It reared back, jaws wide open, teeth glistening. It sank its fangs deep into Edwin's shoulder and he cried out. Though the agony was excruciating, it was nothing compared to the pain of knowing his daughter was gone forever.

The Gates of Perditia

As Thelma caught her breath, she realized that she was no longer in her body. She turned and ran back to the portal of the Nexus, but it was no use—she could not go through. It was like an electrical field that would not allow her to pass. "Dad!" she cried, her voice echoing through the space.

The entryways to the Realms stood before her. It was too late for her. The prophecy had been correct; her death had been imminent. There were no more choices for her now. She had to obtain the Secret and hand it over to Victor if she wanted to save her family, but it would spell death for the world and eventually all the Realms. There was no time to think. She had to complete her task quickly.

Just as she began to pass through the entryway to the Neither Realm, something stopped her, an idea, a spark of hope. Maybe, just maybe, there was a way to foil Victor's plans. She decided to pay a visit to the one person who could help, the only being who could put an end to Victor for good.

The passage to Perditia did not look inviting. As a matter of fact, it looked just like she had imagined it would. The dark stone steps led down into the unknown. The smell alone was enough to turn her stomach. Trying to hold her breath, she began her descent into the nothingness. She held tight to the wall, feeling her way as she slowly stepped down. Finally, directly ahead of her she could see the red flickering of firelight.

She entered into the open passage to see a great stone wall that seemed to be miles high. The heat was heavy. Before her was a small walkway that led to an opening guarded by two massive stone beasts holding sharp axes. Slowly and cautiously, she began to walk toward them keeping her eyes open and aware. Way off in the distance, she could hear wild laughter mixed with yelps. It was as if someone was being put to death by tickling. She knew all too well that tickle torture was no fun at all.

Whap!

The great axes slammed down before her. One of the stone creatures slowly turned its head to look upon her. "You do not belong here," it groaned.

"No," Thelma replied nervously. "I hope I don't. But, I have to get in. I have to speak to someone."

"You cannot speak to the condemned," it replied.

"I have a message for Felix Payne."

"Unacceptable."

"Please!"

But the statue would not answer. Then a small figure stepped out of the darkness. "Felix Payne, you say?"

"Yes, I have to talk to him…now!" Thelma pleaded.

The small thing stepped around the blade of the axe and peeped at Thelma. "I can take you to him…if you don't tell."

"And who are you? How do I know that I can trust you?" she asked.

He was a small red demon-like being, with petite red horns and a pointed tail. He wore a belt with a buckle that had the letter "B" engraved on it, which held up his loose pants. His hooves clicked on the stony ground. "My name is Bumbles," he said, rubbing his hands together.

"Hello, Bumbles, my name is…"

"Thelma Thimblewhistle. Yes, everyone knows Thelma. For you to be here…must be something bad. Must be very bad outside for you."

"Yes, Bumbles. It is bad. I have to talk to Felix. Can you take me?"

Bumbles touched the blade of the axe triggering the stone creature to raise it. It resumed its previous stance without saying another word. Then Bumbles walked to her and took her gently by the hand. "You must never tell. No telling on me."

Thelma held his hand. "No…I promise."

Together, they walked through the gates into a vast area that stretched as far as the eye could see. It was lined with humongous metal doors. Each door was fitted with a bulky metal padlock in its center. As they walked down the corridor, the prisoners could sense Thelma's presence. They beat against their doors, trying to break through and snatch her, but Bumbles held tight to her hand.

"Do not be scared. Bumbles has you," Bumbles said.

They reached a set of five doors that were unlike the others she had passed in that they were larger and fitted with gigantic locks made of gold. Bumbles pointed to the largest door in the center and then backed away. With a gulp, she approached it.

"And what do you want?" called a deep voice from the other side.

"Are you Felix Payne?" From behind the metal doors around her she could hear the other prisoners hiss the name *Felix Payne*.

"Maybe," replied the voice. "What do you want?"

"I have some information that I thought you might find interesting."

"Hardly," the voice replied.

"Do you know Victor Von Hallow?"

At first there was no response. Then the voice said, "Go on…"

"He's supposed to release you soon, right?"

"Who are you? Who has sent you?" the voice said becoming troubled.

"But he's not going to," Thelma confirmed. "Victor sent me to the Neither Realm to get the Secret for him. He wants to use it to become powerful enough to make you and the Boogey Men his slaves."

Mad laughter reverberated from off the walls around her. Apparently, the inmates found her statement amusing.

"Is that so? Tell me, what is your name?"

Bumbles touched Thelma's hand and she looked down to him. He timidly shook his head, warning her not to say. "My name's not important. Do you want to stop Victor or not?"

There was a moment of silence as Felix contemplated what she had told him. Then, he said, "I will require four of my Boogey Men to accompany me," said the voice. "Should you free us, we will not return to this prison." Thelma did not answer. She stood there weighing her options, trying to take the best course of action. It seemed hopeless either way. "Well?"

"I'm thinking!" she said.

"You can free the few of us now before Victor has his power. Or, he can free all of us once he has his prize. Either way, we *will* be free. The choice is yours."

It was true. There was no flawless solution to her predicament. Felix would be roaming the world once again, regardless of what Thelma decided. However, she knew it would be far worse for all of the Boogey Men to be unleashed under Victor's rule. "How do I free you?"

"Only energy that is uncontaminated can unlock these doors. Your soul is pure—I can smell its sickening innocence. Simply touch these locks and they will open. Release my brothers first."

With a deep breath, she walked to the first door. Touching the lock of gold, it began to glow red hot. Then she touched the second lock. One by one, the bolts began to melt away and puddle onto the ground. The doors opened, allowing the shadows to escape. They began madly circling around her while Bumbles clung to her, hiding his eyes. They laughed and cackled as she ventured toward Felix's prison. With a deep breath, she touched the lock on his door and watched as it melted away. The door cracked open with a loud, rusty thump.

"Hide your eyes!" Bumbles called to her. And Thelma did so.

And as the largest shadow escaped with its companions, she cried to herself, ashamed of what she had done.

Felix Comes Home

nna was still wrapped tight in the thorny vines. She wished she could do something, anything to help save Edwin. A glimmer of light caught Anna's eye. It was the sword, tucked neatly in a pile of rubble by the grandfather clock. Anna fought until her face was free of the viney ropes.

"Mimi! Mimi, the sword!" Anna called. "The sword…by the clock!"

Mimi continued to fight against her restraints until she was able to free her arm. Once she had untied herself, she began searching the dark room. She spied the lost sword directly where Anna said it was resting. She took the heavy thing into her hands; however, there was no way for her to get past the monster to deliver it. Edwin was struggling, blood pouring from his wounded shoulder. The monster was about to overpower him.

Taking a deep breath, Mimi yelled for Edwin as she slid the sword straight through the legs of the creature. Edwin caught it before it skated beyond his reach. As the creature came at him with its jaws, Edwin swung the blade hard, cutting its face. As he got to his feet, its claws cut through the air slicing into his arm and knocking him to the ground once again.

"Now, you die!" howled the creature.

With a great *boom*, the portal of the Nexus grew brighter causing the monster to stop just as it was about to take a final bite into Edwin. Effortlessly, it slung him across the room. With a smile on its face, the monster stomped toward the Nexus, prepared to receive the treasure that was to be delivered. "Good girl," Victor said as he began to regain his human-like appearance. But to his surprise, four shadows entered the room through the Nexus and stood on the floor around him. Fearfully, he looked into their black faces and glowing red eyes.

"You are in trouble!" one of them sang.

"What is this?!" Victor yelled.

"Someone paid us a little visit tonight, Vic," said another.

"Said you'd been up to some bad things…plotting against us," another said.

Mimi could see Edwin beginning to awaken, Iggy kneeling by his side. She began to slowly move to them. In a flash, one of the figures was beside her.

"Boo," it spat as it jumped at her. She yelped with fright and when she did a thin, mist-like fog appeared all over her body. The thing sucked the haze off of her in one breath. "Wow! Old lady fear is the best!" the thing giggled. "I've always loved it." Then it belched. "Whew! 'Scuse me! Let's see if we can scare some more juice off of ya, ya old bat!"

"Laugh, Mimi!" Anna yelled.

"What?" Mimi asked, not understanding.

"Do it! Laugh. Think about when my shorts fell down in front of Billy Preston! Remember those pink bloomers I had on? Think back! Do it now!"

Mimi's mind filled with images of that embarrassing moment when Anna was hoping to impress a young man in the neighborhood named Billy, but instead she ended up humiliated when her shorts fell to the ground showing everyone she was wearing huge, pink bloomers with ruffles on them. With a snort, Mimi broke into laughter. Horrified, the thing howled in anguish and rushed away from her, burnt by her laughter. She rushed to Edwin's side.

Suddenly, something else began to step through the Nexus. The massive dark figure dripped with black ooze, its red eyes ablaze. As it solidified, it appeared to be dead, like a decomposing zombie. The flesh from half of its jaw was torn and hanging loosely to the side. Its long, bony digits were lined with sharp talons. It was very tall as it stood upright and peered down at Victor.

"Felix! But, how did…" quivered Victor.

"How did I get free?" Felix interrupted. He pointed to the grandfather clock that lay on the floor nearly demolished. "Well, you were late."

"I…I…"

"Shhhh," said Felix. "It's okay, Victor. I mean, I know you wouldn't betray our little arrangement."

Victor swallowed. "No! I would never…"

"Because I'd have to kill you then, you understand." The other Boogey Men chuckled. Felix morphed into a black fog. In an instant, he rematerialized in front of Victor and forcefully snatched him by his neck. Victor fought against his grip, struggling to break free. "See, I think you were planning to do something very bad…very, *very* bad, Victor. Me…your servant? No, I don't see things that way. And now that we're free, we don't need you anymore."

"But what about the other Boogey Men? How will you free them?" choked Victor.

Felix thought for a moment and then said, "Eh…we'll make others." With a quick thrust, Felix began to rip and tear Victor's soul from his body as he wrestled against him. The Boogey Man tossed his limp, lifeless body to the ground and held Victor's glowing soul to his face. "See how easy that was? You were unwise to think you were smarter than me, Victor. We'll let the Realms sort out what to do with you!" Then he flung Victor's spirit through the portal.

Thelma was quite shocked to see Victor's soul as she reached the entryway to Perditia. He was surrounded by people who held him as he struggled. "No! It's not fair! Let me go! Let me go!" he screamed as they dragged him into the entryway of the Neither Realm.

Whittleton stood with a severe look on his face, scribbling notes into his book. Noticing Thelma, he stomped over to her angrily. "What have you done?! What have you done, Thelma?"

"I…I…" she tried, but no words would come out.

"You've released not only Felix, but his four most powerful commanders as well!"

"She did what she had to do, Whittleton," said a handsome man who approached them. It was none other than Markus Evermoore.

"Markus?" Thelma asked.

Markus bent down to her. "Hello, Thelma. It is so nice to meet you."

"We wish it could be under better circumstances," said the woman Thelma knew to be Maria. She walked over and took Thelma by the hand. "How are you, honey?"

"Well…" Thelma answered. After all, not only was she dead, she had unleashed the Boogey Men back to the world. Tears welled in her eyes. "I'm sorry," she began to cry.

"Oh, honey," Maria said embracing her. Maria leaned back and looked into her eyes. "You did exactly what you needed to do, Thelma. If you would've given Victor the Secret, there would have been no hope."

"Right," Markus added. "That would've been so much worse. Doing what you did was very smart."

"Smart?" said Whittleton in amazement.

"Yes, very smart," said another man. He walked up and stretched out his hand. "I am honored to meet you, Thelma. My name is Chandu."

Thelma shook his hand and realized that she was surrounded by all of the Oracles. "It's you…all of you."

"Yes," said the woman Thelma knew as Adria. "We've seen you before during your first visit. You just couldn't see or hear us then."

"The beings of light," Thelma smiled.

"Yes," Maria confirmed.

Whittleton was becoming impatient. "Yes, this is all very touching, but what are we to do about the Boogey Men?"

Markus stood up and gave Whittleton a hearty pat on the back. "I think I know someone who won't be too pleased that old Felix is out of his cage."

"Where are you taking Victor?" Thelma asked.

"He will be held until he can be tried," answered Whittleton. "Then he'll be delivered to his final destination."

"What about me?" Thelma looked to Maria. "Can I at least say bye to my dad?"

Maria giggled and brushed Thelma's hair from her eyes. "I think we can arrange something."

"In order to get her back, you know what we have to do, don't you?" said Markus.

"But there has never been one so young," said the Oracle named Claudia.

Maria took Thelma by the hand. "Well, there will be now." The others smiled and looked at Maria in agreement. Maria bent down to Thelma once again. "Thelma, in order to get you home, we're going to have to *expand* your gifts."

"What do you mean?" Thelma questioned.

"You'll have to become an Oracle," said Markus. "The only thing is there's never been one as young as you. Most Oracles don't come into power until they turn eighteen."

Thelma looked to him. "Will it hurt?"

The group chuckled.

"No," Maria said with a smile. "It won't hurt, honey. But you'll need to be patient. Like Markus said, we don't know what this will mean for someone your

age. Maybe your powers won't bloom until you're eighteen. Maybe they'll never bloom at all. But it's the only way we can get you through the portal."

"She must go back," Whittleton confirmed.

Maria gave a nod to Whittleton. "Now…you take care of yourself, Thelma. And take care of Marilyn."

Whittleton began to lead Thelma to the center of the others.

"Will I see you guys again?" Thelma asked.

"Sure!" Markus said. "Tell your grandmother that we love her and that we're watching out for her."

Thelma smiled and shook her head.

"We've always been with you. And we will continue to be," Maria added. "Now close your eyes."

Thelma closed her eyes while the Oracles surrounded her and joined their hands. A light began to travel from each of their bodies, slowly entering into hers, filling her with warmth…filling her with power.

The Oracle

With Victor now dead, the vines that held Anna died away setting her free. She phased and floated to where Mimi and Iggy knelt next to Edwin.

"It appears we have some fresh meat, boys!" Felix said as he stared at Mimi, Edwin and Iggy.

"Woo hoo!" shouted one of the fiends. "But that one's already dead!" It pointed at Anna.

"This one, too," said another as it examined Thelma's body.

"Leave her alone!" shouted Edwin.

Noticing Edwin's emotion, Felix walked over to Thelma's body. "What do we have here?" He brushed the hair back from her face and then his dead eyes grew wide. "It can't be!" Reaching behind her head, he lifted her to get a better look. "I never thought I'd see *you* again." Felix turned to them holding Thelma's limp body. "I take it this belongs to you?"

Using the last of his strength, Edwin picked up the sword and stood upright. He pointed the blade at Felix. "Put my daughter down."

Felix laughed. "Put her down? I think I'd rather make a home of her. You know, just for old time's sake. Yes, I think she'll be a fine host. Young, agile, powerful. I mean, I can't take over the world looking like this, can I?" The other Boogey Men laughed. Edwin started to approach him. "Hold him!" Felix snapped.

The Boogey Men vaporized and appeared around Edwin, holding him in place.

"Let her go!" Edwin yelled. Felix smiled and bent down to Thelma's face. A dark energy began to flow through Thelma's nose and mouth as he began to enter her body. Edwin fought against the Boogey Men, but he could not break their grip. "No!"

Thelma's body began to drift into the air as Felix's essence continued to fill her. Her eyes opened showing their darkness. But then something happened—Felix began to cough. He coughed once again and shook his head. The other Boogeys looked concerned.

"What is it?" called one of them.

Thelma's body began to turn upright. Felix choked as he tried to catch his breath. All of a sudden, Thelma's eyes opened. Bright, white light shimmered from them as shock mounted Felix's face.

Boom!

The force of energy which exploded from Thelma's body was strong enough to knock them backward. The Nexus gate once again erupted with light while commanding voices filled the room. A warm wind blew with a fierce strength, clearing the area of debris. Then they heard the voices begin to chant in unison.

"I am *Gerardo* of *Italy*."

"I am *Qua-li* of *China*."

"I am *Chandu* of *Ethiopia*."

Thelma was suspended in midair, arms outstretched, palms facing up, her eyes glowing luminously as she spoke in a multitude of voices of different dialects from across the world. The wind whipped her soft hair wildly to and fro. She floated toward Felix and he backed away in fear.

"Help me!" Felix cried to the other Boogey Men, but they scattered and vanished from the room, abandoning him.

Edwin ran to where Thelma hung in the air. "I am *Adria* of *England*," she continued. "I am *Jacque* of *France*. I am *Claudia* of *Chile*. I am *Markus* of the *United States*. I am *Maria* of the *United States*." She looked down to him like an angel from the heavens. In unity, the voices reverberated through her mouth before finally saying, "*We are the Oracles of the Neither Realm and we welcome you, Thelma Thimblewhistle, Oracle of the Dominion.*"

Felix leapt to strike, but as he did a colossal crimson hand with black claws sprang from within the Nexus taking him in its grip. The Evermoore gate crumpled as the hand of Nickolas pulled the Boogey Man back through the portal. Thelma's body, limp and unconscious, floated into Edwin's arms. He fell to the ground desperately clinging to her. Mimi, Iggy and Anna joined him.

"No…no, no, no, no! I can't lose you, too. You're all I've got!" Edwin held her to him as he rocked back and forth, sobbing.

Anxiously, they awaited a sign, a glimmer of life, hoping to find that Thelma had returned. There was no noise, no breath. Thelma was soaked to the bone and cold to the touch. She slowly lifted her tired head and looked into her father's wet eyes.

"You've got snot all over me," Thelma said with a weary smile.

Edwin cried and laughed with delight as he pulled her close. Mimi held her hands together, smiling from ear to ear as tears of joy spilled down her cheeks. Iggy and Anna cheered and held one another. They had all witnessed the birth of a new Oracle, the youngest Oracle to ever exist. Thelma Thimblewhistle had fulfilled her destiny. She had died to save the dead…and lived to tell the tale.

And all was *right* in the *Realm*.

On Living with the Dead

Thelma laid in bed thinking about her experiences and the tasks which lay before her. It was difficult for her to remember her life before the Neither Realm. She wouldn't trade the friends she now had for anything—even Indiana. She had grown quite fond of her new family, even Whittleton, who could be quite taxing at times.

After finding out her relation to the Evermoores, Thelma was not at all surprised that her grandmother had dormant abilities as an Auditor. Mimi and Anna had a wonderful time talking and laughing about their past and Anna spent a great deal of time telling her all about the wonders of the Neither Realm. Thelma wondered when she was grown and had children of her own if they would have gifts as well. Would that not be wonderful?

Being a kind soul, her father went back to the underground tunnel to rescue the lonely doorknocker he had met while on his adventure. With Victor gone, he could not abandon it. Sometimes Thelma could tell he regretted the decision, especially when he was forced to answer riddles to get into his own house. She suspected that if her father ever completely gave into the Neither Realm, he could become a perfectly fine Visionary. Curiously, he always seemed to be able to tell when the phantomous Pawpaw was around, but that was mostly due to the sneezing fit that would overpower him while in her presence. Thelma found it comical—Pawpaw either loved her father or loved tormenting him.

Though Patty could never know of the Neither Realm, she and Thelma had become close friends. Thelma had made a promise to Whittleton and the others that she would assist them in keeping their world a secret. It was simple to hide something that couldn't be seen in the first place. Granted, there had been a couple of stumbles along the way. Anna once moved a table across the floor by accident, causing Patty to believe it had moved on its own. There was also the time Pawpaw had caught a mouse and carried it through the living room making it appear to float like the rodent was filled with helium.

Since returning from the Realm, Thelma had attempted on several occasions to travel through the wardrobe Nexus to the Neither Realm without Anna, but she didn't quite seem to be able to achieve success. The first few times, she found herself in Mimi's bedroom, falling from her mirror. After that, Thelma felt it best to allow some time; she didn't want to end up in the *morgue* again…or worse.

With Victor no more, Lillian had been promoted to President of Hallow Savings & Loan. Well, now it was called *Oracle* Savings & Loan, a wholly owned subsidiary of Highwater National Bank. The Board was so impressed with Edwin's development of the Merchant Division that they promoted him to *Senior Vice President.*

Thelma had seen Iggy several times since the incident and enjoyed his company very much. Even though he was now free, he decided to remain in the human world instead of returning to his home in the forest—*2503 Webworm Woods, Last Tree on the Left.* The other ghouls made fun of him now that he had a teddy bear, but Iggy didn't care. He was actually paid for his work at the bank now, so he was able to buy a lot of stuffed animals!

Yes, overall, things were going quite well. Thelma wondered what it was going to be like to be an Oracle. So far, with the exception of more confidence, she had not felt differently. The fact was that no one really understood what being an Oracle was like; the powers were different for everyone who had ever possessed them. There was a possiblility she would develop no powers at all.

Though Felix was imprisoned once again, there were still four Boogey Men on the loose, hiding in the night, roaming the closets of unsuspecting children. It was up to Thelma to find them and return them to Perditia, and she would do just that. She had no idea where to begin. She could certainly question members of the dead community. It was also possible that the little demon, Bumbles, would know. She always loved to call on Allister and he was certain to have plenty of information. Maybe she would even find the nerve to ask the Grimm Reaper—that is, if he could find the time to meet with her. After all, Thelma knew Death was a busy guy…

…and a *very* good chess player.

about the author

A.J. Grea is an author and screenwriter living in East Tennessee with his husband of twenty years, three snarky cats, and a meddlesome squirrel who will not stay away from the windows. A lover of 80s horror, he began writing short stories at the age of nine.

One of his first stories, "The Monster Who Ate My Brother," resulted in a parent-teacher conference, during which his mother had to assure the concerned faculty that his siblings were fine.

When not spinning hair-raising yarns, A.J. spends time as most middle-aged comic book fans do--playing video games and collecting childhood toys that remind him of when his only responsibility was being home before streetlights began to glow.

9 781968 152086